Sinner's Choice

by Denese Thomas

Copyright © 2014 by Denese Thomas
Sinner's Choice
First Edition, Paperback
Published 2015
ISBN-13: 978-1484802090
ISBN-10: 1484802098
Library of Congress Control Number: 2014905247
CreateSpace Independent Publishing Platform
North Charleston, South Carolina

Scripture taken from the New King James Version®.Copyright © 1982 by Thomas Nelson, Inc. Used by permission. All rights reserved.

Scripture taken from the Scoffield Reference Bible.Copyright © 1967 by Oxford University Press, Inc. Used by permission. All rights reserved.

Dedication

Heavenly Father, in Jesus' name, without Your direction and guidance, this novel would have never been completed. To You, I offer up my highest praise, and I pray that You find it acceptable in Your sight. Thank You, Father. I love You eternally. I never would have made it this far without Your grace and mercy. Thank You, Father, for walking beside me during the difficult times. Mom, next to Jesus Christ, you are the second greatest blessing in my life. Thank you for raising me to be the woman that I am today. Most of all, thank you for praying for me during a period in my life when I was too foolish to pray for myself. It was through your prayers that God kept me. I love you, Mom.

Acknowledgments

I would like to thank the following people for their love, patience, friendship, and encouragement: Rose Miller, Clifford Jones, Marilyn Lee, Mahlona Muex, Gwen Muex, Anthony Muex, Darryl Muex, Kevin Muex, Reginald Muex, Denise Blanchard, Michael Campbell, Angela Taylor, Joan Glover, Anna Donaldson, Sandra Cervantes-Jones, Charles Ellis, Jesiree Jenkins, David Batteast, Lois Weatherspoon, David Cornell, Richard Long, Kevin Moran, Anthony Caruso, Scott Valentine, Dave Gladden, Homer Hudson, Bennie Blackmon, Courtney Johnson, Eva Miller, Kevin Sanders, Sherdon Douglas, Donnell Walters, and Louise Drayton-Smith.

Chapter 1

"OH! HEAVENLY FATHER, in Jesus' name, if You will please ease my pain."

Mary Ellen Sutton (Ellen) whispered a quick prayer while she lay resting as best she could in her hospital bed. No matter how she raised her feet or lowered her head, the bed just wasn't comfortable. The cold of the bars on either side made the whole room daunting and grim. She tried hard not to imagine how many others had been there before her feeling the exact same way. She concentrated on shallow breathing since her space reeked of other people's blood, sweat, and tears, not to mention that unpleasant aroma of hospital disinfectant. The thought of inhaling it all was disheartening, but she worked hard at not allowing a single negative thought into her head or heart. Desperate to escape the sharp pains that had almost consumed her, she tried to force herself to sleep, but the shuffling of feet outside her room, and the monotone voice over the hospital intercom, prevented her from doing so. Whoever Doctor Jacques Muex was, she wished he would answer his freaking pages.

"A French doctor," she thought for a moment and then mumbled, "He can perform a thorough examination on this ancient, eighty-five-year-old chest and these sagging milk jugs of mine anytime." She chuckled for a quick second until another sharp pain shot across her chest. "Oops! Sorry, Lord. I know that was a sin."

After being in the hospital for well over a month, she thought that she had met every doctor employed by Blanchardtom Memorial

Medical Hospital. A faint grin made its way past her physical pain and onto her face as she contemplated eventually meeting Doctor Muex when he, too, would attempt to drain the last ounce of blood from her feeble body.

Ten years prior, she had first been diagnosed with heart disease, and it had since advanced beyond any worthwhile treatment. Being the unselfish woman that she was, her mind immediately focused on her sons. Even though they were grown men well into their forties and fifties, she wondered what would happen to them after she passed on from this world. But concerns for herself, she had none. She held steadfastly to the Gospel of John that Jesus had gone to prepare a place for her. Having served God faithfully, she confessed Christ as the Messiah at an early age and diligently did His will. She fed the hungry, oftentimes depriving herself so that the least of the poor could eat. She witnessed to anyone who would listen about all that God had brought her through and just how great He was. She was a devoted member of Salvation to All Missionary Baptist Church. She tithed faithfully and temporarily sheltered neighborhood children who were without means or stable living conditions. A tear formed and then slipped down her cheek as she held on to the thoughts of God's goodness. Even when she had learned of her diagnosis, she had praised God and asked Him not to move the mountain but give her the strength to climb it.

Her thoughts were interrupted by footsteps that seemed near her bed. Her first thought was another nurse entering to take her vital signs, but that thought was quickly dismissed upon hearing a familiar voice belonging to someone she had catered to for decades.

"Ma, how are you feeling?"

Full of emotion and in excruciating pain, she couldn't speak; instead, she slowly nodded her head. Any negative response would have only worried her sons, and she didn't want that. She always felt the love of her boys, but being hospitalized for the past month had made apparent just how much they relied upon and truly loved her. Even as adults, they depended on her care and attention more than ever, and she knew this.

She felt the warm lips of her eldest son, Connery Sutton, as he knelt over and tenderly kissed her forehead. Another set of approaching footsteps caught her attention. Instantly, she knew that it had to be her second-eldest son, Harper Sutton, because the brothers were inseparable—like two peas in a pod.

Harper stood at the foot of his mother's bed and smiled at her loving face. He caught a glimpse of a tray of partially eaten baked chicken and mixed vegetables on the serving table.

"Did you eat anything today?" he asked. Before Ellen could nod, he continued, "Are you still in pain? Did the doctors come in today?"

He finally gave her time to respond. A grin crept up through the pain and materialized on her face. She sensed the love in her son's voice. Instead of nodding, she wiggled two of her fingers. Satisfied with her answer, he smiled and then took a chair, which gave him a perfect view of the small, mounted, color television on the wall near the head of her bed.

"Where's Mabrey? He said that he was coming today," Harper asked Connery, flipping through the channels.

"I don't know. Knowing him, he's probably laying up with some woman. I'll deal with him later. I'm only worried about Mom right now."

"I'm hungry. You have any money on you, Connery?" Harper asked, rambling through his rear pants pockets. "I know I had some money on me somewhere," he mumbled while reaching into his front pants pockets, turning them inside out. A large hole appeared in the front right pocket of his favorite pair of faded, worn blue jeans. When he twisted his body sideways, another large hole appeared in the pocket of the right buttock.

"My money must have fallen out somewhere. Do you see any money on the floor over there?" he inquired almost too loudly.

"Keep your voice down. I think Mom is sleeping." Connery whispered just loud enough. Directing his attention at Ellen, he found her resting peacefully.

"She went to sleep that fast?" Harper asked. "They must have given her medicine."

"I don't know, but don't bother her. Turn down the volume on the television so that you don't disturb her." Connery looked sternly at him and then focused his attention back on his mother.

"Will you loan me five bucks, Conn?" Harper always resorted to his nickname for Connery when he wanted something. "I lost my money!"

"Lost my butt cheeks!" Connery snapped. "You have to have money in order to lose it. I forgot that you break into houses for a living. I don't understand, Harper. Please, enlighten me. You burglarize what—two or three houses a week, and you're still broke? Exactly what do you do with the money you get from selling the stash? You don't help Mom out any. I thought thieves lived like fat cats. Hell, look at all those politicians in Congress."

Before Connery could continue, Harper interrupted in that menacing voice that he knew all too well. "When do you ever help Mom? You stinky son-of-a-gun, you receive your SSI check, and you disappear until it's gone. Say one more word about me, and I'll call the got-damn government and tell them your funky ass has been faking all these years. Now who's the thief? And you can keep your money. If we didn't live with Mom, I'd call the damn cops and tell them that you're in possession of a lot of my stolen stash and where they can find it."

As Connery was about to respond, he was hushed by the movement of Ellen's head, but she never opened her eyes.

"She's still sleeping. Be quiet, man," Connery demanded. "Mom doesn't need to hear any of this."

Ellen pretended to sleep while she listened to every word of her son's argument. Under no circumstances did she want them to know she was listening. Drifting back in time, she remembered when she was initially informed that she would never be able to conceive children of her own. Determined not to allow sterilization to rob her of the family she always wanted, she immediately altered her plans toward adoption.

For some unknown reason, she still remembered the adamantly negative responses she received from her family and friends after sharing with them her intentions of adopting: "You never know what you're getting with other people's children," "Most of their parents are drug users and criminals," or "Their own parents don't want them—doesn't that tell you anything?" To this day, those words still pierced her heart with pain.

She took a deep breath and allowed her thoughts to wander back over the years of her sons' lives. Even now, she didn't regret adopting five boys from different walks of life. She gave them everything a single mother of five could give her children. They didn't have everything they wanted in life, but they certainly had everything a child needed. The one thing that she made sure they had plenty of was love. But somehow Connery, Harper, Stanton, Mabrey, and Wentworth Sutton hadn't turned out quite how she planned.

At the early age of seven, Connery Sutton, the eldest of the brothers, had been adopted from Miller-Jones Children's Home in St. Louis, Missouri, as were all the others. He was tall and slender in stature with a dark-brown complexion and very coarse hair. A distinguishing mole that sat on top of the left side of his lip was what made her remember him most when she first began her search for a child. Or maybe it was the compassion she had for him the first time she ever laid eyes on him.

Upon her initial visit to the children's home, she had observed little Connery Martin standing in the play area. He was surrounded by several other orphans who were taunting him and shouting cruel remarks about his lip. Her first thought was to reach out and hug him because she believed that no child should ever have to suffer abuse. But

Connery had proved to be a little fighter, and what she heard escape his suntanned lips made her stare in disbelief. Little Connery just up and started using profanity and words most adults had probably never heard before. Just as she was about to intervene, Connery hit one of the little boys in the jaw. From that moment on, she knew that she had found her first son—a kid who needed rescuing from the environment he hadn't asked to be a part of. Not long after, Connery came to live with her, and the first thing she had done was give him her last name. She almost let another grin surface on her face when she realized that, actually, this was the second thing she had done; the first thing had been to set the ground rules about his foul little mouth.

Fighting furiously to hold back her grin, she thought of Harper, her second-eldest son. A couple of months after bringing Connery home, she had decided to adopt again and knew exactly who that child would be— the little six-year-old whom Connery hit in the jaw, Harper Williams.

Connery's first response upon finding out still tickled her even now. "Leave that black bastard right where he's at," he had demanded.

That turned out to be his first spanking. It saddened Ellen at the time to physically lay hands on her children, but now it comforted her. How she wished that she would have tanned their little bottoms a trillion times more.

"Mom, are you up?" she heard Harper ask now, but she refused to respond. "Mom, are you up?" he asked a second time in a tone one pitch higher but again received no response. Truth be told, she just wanted to lay there and think back on the best years of her life—her boys.

"She must be still sleeping. Leave her alone," Connery instructed, pulling the covers further up to her shoulders. "If she's sleeping, then she's not in pain."

The first day she had arrived home with Harper, she remembered Connery slamming the front door in his face. She could have strangled his little black behind, but love prevented her from acting out her thoughts. But Harper didn't care. He ran over to Connery and embraced him for what seemed an eternity. Connery just stared off into space with despair. Immediately, she sat both boys down and explained to them the meaning of family and brotherly love. She thought that Connery would never make amends with his new brother, but one day the two just clicked. Thinking that her lectures had finally sunk deep into Connery's heart, she was taken aback after accidentally stumbling onto the secret that bound them together as blood brothers. While cleaning out their bedroom closet, she had discovered mounds of electronics that she hadn't purchased. Upon confronting them, Connery was quick to offer Harper over in exchange for clemency. It broke her heart to discover that Harper had been burglarizing neighborhood homes and harvesting the loot in her house.

How vividly she recalled marching Harper over to her neighbor's residence to return his video cassette recorder. Mr. Anderson put the fear of God into Harper's heart when Ellen demanded Harper issue him an apology. Damn the apology, apparently.

"If I catch that little illegitimate, black speck of yours breaking into my house, I'll put some buck shots in his black butt," she recalled him saying. As she was about to correct Mr. Anderson concerning his dialogue in front of young Harper, he slammed the door shut in her face. From that day forward, she had never found stolen goods in her home again, but her motherly intuition told her that Harper hadn't turned from his evil ways. Every night before climbing into bed, she would say a prayer for his safety and ask God to change him.

Silently, she started to thank Jesus. She never looked at it as His not answering her prayers; instead, she knew in her heart that it was Harper's choice to turn from his evil ways. If he took the first step, Jesus would do the rest. But, regardless of how Harper Sutton chose to live his life (she changed his last name as she did all her children), he was still her son, and she loved him.

Her thoughts switched to her middle son, Stanton. The day she brought him home at age six, Connery and Harper were stunned to see that he was Caucasian, but they readily accepted him as their brother. It didn't take long for Ellen to realize that Stanton, like his older brother, Connery, had a mouth on him, which she figured that he, too, must have picked up from his stay at the children's home. But Stanton also loved to drink. Too many nights during his teenage years and early twenties, she worriedly sent Connery and Harper out to search for him. Her worries were instantaneously replaced with anger when she observed them approaching the residence clutching their brother underneath both armpits. Before she had time to question his whereabouts, an irate Connery was swift to disclose the information as he and Harper dragged Stanton inside and up to his bedroom.

"We found his pissy ass in his favorite resting place, the gutter, clenching his best friend as usual. We ought to have let his ass lay there until he had enough sense to get up on his own. Believe me, he has plenty of that antifreeze in his system to keep him warm, and if he freezes overnight, what the hell. Put his sorry ass in a plywood box and bury him in the back yard," Connery had recited a thousand times. She remembered warning Connery that his words might come back to haunt him one day. When Ellen insisted that the boys not lay Stanton down soiled, she was met with grave rebellion from her clan.

"We refuse to wash a grown, white man's balls. We have our own to play with if we so choose to do so." Oftentimes, she had ended up bathing Stanton while two of the boys hesitantly held him up in the tub.

Many times she wondered if the trait was inherited from one of his biological parents. She had never bothered to educate herself with the background of any of her boys; she just knew that they were the ones the moment she laid eyes on them.

An announcement that visiting hours were soon to be over blaring from the intercom gave her the perfect excuse to open her eyes. She did so slowly, pretending to adjust her sight to the bright light illuminating the room.

"Mom, can you hear us?" Connery asked as he and Harper stood over her bed. "We're going to leave now."

As she was about to respond, her younger sons, Stanton, Mabrey, and Wentworth, entered in a hurry. Feeling blessed to have all of her boys huddled over her; she found the strength to speak.

"I love you guys." Her soft, feminine voice could barely be heard over the noise from the nurse's station located just south of her room.

"We love you, too, Mom. We love you, too."

Their response sounded like a symphony orchestra to her ears. Not wanting to cry in front of them, she fought hard to hold back her tears, but one ran down the left side of her cheek.

"Stop crying, Mom. We'll be OK until you get home."

They tried to console her, but her tears flowed like a waterfall. When she reached out to embrace them, the IV needle pained her.

"Gather around my bed." They complied and listened attentively to the words of the one person whom they loved more than anything in the world. "I don't know how much longer I'm going to be with you boys."

"Don't talk like that, Mom. You're not going anywhere, I promise. You'll be home in a couple of days so that we can take care of you," Wentworth proclaimed.

"Listen, boys! I need assurance from you before I leave this world that the five of you will always stick together no matter what. Promise me that."

"You know we will, Mom. We promise you." Their sincere expressions reassured her of everything she needed to know.

"OK! I'm holding you boys to your promise. Remember, I'll be looking down at you from above. Just because I'm not here doesn't mean I can't see you."

"Stop saying that, Mom. We hate it when you talk like that. Nothing's going to happen to you. You'll be home again soon, cooking for us." Wentworth smiled.

Laughter rang out in the room, but Wentworth wasn't joking. His calmly spoken words were to reassure himself. He just couldn't bring himself to imagine life without the beautiful woman who lay in the bed before him. Tears swelled in his eyes, but he dared not allow them to fall in front of his brothers. Gently, he stroked her right foot.

"I'm sorry, but visiting hours are over. I'm going to have to ask you to leave now," an attractive-looking nurse stated as the boys turned around.

"We've got to go, Mom, but we'll be back tomorrow," they stated in unison and then kissed her cheeks.

Reaching into his front pants pocket, Connery produced the car keys to his mother's old sedan, which was parked in the hospital's garage. As they made their way out of the room, Wentworth returned to her bed.

Kneeling beside her, he whispered softly in her ear, "I love you."

"I know, baby. Now go home and get yourself something to eat, OK?"

Nodding his head, he stole one last kiss and then joined his older brothers who were waiting for him in the corridor.

When she could no longer hear their footsteps, Ellen prayed and cried, "Dear Lord, please, hear my cry. Please, hear my cry. I love my boys so much. Heavenly Father, please take care of them after You take me from this world. I need Your reassurance that my boys will be OK. Father in Heaven, I'm not afraid to die. Because of our Lord, Jesus Christ, death cannot touch me. I'll only die once, and through death comes eternal life through Jesus Christ. I pray that I have served You faithfully and that I have found favor in Your sight. Father, I pray for the souls of my kids. Please, Heavenly Father, in Jesus' name, touch the hearts of my boys that they may come to know You and turn their lives over to You. Please, send Your angels to protect and keep them safe as they try to find their way in this evil world. Heavenly Father, I know that You are able to do all things.

You said that if we ask in Jesus' name, it shall be done if we only believe, and I take You at Your word. I stand on a solid rock called Jesus Christ, and through Him all things are possible. Father, I ask that You guide their footsteps, direct their tongues, and make it so that they one day submit to Your will. In Jesus' name, I pray. AMEN."

As she lay there sobbing in the presence of God, a familiar peace came over her, a peace she had felt many times in the past when she had prayed and submitted herself fully to Him. Suddenly, she sensed a presence in the room with her, but when she opened her eyes, she found nothing. Staring into the bathroom through the open door that Wentworth forgot to close, she found it empty also. When her eyes landed on the two chairs by her bed, she saw slight impressions in the seats as if someone or something was resting in them. For a split second, she questioned her sanity. Closing her eyes, she brushed it off as being a figment of her imagination until she caught a second glance. The impressions were now more profound. A quick second of fear struck her, but God's peace quickly came back upon her.

"Peace be still," she said aloud with a joyful heart. "Thank You! I thank You, Heavenly Father, for hearing my cry. In Jesus' name, I thank You, and I give You my highest praise." She adjusted her shoulders on the pillow and then settled in to rest.

→══◉ ◉══←

"That car, being as old as it is, still runs pretty good," Stanton declared as he made a straightway sprint to the refrigerator at home. Without peering over his shoulder, he knew that his brothers were in direct pursuit of him. The house was beginning to show signs of a female's absence, even with Wentworth's efforts to keep it tidy, he thought to himself.

"What's in there?" Mabrey asked as he looked over Stanton's right shoulder. From where he was standing, he could only see half a loaf of bread and condiments, which were neatly placed in the side compartments of the refrigerator door.

"We still have leftovers and some lunchmeat. There's some bologna, liver, cheese, eggs, chicken…," Stanton called out as he took a survey.

"Pull out that leftover chicken for me, Stant." Connery made his way over to the cabinet where he always found the saucers neatly stacked. "That'll do me for the night. If we need to get supplies, I'll stop by the store tomorrow on my way back from the hospital. Where's Wentworth?" He finally noted his absence due to hearing no objections to him eating the last of the deep-fried chicken.

"He went upstairs, I think. I guess he isn't hungry," Mabrey answered without giving Wentworth's absence a second thought.

He positioned himself at the dinner table next to Connery where he settled in for a double-decker bologna-and-cheese sandwich and a cola. He watched Connery gulp down the chicken as if there was no tomorrow. Stanton and Harper soon took their places where they munched on liver, cheese, and crackers.

Chapter 2

WENTWORTH LAY ACROSS the foot of his mother's bed, staring at the pastel wallpaper. The promise he'd made to her replayed in his mind like a taped recording. Even though he was immune to hearing her talk about death, he preferred just about any subject to it. Oftentimes while growing up, he would lay awake at night and contemplate what life would be like without the one person who made everything worthwhile.

He thought about all the struggles he had endured in the past, being a Latino with very little education, and how he hustled to survive by performing temporary odds-and-ends jobs in construction. Sizing himself up, he decided that he had never amounted to much. Truth be told, that was fine with him as long as he found acceptance in the eyes of his elder brothers and his mother.

He recalled the first day he had arrived at the Sutton residence to meet his four brothers. Immediately, he was taken aback by them—Connery especially, because of his foul mouth and hardcore persona. From day one, he vowed to pattern his life after his hero, Connery.

But he refused to fool himself. In reality, he could never fill any of his brother's shoes. Connery was tougher than nails and a gambler and fighter by nature who talked the talk and walked the walk. Harper was a world-class thief, burglar, and liar, and he was just as tough as Connery. Stanton was a stocky, green-eyed drunkard and loudmouth. And Mabry was a smooth-talking, dark, curly-haired, extremely-muscular woman-izer, who made his living in the bedroom. Known around St. Louis as the Italian Lover of the western region, he certainly lived up to his repu-tation. Wentworth's present thoughts were interrupted by loud laughter from his brothers. Curious, he wandered downstairs to find them sitting at the kitchen table engaged in conversation.

"Man, sex sells. If it didn't, most female hip-hop and R&B singers wouldn't have a job," Mabrey proclaimed while sipping on a can of cola.

"Most of them don't have one, and it's their fault. They choose to use their assets rather than their brains to get ahead in that business," Harper replied. "What they don't realize is that their assets can only be spread around for so long until they start to lose their value. Then what do they do?"

Laughter rang out in the room as Harper gave Mabrey a high five.

"Yep! You're exactly right. Then they have no choice but to trap a couple of basketball or football stars by having kids. Gold diggers always target high-profile athletes because they're the easiest cows in the pasture to milk. Hey, they need to maintain that lavish lifestyle so they do what needs to be done. It's sad, isn't it?" Mabrey replied.

Their conversation continued on into the den. After flipping through the channels repeatedly, Connery settled on the classic horror flick, *Dracula*. One by one, they settled in for the night by kicking off their shoes and pulling off their shirts. Wentworth made a pallet on the floor consisting of a blanket and two pillows, while his brothers occu-pied the sectional and lounger. It wasn't long before the television was watching them.

Harper awoke to the sound of the telephone ringing. After canvass-ing the room and finding his brothers sleeping soundly in their same spots, he glanced at the clock on the wall.

"It's four o'clock in the morning. Who could this be?" Stumbling over to the phone, he stretched his fatigued body. "What?"

"This is Blanchardtom Memorial Medical Hospital. I'm trying to reach a Mr. Connery Sutton." The friendly voice on the other end of the phone left Harper unresponsive and momentarily paralyzed with fear.

"Hello? Sir, are you still there? Is this Mr. Sutton?"

"This is his brother, Harper Sutton. Are you calling about my mother, Ellen?"

"Yes, sir. Sir, we need you to respond to the hospital, please."

"What's wrong? Is something wrong with my mother?" Harper insisted in a voice so thunderous that it woke his brothers. Connery, Stanton, and Mabrey huddled around him, while Wentworth dropped his head face down in his pillow.

"Sir, I can't give out any information over the telephone. Are you or someone in your family able to respond to the hospital immediately?"

"We're on the way." He slammed down the receiver and reached for his shirt. "We need to get to the hospital. Something is wrong with Mama."

"What's wrong with Mama?" Wentworth could hardly breathe due to the tightening of his chest. He waited impatiently for Harper's response. "Is she dead?"

"The hospital wouldn't say."

"Well, what did they say?" Connery commanded in a take-charge tone of voice.

Stopping dead in his tracks, Harper stared steadily at his brother. His silence told Connery everything he needed to know. For the first time in his adult life, Connery witnessed tears building in Harper's glassy-looking eyes.

Refraining from asking any further questions, the five brothers threw on their garments and rushed back to the hospital. They were met in the intensive care unit by two nurses who kindly escorted them to one of the waiting rooms on a private floor.

"Where's our mother?" Connery stood erect with his hands folded on his chest.

"Sir, the doctor will be in shortly to talk with you. I can't give you any further information right now. You really need to wait for the doctor."

Connery shook his head in disbelief and then walked out into the corridor. After scanning the hallway from one end to the other, he leaned his slender frame against the doorway and briefly rested his head in his hands before rejoining his brothers.

The ten-minute wait seemed like ten hours before a short, white male dressed in blue hospital scrubs entered the waiting room holding a manila folder stuffed with files. After eyeing the five brothers carefully and noting the distraught looks on their faces, he struggled to find the right words to say.

"Are you gentlemen the family of Mary Ellen Sutton?"

"Yes, we are. Is she OK?" Jumping from his seat, Wentworth stood within inches of the cardiologist. "Is Mama going to be OK?"

"I'm deeply sorry to have to inform you, but Ms. Sutton passed away. We did everything we could to revive her, but we…we just couldn't."

"Did she ask for us?" Wentworth inquired.

"She didn't, sir. She passed away in her sleep. We're almost certain that it was a massive heart attack. Once I finish preparing all the paperwork, the body will be turned over to you gentlemen. Once again, I'm sincerely sorry for your loss. Do you gentlemen have any more questions for me at this time?"

Silence fell over the room as if it wasn't occupied. Wentworth's attempts to process the devastating news that had just been handed him was to no avail. Slowly, his legs weakened until they gave way, sending him crashing to the carpeted floor. Tears swelled in his eyes as he looked over at Connery for comfort, but he found his brother sitting partway in a chair with his face completely buried within the palms of both hands. A heart-wrenching yell, followed by loud banging resonated from behind him. Turning toward his other brothers, he observed Mabrey kneeling down in a praying position, banging his fist against the wall. No longer able to fight back his tears, they streamed down his cheeks.

"Mama, what happened? We need you so much. I can't find my way without you here to guide me."

Wentworth allowed his head to fall face down on the floor. His heartbreaking pleas prompted Stanton to kneel down beside him and gently stroke his back.

"I'll leave you gentlemen alone." The cardiologist turned slowly to leave, but he was stopped by one last question from Connery.

"Can we see her one last time?"

"Sure you can. Give me a minute, and I'll have one of the nurses escort you."

Connery didn't verbally respond; instead, he nodded his head and then stared off into space.

Minutes later, they were led down several winding corridors until they reached the emergency room. A bitter silence loomed over the cluttered room as they took their places around the nude body of their mother that was covered by a single white sheet. Standing near her head, Wentworth stroked her curly blond hair, which fell just shy of her brows. Expecting her to wake at any moment and display her award-winning smile, he was brought back to reality when Mabrey leaned over and rested his head on her chest.

Connery, being the strongest of the brothers and knowing what his mother expected, somehow managed to pull himself together. Mustering up the last of his inner strength, he forced himself to speak.

"We had better get going. Mama wouldn't want us falling apart like this. You know what she always said about death: if a person dies in the Lord, rejoice over their homecoming, because they are experiencing a joy unimaginable."

At that moment he was interrupted by the attending nurse. "We can release the body over to you now. You're free to contact the funeral home who'll be handling the arrangements. If you need any assistance, please don't hesitate to ask. My name is Kay, and I'm just down the hall. Please, take your time; there's no rush. And I'm so sorry for your loss. I wish all of you well." Without further hesitation, she turned and exited the room.

None of the brothers wanted to make the first move toward the door, not even Connery. Their bodies were glued to the bed that supported their precious mother's lifeless body. Walking away felt too much like abandonment, even if her body was spiritless. Realizing that he had to find a way to get his brothers out of the hospital soon or they would never leave, Connery acted.

"Hey, we need to go home and start making arrangements. I know it's hard to say good-bye, but we've got to let go. She's no longer with us; she's in a better place now. All we can do now is honor the promise that we made to her. Come on; let's go home."

One by one, they kissed her forehead and said their good-byes. Wentworth searched deep within himself for the strength to walk away but came up empty. The thought of his rock and pillar never walking through the front door of their residence again tormented his already weary soul. That beautiful smile that had warmed his soul over the years better than chicken noodle soup was now gone. She was his best friend and angel. More than anything, she was the only person qualified, in his eyes, to hold the royal title, Mama. It wasn't until he felt Connery's touch that he turned away.

The walk down the corridor and out onto the parking lot seemed endless. Sensing that none of his brothers wanted to be the first to enter the vehicle, Connery opened the door and made his way into the driver's seat. Not until then did the others follow suit and claim their spots.

Upon arriving home, they made their way into the den of a house that no longer held that home-sweet-home feeling they had come to know for the last four to five decades. All that seemed to stand now were four empty walls, except for the decades of memories that were, for now, too painful to recall. The personal touches that Ellen had put into decorating the house, like her hand-painted ceramics, somehow no longer held their attractiveness, and the pastel-colored walls were made gloomy by heavy darkness. All that remained was emptiness.

⋯⊱═⊙ ⊙═⊰⋯

Connery finally returned from the funeral home around twelve that afternoon. He was grateful to learn that Harper had contacted Salvation to All Missionary Baptist Church and arranged funeral services as instructed. That allowed him time for a short breather. Knowing that his younger brothers were not up for the task, he tried to handle as many of the arrangements as possible. After observing Harper, Stanton, and Mabrey seated at the kitchen table conversing over coffee, his mind quickly turned to Wentworth.

"Where's Wentworth?" he asked, while putting two teaspoons of nondairy creamer into his cup of black coffee.

"He's upstairs going through Mama's wardrobe. You told us to pick out something for her to wear," Stanton responded in a dull, dry voice. "He's been up there for quite some time now."

Of all his brothers, Connery knew that Wentworth was taking their mother's death the hardest. Maybe it was because he was the youngest, or that he was closer to her than the rest of them. After all, Connery thought as he took three quick sips of coffee, Ellen had always taken more care with Wentworth than she had with any of them. Without a word, he excused himself from the table and ventured off upstairs to his mother's bedroom to check on Wentworth.

He observed Wentworth sitting on the bed, bending over to look through one of the drawers in the nightstand. Beside him was a beautiful silk-and-lace white dress that had been meticulously positioned in the middle of the bed.

"You picked out the white dress for Mama?" Connery inquired hesitantly, not wanting to disturb his brother.

"Angels wear white," he responded while continuing his search in the drawer. "That's what Mama always said."

A chuckle echoed from Connery's mouth as his mind journeyed back in the past to the millions of quotes Ellen had cited over her life span. "That is what she said, isn't it?" he smiled. "Do you need me to help you? What other garments do you need to find?"

"Ha! Ha! Ha! Ha! Ha!" Wentworth fell backward onto the bed, sending his legs soaring in the air. Clutching his stomach and rolling sideways, he collided with the floor.

"What are you laughing at?" Connery looked on curiously as Wentworth's laughter escalated with mixtures of moans and groans. "What's so funny?"

He held up a pair of his mother's hefty, pink panties, which were trimmed in white lace. After making several failed attempts to verbally communicate with Connery, he gave up.

"Mama's going to get you," Connery stated laughing as if she still existed. For a split second, he almost returned to grieving mode, but he quickly refocused his attention back on Wentworth who was still holding the undergarment in his hand. Connery couldn't help but laugh with him. A warm sensation filled his body. He made his way over to the bed and kneeled down on both knees.

"Mama was a stout woman, wasn't she?" he jokingly asked, watching his younger brother enjoy a well-needed moment of blissfulness. "You're so damn silly. You know Mama can see us, don't you?"

Still consumed with laughter, Wentworth nodded his head up and down while rolling around on the floor in a fetal position.

"What's all that banging noise?" Mabrey asked as he, Harper, and Stanton made their way into the bedroom.

"What are these big things?" Mabrey yelled. "Are we redecorating Mom's room with new curtains? Are these really Mom's big drawers? Was she really that heavy?"

When he put the panties over his head, the elastic waistline fell down to his neck. "Damn, Mom!" he stated and then fell down on one knee laughing.

Stanton shook his head in disbelief, but he continued to enjoy the moment of laughter. Grabbing the panties from Mabrey's head, he folded and then placed them on top of the white suit. "Stop laughing at my mother's bloomers. She can't help it if she loved to eat."

Another round of laughter erupted in the room. They surveyed the worn-out Bible sitting on the nightstand next to her bed and the wooden cross hanging on the wall alongside numerous pictures of Jesus. Silence fell over the bedroom as memories of their childhood came flashing back.

"To be absent from the body is to be present with the Lord. I can't tell you how many times I've heard Mama say that. She's with her Lord now," Mabrey stated in a tone not much louder than a whisper. "I wish I could see her just one more time just to let her know how much I love her. Anyhow, if you've gotten all her things together, I'll take them down to the funeral home. Just make sure she looks good, OK, Went?"

"I've got it," Wentworth answered, carefully placing the items in a travel bag.

"I'll tell you what, let's all take it down there and then get something to eat. I can use a greasy, double cheeseburger right now with a large order of cheese fries," Connery stated, making his way out of the bedroom.

"Sounds like a winner to me, big brother," Harper replied, smacking his lips. "It'll sound even better if you foot the bill."

"Do you ever stop trying to get over?" Connery asked with a smirk on his face. "Must you always try and get over on people?"

"Hey, you're the oldest. What did Mama say? I do believe she told you to take care of us, you sapsucker." He elbowed Connery in the kidney, causing him to stumble forward and go down with a crash.

Seeing the two go at it, the others laughed when Connery grabbed for the wall in order to balance himself. The thought of his younger brother getting a shot in on him made him giggle. Standing erect, he eyed Harper like a vulture that waited for the right moment to strike back. "Mama said for us to stick together, fool, and I've got your sap, you sucker," he shot back and then joined in on the laughter.

"Well, both of you suckers can buy me a cheeseburger," Wentworth jokingly pushed through them and headed downstairs with his mother's attire grasped tightly in his hand.

"Keep dreaming," they yelled simultaneously, following him out of the bedroom.

"Don't lose Mama's big drawers. We can't let anybody see those," Mabrey joked.

"I can almost guess what Mama is saying about us right now," Connery added. "Lord, look at those silly boys of mine. They're throwing my underwear all around the room and putting them on their heads. What has gotten into those fools of mine?" he mimicked in a tone almost identical to hers.

Chapter 3

ELLEN FOUND HERSELF immersed in pure darkness. Believing that she was dreaming, she closed her eyes and then reopened them only to discover that it was real. Scrambling in circles, she sought to touch a solid platform. Fear overwhelmed her as she began to comprehend that there was nothing supporting her—just air. Never before had she been afraid of the dark, but this was a peculiar kind of darkness.

Heart-wrenching wails screeched two feet in front of her, stopping her dead in her tracks. Something soared by the right side of her body, causing a gust of wind to swiftly brush over her right shoulder. Panicking, she drifted backward to escape it.

"Jesus, please, help me. I need You, sweet Jesus, because I'm afraid. Take my hand and guide me through this," she begged while tears rushed down her face. "I'm lost. Where are You, Jesus? You said in Hebrew 13:5 that You would never leave us or forsake us. You said that You would always be there to the end. I need You now, Jesus. Please, take my hand and guide me, Father." She formed her hands in a praying position.

She observed a faint light in the distance that seemed to be nearing her location just as another toe-curling scream blared from within the darkness, causing her to tremble. Refocusing her attention in the direction of the light, she noticed that it had expanded. Another tormenting scream blasted directly above her head, followed by a gust of wind, which caused her hair to blow fiercely.

"Lord, please, help me," she prayed again as the howling became more frequent and intense. Gusts of wind swirled all around her as if she had been swept up by a miniature storm. She desperately wanted to see who or what was creating the nerve-rattling shrieks, but the dense darkness left her completely blinded.

"No! No! No! No!" a strange and abrasive voice roared out of nowhere.

Planting both hands on her ears in an attempt to block out the frightening screams, she shut her eyes a second time. Sobbing uncontrollably, she couldn't wipe the tears from her cheeks fast enough. Petrified, she began quoting the 23rd Psalm.

"The Lord is my shepherd, I shall not want. He maketh me to lie down in green pastures; He leadeth me beside the still waters."

Intimately speaking to the Savior, she stretched her hands upward. "Father, I know that I'm Your child. You said that I had nothing to fear. You promised to protect and keep me always, and Jesus, I take You at Your word. Father, You said to be absent from the body is to be present with You. I don't see You. Where are You? Your word is infallible."

"Open your eyes," a soft voice whispered from within the darkness and amid the terrifying screams.

Even more paralyzed by fear, she refused.

"Open your eyes, Mary Ellen Sutton. Thou art safe," the voice reassured her.

Not sure what she would encounter, she complied, and what she saw before her sent warm vibrations through her trembling body. In amazement, she stared at the lovely scene. Before her were four baby cherubim with glistening faces and snow-white garments. Their eyes were fiery, their hair was like gold, and an aura of light radiated from their bodies. Flapping their wings, they smiled warmly at her. They were the most beautiful creations that she had ever seen.

One of them held within his hands a small, solid-gold book, which was bound by a rope made of extravagant pearls. Upon opening the book, rays of light projected from the ruby-and-emerald-covered pages. Ellen couldn't see what was written in it but looked on as the angels read the contents silently, all the while gazing at her.

"Hello, Mary Ellen Sutton," they greeted her.

She didn't answer; instead, she continued to stare in amazement.

"You art Mary Ellen Sutton?" they asked in the same soft, loving, and patient voice.

It took her a few seconds to realize just who she was. Chuckling, she nodded her head. It had been decades since anyone referred to her as Mary Ellen—so long that she simply forgot her first name was Mary.

"Yes!" she responded, still admiring the beauty of the angels. "I'm Mary Ellen Sutton."

They redirected their attention back to their book. Moments later, she observed them eyeing each other and then nodding their heads up and down while circling her.

She tried to track their every movement, but they were moving at too fast a speed. Finally, they faced her with picture-perfect smiles. Their white wings flapped about.

"Mary Ellen, doest not be afraid. Our Lord, Jesus Christ, hast sent us to accompany you on your journey."

"My journey?" she stuttered, looking around.

"Yes, your journey. We were instructed to accompany you on your journey to Heaven."

"Thank You, Lord Jesus. I thank You so much, Father." She lowered her head as tears of joy rolled down her face. "Holy is Your name, Jesus. You are worthy of praise." Forming her hands in a praying position, she placed them near her mouth. "I love You, Lord Jesus, with all my heart and soul. I have longed to be with You in Paradise. Thank You, Lord!"

The angels looked on while she gave praise to the Lord and then bowed their heads in silence. Looking up, she realized that they had joined her. "Praises be to our Lord in the highest. Holy is Thy name, for You art worthy to be praised," they sang in perfect harmony while rocking from side to side. "Holy is Your name forever and ever. AMEN."

"That was beautiful," she complimented them.

"Are you ready, Mary Ellen?" they asked as two of them positioned themselves at her feet and the other two at her shoulders. "The journey ahead is a lengthy one."

She took a deep breath. When the cherubs at her shoulders started to ascend, she felt her body gliding effortlessly. The radiance from their bodies faintly illuminated the passageway when they did so. Minutes into their journey, another heart-stopping screech exploded from within the darkness, prompting her to ascertain that the angels were still present.

"Doest not be afraid. Our Lord is with you."

"What are those scary sounds?" she asked, staring out into the darkness.

"Observe, Mary Ellen." Their bodies glistened more intensely.

When she looked around, she observed thousands of pairs of transparent angels with serious expressions on their faces descending into the darkness. Between them were humans of every ethnic background, and they were bound by their hands and feet with heavy, metal chains. She looked down as far as she could until her view was clouded.

"Where are they going?" she asked after observing no other angels ascending upward.

"They are en route to Hell."

Hesitantly, she asked. "Why am I the only person ascending and so many are descending?"

"Our Lord said that many shall enter into the gate that is wide with a broad way. That gate leadeth to destruction. But few shall enter into the straight gate, which way is narrow, and leadeth unto life. Few shall find that gate."

Attempting to regain her composure, she inhaled a deep breath. "Lord Jesus!" she whispered to herself and then lowered her head with a heavy heart. Staring straight down, she attempted to steal a peek into Hell but was again blinded by darkness.

The cherubs at her shoulders looked at her and smiled. "You can't see into Hell, Mary Ellen, for it is a horrendous place that the human eye cannot bear sight of."

From that point on, focusing on the journey ahead was almost impossible. She found herself saying a silent prayer for all the lost souls descending into Hell.

"Is there anything that you can do to help them?" she pleaded.

"I'm sorry, Mary Ellen. It's not our Lord's will that any should perish, but their names were not written in the Lamb's Book of Life. Remember, our Lord spared not the angels in Heaven when they sinned but cast them down to Hell."

Her heart sank in sadness when she envisioned all the lost souls spending eternity burning in fire and brimstone. How can anyone want to end up that way, she thought to herself? How can anyone spend their entire life on earth and not heed God's warning? Thinking back on all the times that she had disobeyed God, she realized that she, too, could have ended up like them.

"Thank You, Father, for never letting go of me. No matter what, You never let me go. Thank You!"

She continued to commune with the Lord until she observed a dreadful, dead-looking, Jewish male with a deeply sunken face in chains, descending into Hell. His pants were shabby looking, and his T-shirt was filthy and badly ripped into shreds.

"Please forgive me, Jesus. I'm so sorry. I repent of my sins. No! No! No! Please forgive me," he shouted.

When he passed Ellen, he looked straight into her eyes. The look of anguish on his face was more than she could bear; therefore, she lowered her head until he was out of sight.

"What did he do?" she asked as her body quaked from the annoying look.

"He was blessed with great, great wealth, but he fell into temptation. Instead of laying hold on eternal life, he built his trust in uncertain riches. He stole from and enslaved the poor but received the rich. Many who came to him in need were turned away. He fed not the hungry, clothed not the naked, and housed not the homeless. He was blessed, Mary Ellen, that he may be a blessing to many. When he died, he bestowed all of his riches unto his pets. When he chose to err from faith, money became his god."

Another one of the angels turned to her and said, "Our Lord said that a rich man shall hardly enter into the kingdom of Heaven. It shall be easier for a camel to go through the eye of a needle. He said, 'Lay not up for yourself treasures on earth, where moth and rust doest corrupt, and where thieves break through and steal. But lay up for yourself treasures in Heaven, where neither moth nor rust doest corrupt, and thieves doest not break through and steal.' Our Lord said that where your treasures art, there shall your heart be also. He loves a cheerful giver. Remember, Mary Ellen, the love of money is the root of all evil."

"He wasn't dressed as if he was rich," she replied.

"Remember, you brought nothing into this world, and it is certain that you can take nothing out."

"I read that in the book of Timothy."

"That is correct, Mary Ellen."

"What are your names? Oh! Please, excuse my manners. I forgot to ask." She laughed. Her cheeks turned rose-red.

"My name is Peace."

"My name is Meek."

"My name is Humble."

"My name is Truth."

"You're all named after Jesus—how beautiful."

Ellen closed her eyes and attempted to visualize the magnificence that awaited her. She thought about what she would say or do upon laying eyes on the Savior: kiss His hand, kneel down and kiss His feet, praise His name, or shout. She figured that she might even pass out and have to be revived.

Anticipation got the best of her, but she was abruptly brought back to reality when another chilling yelp roared several feet ahead. A middle-aged, Native-American male, covered with lesions and with widely dilated eyes, swooped down.

"Help me! Help me! I know now!" he cried out in a terrified and appalling tone.

"What did he do?" she asked Peace.

"He simply did not believe."

"Well, that alone will earn you a free, first-class ticket down there, won't it?" Sadly, she shook her head from side to side.

"You must believe, Mary Ellen. You must believe."

Seconds later, a stocky black man with salt-and-pepper hair swiftly passed them. Remembering the haunting look on the face of the rich man, she avoided eye contact. Instead, she focused on the cherubs at her side. Only after he passed did she attempt to steal a quick peek.

"What about him? What did he do, Peace?"

"He wouldn't forgive his father for physically abusing him as a child. He resented his father's actions and fled his abuse at an early age, hardening his heart toward him as he aged. His father, recognizing his sins, pleaded with his son for forgiveness, but his pleas were rejected. He lived his life hating and never forgiving, and he breathed his last breath unforgiving. Mary Ellen, our Lord said that if you forgive men of their trespasses, your Heavenly Father will also forgive you. But if you forgive not men of their trespasses, neither will your Father forgive yours. He said to put away all anger, bitterness, malice, and wrath, and to be kind, tenderhearted, and forgiving to one another—not letting the sun go down upon your wrath. Mary Ellen, our Lord said to love your enemies and bless them that persecute you and not curse them."

The next minutes were spent chatting about Paradise. She thought about all the prophets, the women of the Bible, and even the disciples she had read about. There were so many inhabitants of the Old and New Testaments that she wanted to assemble with, but the one person whom she desperately wanted to meet, after God and Jesus, of course, was the thief on the cross. Researching the contents of the Bible in her mind, she realized that his name was never mentioned, only his occupation. To her, he symbolized just how forgiving Jesus is. Here, a thief, within minutes of dying and facing a lifetime of torment was saved because he acknowledged Jesus as the Messiah, admitted that he was a sinner, and asked for forgiveness. She desperately wanted to know his name and what prompted him to ask Jesus to remember him in Paradise.

"I will love more. I promise. Give me one more chance to love everybody. Please! Please! Give me one more chance, please. I can change."

Ellen's thoughts were interrupted by the sound of a very soft and remorseful voice.

"Peace, I take it that he didn't love?" she asked as a young, bald, white male coasted by her. Engraved on his upper arm was a large tattoo of a swastika. The remorsefulness in his voice and the look of anguish on his face saddened her heart. "What is his history, Peace?"

"He likened unto his own kind, reserving love for his own race and fearing that which was foreign to him. Our Lord, Jesus Christ, said from the beginning to love one another. Mary Ellen, there is no fear in love, but perfected love casts out fear, because fear hath torment. Our

Lord says, 'He who is in light and hates his brother is in darkness, walks in darkness, and knows not where he goes because the darkness has blinded his eyes. If a man says he loves God and hates his brother, he is a liar. How can he love not his brother whom he hath seen, and love God whom he hath not seen? He who loves God loves his brother also, for God is love."

"I understand," she responded, nodding her head up and down.

Just then, another deafening and beastly cry blasted rearward of her. Her heart raced over a hundred beats per minute, and she abruptly stopped in her tracks. The cherubs halted their journey.

"Can I return and warn my friends?" An Asian male bound in chains begged the two angels stationed at his side. His ashen skin had nearly lost all its pigment, his eyes had sunk like small craters, and his flesh had shriveled, visibly showing his skeletal frame. "Let me warn them so they won't end up like me. If they hear my cry, then they will heed my warning," he pleaded as his appalling voice faded into the darkness.

"Why is he going to Hell, Peace?" Ellen inquired again.

"He lusted after strange flesh, Mary Ellen."

"He lusted after strange flesh," she repeated to herself.

Being elderly in age and growing up in a traditional era, she couldn't quite comprehend just what Peace was saying. A puzzled look covered her face. She looked at him, struggling to understand.

"Yes, he lusted after strange flesh. He found pleasure in men, the kind that should be found in women. He was ministered to by many saints who sought to set him on the path to righteousness, but he refused to heed those warnings. He chose to live life in his favor rather than our Lord's. Mary Ellen, our Lord gave him over to vile affection, where he dishonored his own body, burning in lust. Knowing the judgment of our Lord, anyone who commits these things is worthy of death. Do you remember Sodom and Gomorrah?"

"Oh! I see, Peace. You're talking about that kind of strange lust. I see now." She chuckled from embarrassment. "As you get older, it takes the brain a little longer to comprehend." She burst into laughter.

"That's OK, Mary Ellen."

Again, she inventoried the thousands of souls descending toward Hell. Scanning her surroundings, she observed from a tad of a distance a young-looking, black male whom she estimated to be somewhere around twenty years of age. He, too, was screaming and displayed an agonizing facial expression that sent chills up and down her spine. As he neared her, she observed him to be much younger. Just as she formed her lips to inquire about the youth, she was cut off by an angel soaring at full speed. He was much larger in stature than the cherubs and was ascending toward Heaven. In his hands was a white bassinet with a shimmer of light projecting from it.

As if time had stood still, all the other angels paused for him, and a dead silence fell over the lost souls. Backing away, they cleared a pathway for him to soar. When he passed Ellen, she couldn't help but notice the loving look on his face as he cradled and transported the bassinet with exceptional care.

She also caught a glimpse inside the bassinet. Lying still under a milky-white blanket was an infant. She wasn't able to determine the sex but observed that the dark-haired baby seemed to be sleeping peacefully. Soaring rapidly and silently, the angel allowed nothing to disturb him. Only after he had disappeared did all the other angels carry on with their assignments.

"It's always a tragic event when a baby dies," Ellen stated as she continued to survey the lost souls.

"She was stillborn at birth. The angel, Galilee, is transporting her to Paradise where our Lord shall restoreth her soul," Peace informed her. "She shall reside eternally with our Lord."

She smiled at Peace, regaining sight of the youngster. "Peace, how old is that kid over there?"

"He's sixteen."

"He died so young."

"He disobeyed his parents, cursed their name, and stole from them. He rose up against his father and smote him. In the Ten Commandments, our Lord's law says to honor thy father and thy mother that thy days may be long upon the land. Our Lord also said that if any shall smite or curse their father and mother, they shall surely be put to death."

"Peace, are all the deceased heirs to the throne in Heaven?"

"Yes, Mary Ellen, but many souls are resting behind our Lord's altar awaiting His return."

"Why is it that my soul isn't resting behind the altar?"

"Mary Ellen, the sons of God dare question our Master's authority; we simply carry out His will. Perhaps our Lord has a task for you. Perhaps He wants to talk with you or teach you something. It could be that our Lord wants you near Him now. Whatever the matter, our Lord's will be done."

They continued on their journey, engaging in deep conversation. As the history of hundreds of lost souls was disclosed, Ellen desperately wanted to reach out to them with a hug, but she knew there was nothing that she could do. She tried focusing on the prize at the end of the journey, but the howling kept sounding from every direction. Suddenly, it dawned on her. The cherubs knew who she was upon their initial encounter.

"They never asked me my name," she mumbled to herself as she thought back. "Peace, how did you know I was Ellen?"

He stared at the other cherubs, and they all smiled at each other. None of them dared to speak but looked lovingly at her for the longest time.

"What? What is it, Peace?" Ellen asked, studying their facial expressions. "Have you been with me before?"

They remained silent as she waited impatiently for an answer.

"Have you been with me before?" she asked a second time.

"We've been with you, Mary Ellen," Truth admitted. His plush wing brushed gently against her ankle.

"I mean before now."

"Yes! Before now."

"When were you with me?"

He didn't respond; instead, he made eye contact with Humble. After eyeing each other, they looked at Ellen. "Mary Ellen, Satan had strongly desired to sift your life for a time because your faith could not be shaken," Truth began to share with her what she desired to know. "He commanded many demons to earth to destroy you, but our Lord would not allow him to have you. Our Lord looked down on you with favor."

"Mary Ellen, on the 6 of May, 1970, you were crossing the street at Broadway and Chestnut—"

"I was almost killed by a car," she interrupted after vividly recalling the incident. "It was coming straight at me and proceeding so fast, but it lost control. The car swerved out of control. I don't know how it missed me."

"Our Lord sent us to protect you. Our Lord blocked it," Truth smiled at her.

"The car swerved," she mumbled.

"It could not pass by us," Meek replied.

Tears swelled in her eyes again. The incident still impacted her so that she covered her face with her hands and wailed. "Oh, Father!" she said. "I praise Your Holy name. Thank You!"

In an attempt to stop her hands from trembling, she tucked them beneath her armpits and stared off into the darkness only to be reminded of the many souls Satan was able to obtain. Quickly, she directed her attention back to Truth.

"What else, Truth?" she whispered.

"Mary Ellen, you were walking home on the 6 of July, 1971. Satan disabled your car at work; therefore, you caught city transportation. You noticed not a tall and stocky man walking behind you. He sought to rob you of your belongings and take your life with a knife. Your neighbor, passing by, picked you up and drove you home."

"I don't remember that."

"Our Lord blocked it."

"You were there?" she asked.

"We were there."

"Mary Ellen, Satan desired you at your death, but our Lord would not allow him to touch His anointed."

"The impressions in the chair, were they you?"

"We were there, Mary Ellen," Meek reassured her. "We waited until you crossed over, where we were reunited to accompany you on your journey."

"Mary Ellen, on—" Meek was about to continue but was interrupted by heavy sobbing.

"I understand, Meek," she replied.

"It's OK, Mary Ellen."

It became clearer and clearer just how much God had done for her. In her lifetime, she had always given great thought and much praise to the Lord for all the trials and tribulations that He had brought her through, but she hadn't given a lot of thought to unforeseen misfortunes that never impacted her life because of God's intervention. For a minute, she thought back to a moment on earth when she attended Sunday service, and Reverend Shannon Reed preached a sermon titled, "God Blocked It." Her heart rejoiced. A part of her was curious to know more, but she decided that she was content with what she had already heard.

"Forgive me, Lord Jesus," she stuttered, trying to regain her composure.

"It is OK, Mary Ellen," Meek assured her. "Our Lord knows your heart."

She spent the following hours sobbing over God's goodness while the cherubs remained silent. At times, she smiled while wiping away her tears, and at other times, she bowed her head in prayer.

"Are we almost there?" she asked after realizing that they had been travelling for quite some time.

"Almost," Peace replied. "We still hath a bit to go."

She turned back to the lost souls. By now, it had become easier for her to watch as they descended, and even the frightening expressions on their faces became bearable. To her, the scene displayed as large raindrops in a heavy downpour of rain. In the midst of all the lost souls, she caught a glimpse of another person ascending to Heaven. The black male was also ripe in age, bald on top, and was being escorted by four cherubim.

"Peace," she exclaimed with enthusiasm and then pointed to her left. "He's ascending, too."

"That is correct, Mary Ellen."

"Who is he?"

"He's a man of God, Mary Ellen. He submitted himself fully to the will of our Lord and walked by faith. He committed his life to ministering to all who would listen, winning over thousands of souls for our Lord. He fed the hungry, clothed the naked, and visited the sick and imprisoned. He honored his father and his mother, that his days upon the land were long. He kept his marriage bed sacred and remembered the Sabbath, keeping it Holy. He bore not false witness against his neighbor and fasted and communed with our Lord much. He did not kill or steal and acknowledged no other God but our Lord."

She unconsciously clapped her hands and praised the Lord because the works of the elderly man overwhelmed her heart with joy. So consumed, she almost overlooked a narrow stream of light just ahead of her, but the indescribable luster of the light and the cherub's facial expressions told her that they were nearing the end of their journey. Watching attentively and not wanting to miss anything, she refused to blink. Entering into it, she felt a soft texture that closely resembled clouds. Standing at the boundary of darkness and light were Seraphim Angels who were all adorned in white attire with eyes both in the front and rear of them. On both sides of them were angels holding chains. Kneeling before the angels were souls who displayed that same ghastly expression she had witnessed too many times during her journey. Behind the angels was a narrow stream of light that shined like nothing on earth. Expecting to stop in front of the angels like the others, she was surprised when they passed by and entered into the beautiful light. She found herself being lifted upward until they came to the end of it. Situated straight ahead of her about fifty yards were very large gates. They were immaculate, pearly-looking, giant in height, and spanned farther than the human eye could see.

"You can walk now, Mary Ellen," Peace instructed as they neared the gate.

Her heart pounded. She was well aware of that gate. A smile lit across her face when she observed several angels standing outside.

"Jesus! Jesus!" she shouted and then bolted for the front door. As she did so, it opened, and a very large angel, standing over fifty feet in height, walked out. His garment, hair, and eyes radiated like the sun, and his wings were gigantic. After Peace handed him his book, he opened it and silently read the contents.

"Doest thou attest that she is Mary Ellen Sutton?" he asked in a tone of voice that roared like thunder.

"I do," Peace smiled and then looked at Ellen and nodded his head up and down.

Staring at her, the colossal angel smiled. "Come in, Mary Ellen Sutton," he instructed.

When they all entered the gate, it closed behind them with extreme force and was secured by an angel shaped in the form of a flaming sword. Inside, angels lined up along the gate.

"Well done," the angel informed the cherubs.

Peace, Truth, Meek, and Humble nodded and then smiled back at the large angel. Their journey had come to an end.

"Our job is done, Mary Ellen," Peace informed her and then flew away.

Ellen wanted to call out to them, but she remained silent. She was immediately approached by another angel who was a bit larger than the cherubs. He was also dressed in snow-white attire, and he, too, displayed a beautiful smile on his face. "Welcome, Mary Ellen Sutton," he stated. "I am Bethlehem."

"H-he-hello!" she stuttered.

"Come with me," he replied and then held out his hand.

"Am I going to see God and Jesus?"

"In time," he responded.

"OK!"

After taking his hand, she was led down streets made of pure, sparkling, transparent gold. They passed many structures: enormous castles and beautiful temples, but most were mansions. There were millions of gorgeous mansions, and many looked to be unoccupied. Each had its own elaborate designs and was accented in precious gems. Everywhere she looked, she saw angels going about their business. Out of the corner of her eye, she observed the elderly, black male that had ascended to Heaven. He was being led down another street by an angel.

"The gigantic angel at the Pearly Gates—was that Michael?" she asked as they strolled down the street.

"No. That was Raphael."

"He's really big."

"Wait until you see Michael," he replied with a grin.

Bethlehem led her to a one-story building that had large, golden stairs in front, huge columns embedded with jewels, and several uniquely sculptured doors. It spanned for blocks. When Ellen entered the building, she observed a large spa, which was also surrounded by huge columns. Over the steaming water was a rainbow of rich colors that stretched from one end to the other. A sweet aroma filled the air, and angels flew about, tending to their duties.

"Step in, Mary Ellen," Bethlehem instructed.

She quickly disrobed and then stepped into the water. At once, the soothing, bubbly water rejuvenated her.

"Where am I?" she asked.

"The Fountain of Revitalization."

Two angels flew down and stood on both sides of her. Gripping her arms and supporting her back, they dipped her body in the spa, and when she emerged, she felt reborn.

"I feel renewed."

"Thou art renewed," Bethlehem replied. "You can come out, Mary Ellen."

After stepping out of the spa, the angels clothed her in a solid-white robe that was held in place by a white sash, and sandals were provided for her feet.

"Can I see my Savior?" she begged.

Bethlehem held out his hand and smiled, "Come with me."

He led her back down the golden street until they came to a massive temple somewhere in the middle of Paradise. It was a majestic temple fit for only a King. Words could not describe the beauty that it displayed. Throne Angels flew all around the temple, and two large Seraphim Angels stood at the door. From within, the glorious sounds of hymnals were being harmonized. They approached the front entrance.

"Take off your shoes, Mary Ellen, before you enter. This is our Creator's Holy Temple, and the ground on which you stand is very Holy," Bethlehem instructed.

She quickly removed her footwear and then took a deep breath. The angel at the door smiled at them and then allowed them to enter. Once inside, Ellen observed several Elder Angels sitting in decorative chairs aligned in rows. Flying around a huge throne were Throne Angels. Nothing could have prepared her for what she witnessed next. Seated on His throne was who she had lived for and cherished the thought of all her life, our Heavenly Father. Words could not describe the Creator. Tears gushed down her face as she kneeled down and lowered her head because she did not feel worthy to behold the awesome sight of Holiness. Everyone in the temple kneeled down, bowed their heads, and then sang songs of praise.

"Praises to the Lord, for He is Holy. Glory be to God in the highest, for He is worthy to be praised. Hallelujah! Hallelujah! Praises be to the King of Kings. You art worthy to be praised."

The next hours were spent in joy in the temple, praising the Holy Father. After the praises concluded, everyone began to leave the temple except the Elders and Throne Angels. Ellen felt like staying there forever and praising the Lord, but she followed Bethlehem out of the temple.

"Come with me," he instructed her. They walked for several minutes down the street. From afar, Ellen spotted a man dressed in a solid-white robe standing in front of one of the temples surrounded by angels. She trembled after she observed His hair to be like that of lamb's wool. Without a doubt, she knew it was the Messiah.

"Jesus! Jesus!" she yelled and then bolted toward the Son of Man. Upon reaching Him, she dropped down on both hands and knees and bowed her head. Immediately, the large holes in both of His feet caught her attention, causing her mind to revisit the cross. Trembling with unimaginable joy, she gently stroked the holes with her fingers. Tears streamed down her cheeks and onto His feet. Too overcome by emotion, she couldn't speak. She just wiped the tears with her hair and garment. Without thinking, she kissed His feet and shouted out with joy.

"Jesus! Jesus! Thank You, Jesus. You made this sacrifice for me. Thank You, Jesus. I love You, Lord. I praise Your name." She clung to His feet for dear life and cried. "I have waited so long to look upon Your

Holy face—a face I'm not worthy to behold. I praise Your name forever. Sweet Jesus! Thank You, Lord."

"Mary Ellen!" His calm, soft, and gentle voice stated. His soft, velvety hand touched her shoulder. "Get up, Mary Ellen."

Raising her head, she observed Him holding out His hand to help her up. She observed the large, three-quarter-inch hole with withered-looking tissue directly around the edges. She grasped His hand and placed it on her cheek. Closing her eyes, she rocked from side to side.

"I'm all right now, Lord. I'm all right now," she cried, refusing to let go of the hand that had born the sins of the world, the hand that had bled for the remission of sin.

So moved with emotion, she didn't see Jesus crying with her or feel Him touching her hair. He stood there and listened attentively and joyfully to her shouted praises and sobbing. Touched by her sincerity, He gently wiped her tears away.

"Mary Ellen!"

"Jesus!" she replied instantly.

"Mary Ellen!"

"Jesus!" she shouted back.

Jesus could do nothing but laugh as she clung to Him and refused to let go, and the angels rejoiced over her happiness.

"Get up, Mary Ellen," Jesus finally got the chance to say.

"Lord, I'm not worthy."

"It's OK," He assured her and then helped her to her feet. "I know you love Me, Mary Ellen."

"I love You, Lord. I really do," she proclaimed, still clinging to His hand on her cheeks. "I truly love You."

"Today, you art here with Me in Paradise."

"And I'm never leaving, I promise. I'm staying with You forever. You are so beautiful."

"I must go, for my Father is calling Me," He stated. "Bethlehem will show you around." He kissed her on the forehead and proceeded to the Holy Temple.

After the angels introduced themselves and welcomed her to her new home, they spent the next hours escorting her around until they came upon an elderly, but brawny-looking, tanned man with long, dark hair, a long, coiled beard, dressed in a white robe.

"Hello!" Ellen greeted the stranger and hugged him.

"Hello, Mary Ellen!" he returned the greeting.

"What is your name?"

"I'm Noah."

"Noah! How are you?"

"Well, I'm still tired from building that big boat."

"Huh!" she whispered with a puzzled look on her face.

"I'm still tired from building that boat. When the Lord first instructed me to build a boat, I thought He was talking about a toy one. When I learned of the measurements, I said 'Really? You're kidding, right?' Do you know how long it took me to build that boat? I wanted to tell the Lord to just drown me with the rest of them because I can't do it."

Tongue-tied and in disbelief, she stared dead-on at the solemn look on his face while searching for the right words to respond with.

"I'm kidding, Mary Ellen. I'm wonderful," he yelled as the angels laughed at her facial expression.

Realizing that he was pulling her leg, she shook her head and embraced him with another hug.

"Welcome, Mary Ellen."

"Thank you!"

"I'll see you later. I'm on my way to meet Adam."

"OK," she replied and then continued her tour of Paradise with the angels.

"There is someone you should meet," Bethlehem stated as he and Ellen bade the angels farewell. They walked for what seemed a mile until they came upon a slim, good-looking man, sitting on mansion steps reading his Bible.

"Hello!" Ellen greeted.

"Hello!" he stated and hugged her. "You must be Mary Ellen."

Ellen looked at Bethlehem, waiting for him to introduce the stranger who had warmly greeted her.

"You wanted to meet the thief on the cross, Mary Ellen," Bethlehem stated.

"How did you know?" she asked, surprised.

"Our Lord knows all our thoughts," he responded.

She reached out and hugged the thief. They both laughed out loud. Bethlehem bade them farewell and then left to attend to his duties. They sat on the temple steps, laughing and holding hands like siblings.

"What is your name?" Ellen asked. "The Bible never mentioned your name."

"I know! I wasn't quite as popular as the rest," he laughed. "My name is Phillip."

"Phillip," she repeated with a smile. "I have to ask you. What made you repent of your sins on the cross?"

He smiled, took a deep sigh, and then looked away momentarily as if to relive that day all over again. "There was something about Jesus that touched me. One look at Him and my whole life changed. For the first time ever, I had hope. I found the peace and joy that I had searched for my whole life. I couldn't explain it then, but I know now. Mary Ellen, I deserved to be on that cross, but Jesus was an innocent man. As I hung on the right side of Him, I heard Him pray for the world, the people, who crucified Him. He never mumbled one word against them, only prayed for them. It was then that I obtained the true meaning of love. Why He loves us so much, I don't know. But if anyone has any doubt about His love, I'm a living testimony as to how much He cherishes us. Believe me, I know firsthand just how merciful He really is. I witnessed His battered body." He paused. "They beat Him nearly to death. Mary Ellen, He could barely stand." Tears rolled down his cheeks. "To this day, I'll never understand how an ordinary man, and yes, He suffered as an ordinary human, could withstand the brutality the world executed upon Him. Truly, it's beyond my understanding. But He paid the price."

"For us," Ellen interrupted.

"Yes, for us," he repeated. "They hurled jeers at Him from every direction and mocked Him endlessly." Reaching into his pocket, he pulled out a crystal, sculptured cross. "I died, but I inherited eternal life. He gave me this cross and instructed me to go on to Heaven and show it to Michael. It's been with me ever since, and I hold it dear to my heart." Intentionally changing the subject, he inquired, "Have you found your way around yet?"

"I'm just getting started."

"Well then, let's get started." Slapping his hands on his knees, he stood erect.

"I was a terrible man," he shared as they walked down the streets of Heaven. "I started stealing early in life, and it soon became my only goal for living. If it wasn't nailed down, I swiped it, and if I could pull it out of the ground, it went missing. I was too foolish at the time to understand the judgment I was bringing upon myself, but I made that choice. I almost allowed Satan to trick me out of eternity with Christ." He sighed. "But the man you see today is a new creature in Christ. Through God's grace, I am a born-again Christian."

"Did you know the other man who hung on the cross?"

"No, but I'm quite certain of his whereabouts. And I don't believe that he's happy right now." They laughed. "It was the grace of God that stopped me from mimicking his actions, or he and I would be miserable together right now." They laughed again.

"Welcome, Mary Ellen!" an unfamiliar voice startled her. "I'm Moses."

"Moses, how are you?" she asked.

"Well, my back is still hurting from carrying those tablets down Mount Sinai. And when I reached the bottom, those disobedient children of Israel made me angry. I became so angry, I threw the tablets down and broke them. The Lord made me walk all the way back up Mount Sinai, get new tablets, and then carry them all the way back down the mountain again. As the younger heirs would say, I think I have a touch of arthur-itis (arthritis) in one of my hands and back. Do you have any Bengay or Icy Hot on you, Ellen? These old aching bones of mine could use a good rubdown right about now."

"I'm not falling for it again." She shook her head.

"Noah or Abraham must have told you their jokes already."

"It was Noah."

"I should have known it was Noah."

"Art thou telling jokes again?" Jesus asked as He approached them.

"I am, Lord, but Noah got to tell his first. Mary Ellen, I bet you didn't know that our Lord has a sense of humor, did you?" Moses asked.

"No, I didn't."

"He laughs, too. People on earth, when they think of our Lord, they think of this straight-faced and totally serious God. For some reason, they feel as if they have to stand at attention and talk perfectly when they address Him. But that isn't so. They really don't know Him, and they fear what they don't know. If they'd invite Him to watch a movie with them, His presence would be there. If they'd invite Him to share a meal at their dinner table, He'd take a seat. Tell Him a joke, He'll laugh. He longs to share those moments with them. But they know not because they know not Him. If they would only take the time to get to know Him, they would find that they can talk to Him with ease and confidence, and they can be themselves. He's a great listener and a lovable

Messiah." Moses hugged Jesus, kissed Ellen on the forehead, and then bade them a farewell.

"Ellen, come with me," Jesus instructed.

She was led down a pathway aligned with immaculate mansions until they came upon one with a loud din coming from inside. Jesus smiled and then led her up the stairs. When they entered the room, it became silent.

"Is that really you, Mama and Papa?"

She could hardly get the words out of her mouth over the lump that had formed in her throat. She always knew that she would see them again someday, and that day was now staring her in the face. Jesus silently slipped out of the room because His Father had urgently called Him to His side.

"Thank You, Lord," she turned to say but found that Jesus had left. Like a child, she ran and collapsed in their arms. "I've missed both of you so much and have longed for this day. When you died, a part of me died with you."

"It's OK, baby. We're back together now for eternity," her mother stated, stroking her hair.

"Look around, kitten," her father said. "Do you remember any of these strange folks?"

Scanning the room, she laughed. "I forgot you guys were standing there." Everybody laughed, while the handful of family members greeted her.

"It's about time you made it here," her cousin Trey said. He wrapped his arms around her midsection. "For a minute there, I thought you were going to stay down there forever."

"Well, I didn't have much choice in the matter. I couldn't come until the Good Lord called for me."

"Well, He called for me sort of early in life—at thirty-nine, that is," Trey continued. "I must admit, I was a bit appalled at first, until I got here. Now, I wouldn't have it any other way."

The next hours were joyous as the Sutton clan welcomed her home.

Chapter 4

Wentworth lay on the edge of his mother's bed massaging his temples. The funeral lasted for hours and was attended by hundreds of friends and family members paying their respects. Their kind remarks reinforced what he already knew about her, and seeing family members he hadn't seen in decades was rather therapeutic. Truth be told, he was appreciative that it was over because every phase of it carved a deeper wound in his heart. Now he could sit down and begin the difficult and lengthy process of healing, if it was at all possible. Rubbing his nose on her pillow, he inhaled the scent of her citrus hairspray that still lingered on the cotton sheets. Cuddling the pillow in his arms, he glanced at their family photo on the wall.

"Are you OK, Wentworth?" Connery asked as he passed by.

"Yeah, I'm OK."

"Are you sure? Do you want to talk?"

Taking a deep breath, he rolled over. For a minute, he eyed his older brother. He admired his resilience and willpower in the handling of their mother's death right up to the funeral. It was Connery's take-charge attitude that had overseen every detail of the arrangements. To Wentworth, he seemed to take it all in stride. Like a Timex watch, he kept on ticking. When they lowered Ellen's body into the ground, he never allowed a tear to escape; instead, he consoled his brothers. His strength was the foundation for how he, Mabrey, Stanton, and Harper had pulled through this ordeal. He wanted to commend Connery on his vigor, but he didn't want to sound weak.

"What's on your mind?" Connery asked.

"Do you ever pray?"

"No."

"Why?"

"I've never had a need to."

"Do you believe in Jesus?"

"I don't know. I believe He exists, but I believe in myself. I've never had any need for Him; I rely on myself. I guess I'm one of those disobedient children Mama always spoke of." Connery smirked.

"Why don't you have any use for Him?"

"I've always carved out my own way in life, I guess. I've fought my own battles and made my own luck. If I've learned anything from living in this world, it's that it depends on you. I've heard people say that they were waiting on Jesus to answer their prayers. Twelve months later, they're still waiting. That's why I answer my own prayers. The way I see it, Jesus takes entirely too long for me. I can answer fifty of my prayers by the time He answers one."

"Mama use to say that," Wentworth laughed.

"Yep, I remember," Connery replied. "The Good Lord sure is taking His sweet time on this matter." Imitating his mother, he placed one hand on his hip and then swayed his head from side to side.

They laughed.

"So, how are you holding up?" Connery asked, examining his brother's demeanor. "How are you really holding up?"

His first thought was to say OK, but Wentworth knew that Connery wouldn't go for it because he could read him like an open book.

"I'm here, I guess," Wentworth shrugged his shoulders.

"So in other words, you're sinking fast, right?"

Searching for the right words to say, he came up empty. Turning away, his eyes rested on his mother's Bible on the nightstand.

"It's OK to mourn, Wentworth. You do know that, don't you?"

At that moment, he broke down. "I miss my mama, Conn."

"I know you do. I miss her, too." He placed his hand on Wentworth's shoulder. "I miss her, too."

"I'm not as tough as you, Connery," Wentworth finally admitted. For a moment, it felt as if a ton of bricks had been lifted off his shoulders. "What are we going to do?"

"Exactly what she said for us to do. We're going to cling together like an unbreakable chain of five unyielding links. We'll lean on each other for support at our lowest points and hoist each other up at our highest points. We're going to stick together and get through this."

"At least you sound convincing," Wentworth replied.

"I didn't say that it would be easy. I'm saying that it's attainable in time."

"Have you ever felt that you needed something more than this world has to offer?"

"No, but you're not me. Listen, Mama has always said that when a man has reached his pinnacle, but his soul continues to thirst and hunger for something more, it's Jesus that he seeks."

"What do you know about Jesus?" Wentworth laughed.

"I never said that I didn't know about Jesus. I know His history very well," Connery divulged in a factual tone. "What I said was that I depend on me."

"Did Mama teach you about Jesus when you were younger?"

"Believe me when I say that I've listened to her for countless hours as she preached the Gospel. That's all she knew how to do." Connery laughed. "But I've also read the Bible."

"When did Satan start reading the Bible?" Wentworth fell to his knees in laughter.

"I set myself up for that one, didn't I?"

"Hey, you said it, not me."

"For your information, dumb ass, Satan knows the Bible very well. Keep in mind that he was an archangel before being cast out of Heaven. How do you think he deceives so many people? He twists God's word, right? Think about it for a minute. How can he twist God's word if he doesn't know it? Did he not twist God's words when he spoke with Eve in the Garden of Eden? How do you think he was able to convince her to eat the fruit? It makes sense now, doesn't it? He's labeled the Great Deceiver and the Father of All Lies, is he not?" He paused. "And yes, I know what the Bible says because I've read it for myself from Genesis to Revelation and more than once, might I add. I may not heed His word, but I know what it says.

Now listen, I'm going to share with you the best advice Mama ever cared to share with me. Find out for yourself what is in the Bible so that no one can lead you astray. Know it for yourself, Wentworth. I'll give you the perfect example as to what I'm talking about. Take the Guyana Tragedy. Over nine hundred people lost their lives because they listened to one man's interpretation of what the Bible says. One man, Wentworth—one false prophet led all those people astray. How? It's because they failed to find out for themselves. The Bible says to test the spirits, right?"

"That's what Mama always said."

"True, but that's what the Bible says. You'll know them by their fruit whether they confess Jesus Christ is come in the flesh, or if they deny it. The word says know them who are of the spirit of truth and them who are of the spirit of error."

"You sound like an old preacher," Wentworth joked.

"No! I'm just a man who has lived and learned a couple of life's lessons along the way for myself. So, are you rummaging around trying to satisfy a thirst you can't quench?"

"I don't know what I'm doing. For the first time in my life, I feel as if I'm surrounded by uncertainty. That guidance that I depended on for so long is no longer there, you know. Mama was always there to clarify what I didn't understand, especially the spiritual things. She always said that one day we would all realize just how much we need Jesus."

"Do you think you need Jesus?"

"I don't know what I need. Even if I did, I don't know how to approach Him," Wentworth admitted, taking another glance at the Bible on the nightstand.

"Just come as you are: beaten and low in spirit, right?" Connery asked. "That's what the Bible says, right? Mama said to just call out His name, right?"

"Yeah, that's what she said."

"If you seek Him, He'll make sure you find Him; and if you forsake Him, He'll cast you off forever. That's what the Bible says, right? If you ask, it will be given unto you. Doesn't it say to seek and you shall find, and to knock and it shall be opened unto you?"

"That's what Mama always said."

"Find out for yourself if that's what you want," Connery encouraged. "Hey, you have a Bible within your reach. Pick it up."

As Wentworth thought on Connery's advice, a powerful and destructive force spoke to him from within and persuaded him otherwise. He sat there, studying the silver etched letters centered on the front of the bonded leather, and as he did so, a calm, righteous, and more powerful force from within instructed him to pick it up. Baffled, he struggled between the two.

"It's your choice," Connery advised him, picking up the Bible and placing it on the bed beside his thigh. "It's your choice."

"You said that you didn't have any use for Jesus, Connery. Do you ever think that someday you might have to call on Him?"

"I've learned to never say never because I just might. I just pray that if I do, it isn't too late for me."

"You and pray are two words that shouldn't be used in the same sentence," Wentworth joked.

"I need a damn drink." Connery made his way out of the bedroom. "Are you coming?"

"I'll be here for a while."

"OK, I'll find those other three degenerates. They certainly won't refuse a drink. Let me seek them that they may be found."

Wentworth grinned and then laid his head on the pillow. Briefly, he held up the Bible in one hand but quickly placed it back on the bed. He wondered if his other brothers knew as much about the Bible as Connery did and if so, why they hadn't bothered to share it with him.

The smell of Ellen's hairspray brought back memories of happier times and all her teachings. At a snail's pace, he retrieved the Bible, and with one turn of the page, found himself in the New Testament. Reading from the Gospel of Matthew, he scanned over the Immaculate Conception of Jesus Christ, His baptism by John the Baptist, His ministry, disciples, and death.

"I don't know what to say to You or how to say it," Wentworth began praying. "I really don't know who You are. Mama said that You are a comforter, a friend, and a Savior, and to just call out Your name." He paused. "Jesus, I need You," he cried out. "I'm lost right now. I don't know what You can do with someone like me, but I'm here. Whatever You need me to do, I will. I realize that—that I need You, Jesus. I truly need You. I'm a sinner, and I ask that You please forgive me of my sins and come into my life."

Falling out of the bed and onto his buttocks, he cried like a baby. Grabbing one of the pillows, he squeezed it tightly to his chest and then rocked back and forth.

Ellen stood at the front of the Pearly Gates looking out at the elongated and richly colored rainbows that occupied the outer compound of Paradise. They complemented the radiant blue firmament and fluffy, white clouds like a masterfully crafted painting. It was a picture-perfect setting that never disappeared or lost its beauty.

Everything operated in an orderly fashion, according to the will of God. Angels entered and exited Paradise, going about their daily assignments of answering prayers for those on earth. Ellen's heart rejoiced each time she witnessed an angel leaving, because she knew that they were en route to help, heal, protect, or provide for someone who needed God's intervention. Someone, somewhere, was about to receive a blessing.

"Well, hello there. We finally meet," a voice echoed behind Ellen.

"I remember you. You're the preacher I observed ascending to Heaven during my journey," she responded and then extended her arms outward to embrace him.

"There weren't many of us going up, were there? My name's Earl."

"I'm Ellen."

"Have you found your way around yet?" he asked.

"I think it'll take an eternity to totally view Paradise."

"Well, then, my sibling-in-the-Lord, why don't we explore our new home together?"

Just as they started their tour, Paradise halted. The heirs and angels let out hearty cheers and then started clapping. They embraced each other with hugs, and then came more praises.

"Earl, what's happening?" Ellen asked.

"I'm not sure, but let's find out. What happened?" he asked one of the angels standing in the street.

"Another soul hast come to Christ," the angel, Alpha, responded.

"Praise God Almighty!" they shouted simultaneously and then joined in on the celebration. "Thank You, Lord."

Trotting down the path, they came upon a temple with its windows ajar. Inside were pews aligned in double rows, occupied by Heaven's heirs. Near the altar stood an angel lecturing with an open Bible in his hand, and the heirs were recording data in their note pads. Earl became so content that he contemplated entering and booting the angel out of the way.

"Look! There's Jesus sitting in the Garden of Sinai," Ellen stated. She grabbed Earl and pulled him down the path.

As they neared the captivating garden of flowers and fountains, they observed Jesus sitting on a velvet bench. Sitting in the grass all around Him were hundreds of wide-eyed tots. Each had their eyes planted on Him while He read them a story from the Children's Bible. When He held it up to show the pictures, they rolled around in the grass and clapped their hands; it delighted Jesus.

From the corner of her eye, Ellen witnessed Peace flying toward Jesus' location with a small bassinette in his arms. Sensing his presence, Jesus stopped story time, placed the Bible beside Him, and looked to the air. Kneeling down in front of Him, Peace opened the bassinette. Inside was a blond-haired toddler around two years of age whose body was badly beaten and bruised. Lifting her from her temporary resting place, Jesus laid her on His lap, and when He did so, her head drooped to one side. Her neck had been broken during a brutal beating that she suffered at the hands of her mother. Overwhelmed with tears, Jesus lifted His head toward the sky and sobbed uncontrollably. His heart ached. By now, the other children had neared Jesus' lap and were drawn to the lifeless body. Placing His hand on the baby's head, Jesus spoke in Hebrew. The bruising and swelling immediately disappeared from her tender skin, and the fractures in her neck healed.

"Awake," He commanded.

After opening her eyes, she looked up at Jesus, smiled, and then touched His robe. Sitting her upright, He leaned down, kissed her forehead, and then placed her on the grass next to the other children who welcomed the newest heir with hugs and kisses. She found a spot in the grass near the Savior and sat down with the rest of the children, and story time continued. Not long after, shrieks of laughter rang out when Jesus chased them around in the garden. Ellen couldn't help but cry at the touching scene.

"Can you imagine not being here with our Lord?" she asked Earl.

"I wouldn't want to imagine it," he replied. They took a bench directly outside of the garden. For the next couple of hours, they watched Jesus entertain His children.

The fiesta was interrupted by an angel who consulted with Jesus briefly and then hurried on his way. Jesus quietly excused Himself from the garden and began walking toward His Father's temple.

"Jesus!" Ellen called out and then sped to His side.

"Mary Ellen, my Father hast summoned Me. I must go." Wasting no time, He kissed her forehead and then quickly departed.

As she and Earl passed the Holy Temple, they observed angels guarding the door. No one was allowed in the temple when Jesus talked with His Father—not even the angels. Seven hours dragged by before He departed His Father's throne, and immediately after doing so, He summoned five legions of angels to the Garden of Israel. Cherubs secured all entrances while they spoke, and upon conclusion of the assembly, the angels made haste, working diligently to complete their assignments.

"What's going on?" Ellen anxiously questioned Earl after noticing the blank expressions on the angel's faces.

"I don't know," he replied.

"I must find Peace," she mumbled and then bade him a farewell before heading toward the front sector of Paradise.

An uneasy feeling came over her as thousands of angels riding in solid-white chariots passed her en route to the front gate, and others prepared gorgeous white horses for travel. Superior angels kept a close eye on their squadrons and checked frequently to ascertain that the

Messiah's orders were completed as commanded. Ellen finally spotted Peace in the Garden of Sinai tending to the children.

"Peace!" she yelled, half out of breath.

"Mary Ellen, you look worried. Art thou OK?"

"Why are thousands of angels preparing horses and chariots at the front gate? Jesus is preoccupied and the angels look so serious. What's going on? Are they going somewhere?"

"Yes, Mary Ellen, they art. 'Tis that time," he advised her. Tapping the bench with his hand, he beckoned her to sit beside him.

"You mean the Rapture, don't you?"

"That is correct, the Great Tribulation. Our Lord is faithful to His word, and He is returning to earth for the sole purpose of retrieving His church; for He shall not have them suffer through such turbulent times. It's now the time of evil, and the Man of Sin shall come to power for a short while."

She reflected back on the earth's present state. "The signs were visible, weren't they? Just as Jesus said that they would be in the last days: false prophets, wars and rumors of wars, famine, pestilences, earthquakes in diverse places, hatred, betrayal, iniquity, fearful sights, and signs from Heaven."

"Truly, the last days of man art at hand," he assured.

"But so many of them will be caught off guard."

"Mary Ellen, our Lord said that of that day and hour that the Son of Man cometh, no one will know, only our Creator Himself. He warned that thou should stay watchful, alert, prayerful, and careful not to fall asleep, because that day would come as a thief in the night: unknowingly and unexpectedly. Many shall be caught unprepared to meet Him as was the case in the days of Noah. They shall ask where the promise of His coming is. Be mindful that He is not slack concerning His promise as many believe but is long-suffering, not willing that any should perish. They're ignorant of this one thing, that one day with our Lord is as a thousand years, and a thousand years as one day. But know that it's not His will that any should perish."

"Thank you." Ellen kissed Peace on the cheek and then made her way to the Pearly Gates.

The huge convoy incited uneasiness in her. Finding a secluded section, she made a seat in the grass, leaned her head up against the gate, and released a deep sigh. Knowing that so many would be left behind in the Rapture gravely troubled her spirit. Trembling, she thought of her boys. A vision of them burning in fire of brimstone flashed in her mind. Facing the realization that she would have to spend eternity without them was more than she could bear. She broke down.

Knowing all things, Jesus put away His labor and headed toward the front gate to comfort His child. "Why doeth thou fret?" He asked her.

She couldn't answer but could only look upon His loving face. Unable to stop her tears, she did what she had always done when she found herself burdened: crawl to her Rock and cling to Him. Sobbing at His feet, she kissed them passionately.

"Lord, please," she finally managed to utter.

"Stand up, Mary Ellen," He instructed. Kneeling down, He seized her by both arms to help her to her feet. "Why doeth thou cry?"

"My boys, Lord," she pleaded.

"Mary Ellen, weep not," He instructed.

"Lord, if it be Your will, please, bless me to have just one of my boys with me in Paradise."

"Mary Ellen, I've heard your cries," He responded. Speaking no further on the matter, He changed the subject. "Come with me." Taking her by the hand, He led her outside the gate.

Learning early in life never to question His word, she tried to stand on her faith. "Where are we going?" she asked.

"I remembered thy prayer. Thou asked Me if thou couldst one day walk as the children of Israel when they fled Egypt."

"That was so long ago," she responded in awe.

Stretching forth His hands, wondrous blue-and-turquoise tides emerged, forming the Red Sea, which spanned outward over thirteen hundred miles in length and over two hundred miles in width. Drawing his sword, Raphael pierced the surface, and it parted to form a path as it had in the days of Moses. The waters rose on both sides to tremendous heights, exposing the seabed, which displayed fine, crystalline, white sands, colorful seashells, plant life, coral reefs, and boulders of various masses.

By now, the heirs of Heaven, both young and old, had taken note of the incident and rushed outside the gate. Mesmerized, they looked on in awe as Jesus brought forth amazing sea animals of all kinds. Seals, sharks, whales, and dolphins all swam together in harmony while schools of fish swam in formation.

Ellen had already journeyed to the edge of the water where she waited for the Messiah to give the OK. With one nod of His head, she kicked off her sandals and hit the sand running like a little kid, yelling and screaming out His name. It was all the other heirs needed to see. Before long, the parting-of-the-sea was populated with thousands of Jesus' children.

"Thank You, Lord. Thank You, Lord," they yelled.

Standing with the angels, the Messiah watched as His children walked, ran, swam, and crawled about, while sea creatures swam to the passageway to solicit warm embraces and piggyback the little children on treasure hunts.

"I remember this well, Lord, only we weren't laughing then," Moses commented. "I remember You holding back Pharaoh's fierce army with fire while we crossed this sea. Just when we thought there was no way, You made one."

All the biblical giants: Daniel, Abraham, Joseph, Isaac, Sarah, Esther, Lot, Elijah, Elisha, Abel, Sampson, Paul, Matthew, Jonathan,

Isaiah, Joshua, Jeremiah, Ezekiel, Shadrach, Meshach, Abednego, Jonah, Joel, Amos, Obadiah, Micah, Shem, Ham, Japheth, and others gathered to rejoice at the joyous sight.

"Come, Father," Shem yelled out to Noah when he passed by.

"Thanks, son, but I've seen enough water in my lifetime—if I'm not mistaken, forty days and forty nights, not including the year we spent in the ark while the waters receded," he joked. After winking at Jesus, he then journeyed on his way toward the other end of Paradise.

Ellen set out to walk the entire passageway, wading through the cool water. Every now and then, she turned to see how far she had wandered out. Under different circumstances, she might have been tempted by fear to turn back when the gates became more and more indiscernible, but getting lost was a thing of the past and fear had no place in Paradise.

Jesus and the angels reentered Paradise to be about their work in preparation for the Rapture. Every hour that passed on earth drew nearer to the long-awaited day of the glorious appearing of Christ. After several hours, Jesus called His children from the water, and it diminished.

After the completion of all duties in accordance to God's will, He reentered His Father's Holy Temple where He kneeled down, bowed His head, and prayed. There, He received final orders as to the date and time in which He would return to earth. Until then, it was an appointed time that only the Creator had known.

Several hours later, the Gates of Heaven opened, and then came a thunderous roar as the mighty army of God led by His beloved Son began its journey. Jesus, in His white garb and in all glory, sat royally on a blazing horse. On both sides of Him and in chariots, were two arch-angels: Michael at His right and Gabriel at His left. Surrounding them were legions of angels maneuvering horse-driven chariots of fire.

Meanwhile, back on earth, the gorgeous, blue sky hovered above and the sun sparkled on the warm, seventy–degree, Sunday morning as people went about their normal daily activities. Mothers sat nearby on park benches watching their children soar on swings and climb on monkey bars, while motorists rushed down the crowded freeways at high rates of speed in an attempt to get nowhere fast. Aircrafts soared above en route to local, international, and exotic destinations, while screeching tires, beeping horns, and blaring car radios filled the otherwise peaceful aura of the day.

Birds flew about chirping as they left their nests in search of food, and homeowners sat lazily on their front porches reading magazines, sipping coffee, and waving at each other in passing. Telephone lines exploded with family members reaching out to each other, while some of God's devoted followers gathered to worship, and others hit the pavement, travelling door-to-door in search of anyone who would take a minute out of their busy schedule to listen to the Good News. Shopping centers operated at half capacity. Consumers browsed the endless aisles of merchandise in challenging economic times, while shoplifters walked nervously about retail shops in search of profitable merchandise to conceal beneath their clothing. Partygoers stumbled through their front doors in search of the first place to lay their heads, while others awakened nude to strangers and strange surroundings.

The Sutton brothers sat lazily in the TV room. The sports channel broadcasted live from the arena in Los Angeles, California, and boos rang out after the home team took an eight-point lead at the half. Potato chip crumbs littered the floor, and the trash receptacle slowly made its way up from half-empty.

Without warning, an intense light suddenly appeared in the sky. Originating out of the east region of the globe and with a luster that overtook the sun, it spread with epic proportion well into the west. The light grew larger and brighter and it appeared to be coming closer to earth.

Wildlife froze in its tracks, birds chirped no more, mighty lions of the earth were afraid to roar, and bees ceased buzzing. The eyes of every animal beheld the light, and the creatures bowed down to it. Among the human race, God's church stood; they knew what that light meant. Confident, they stood prepared and ready.

Coming in the clouds, surrounded by His mighty army, was the Son of Man, the King of Kings, The Alpha and The Omega, the Bright and Morning Star, the Host of Hosts, the Lily of the Valley, the Good Shepherd, the Tender Lamb of God, the Great I Am, Christ, the Messiah, the Prince of Peace, hovering above Jerusalem. He brought with Him the souls of the sleeping.

He sat Holy on His horse, looking down on a fallen world that was once His Father's perfect creation. But now, it had turned away from the truth and likened unto its own foolish manner and evil hearts. Satan had corrupted the once spiritual and peaceful dwelling. Remembering why He had returned, He called for His flock.

"Rise," He commanded in the Hebrew tongue with the voice of an Archangel and with the force of a thousand earthquakes that rattled the earth down to its core.

The redeemed watched as mausoleums rolled back their sealed entrances to the most sacred tombs, and the ground unearthed its coffins six-feet under. Ashes came together to once again form the structure of man in God's likeness, which had been dissolved by cremation, and the waters parted to reveal countless vanished souls that time had forgotten. The dead stood up in their tombs with their eyes planted on the Messiah. But not all were sleeping. Scores of souls failed to rise because they hadn't died in Christ; they were surely dead.

When Jesus, in the Hebrew tongue, commanded the appearance of the sleeping to take form, they were given new bodies and their souls were restored. Their moth-eaten garments were replaced with solid-white garbs that mimicked the Messiah's, and sandals adorned their feet. The living were also given new bodies.

With the sleeping now standing among the living, they were all caught up together in the clouds. Where there had been two people standing on earth, suddenly there was one. Passengers, as well as drivers in vehicles, mysteriously disappeared. Conductors manning trains vanished. Telephone conversations were abruptly cut off. Babies, infants, and kids under the age of understanding or accountability where taken from their parents and caught up with Christ, as were the poor, humble, and meek. Surgeons were stricken with fear after their patients mysteriously vanished from the operating table directly before their eyes. Wives were snatched from their husbands and husbands from their wives. Redeemed murderers, rapists, thieves, and other imprisoned followers of Christ vanished from their cells. Tears of joy filled every grateful eye because their prayers, hopes, and dreams had finally come to pass.

"Thank You, Lord. Praises be unto Your Holy name," they yelled. "Holy is Your name."

Jesus' long-suffering to be with His redeemed had finally come to an end. With His church and the army of the Lord by His side, they set out for Paradise. As unexpectedly as His light appeared, in like manner did it also disappear. The only eyes remaining to bear witness to His glorious appearing were the eyes of the beast. The redeemed had been snatched up in the Rapture, the worldly and evil men (fornicators, murderers, liars, thieves, boasters, blasphemers, unholy, unthankful, proud, trucebreakers, false accusers, traitors, heady, high-minded, unrighteous, idolaters, adulterers, drunkards, revilers, extortionists and the disobedient) were left in ignorance.

An aerial view of the globe immediately following the Rapture showed no apparent change in its population because its inhabitants continued to overpopulate its perimeters from one corner of the globe to the other. The size of the raptured in comparison to the ones left on earth resembled that of a single granule of sand. Jesus' numerous warnings to the world concerning His return had been taken lightly in the hearts of men, and His commandments had been blatantly disregarded. Because they chose to enter the wide gate with a broad way, many were caught unprepared, just as He had warned.

Christ's ten percent stake of the world's six billion eight hundred million people seemed drastically irrelevant as He journeyed back to Paradise with His six-hundred-eighty-million followers. They were the few who had obeyed His commandments and strived zealously to enter the straight gate. They really loved Him because they kept His commandments, dressed in the whole armor of God, girded their loins with truth, and kept their breastplate of righteousness intact. They had resisted the world, living in it but not of it, and had endured to the end. Ultimately, six-billion-one-hundred-twenty-million souls were left behind because they had turned away from the light.

Most frightening of all was that the most powerful force present on earth (God's Spirit) that governed all things, maintained control, limited evil, and restrained the mystery of lawlessness, whose works began in the apostolic days and had continued on into the present, was taken out of the way. Evil was permitted to roam freely on earth, deceiving, conquering, and destroying all that it desired.

→═══ ═══←

"I hate those damn Lakers," Harper yelled as he watched the dominating team make their way back to the locker room. "If Michael Jordan was still playing, the tables would be turned. The Bulls would kick dust from the Lakers' rear ends."

"The *old* Chicago Bulls would kick dust from their rear ends. Be very clear on that. The current Chicago team can barely dribble the damn basketball," Connery replied, shaking his head in disgust.

"Man, basketball will never be what it use to since the old players left. Jordan, Barkley, Magic, Kareem, Drexler, and Bird defined the game. These new players today haven't a clue what it means to really play basketball," Stanton added.

"Give them a chance. They're young. They just need to mature and grow into the sport. There are some great, young players out there today," Mabrey added, reaching for another handful of chips.

"You give them too much credit," Connery disagreed. "We'll never get to see how good they really are because they can't keep their asses out of prison long enough. Wentworth, throw the chips up here," he continued all in one breath. Seeing the large handful that Mabrey had taken, he waited impatiently for Wentworth to pass the bag. "Throw the chips, you bum," he repeated.

Looking down on the floor beside the sofa, he found Wentworth to be nowhere in sight.

"He was lying right here. I didn't see him get up, did you?" Connery asked his brothers.

"I didn't," Harper replied, sticking his head down the corridor. "Maybe he went to take a piss."

"Wentworth," Stanton yelled. Exiting the den, he began searching the first floor of the residence. "Wentworth, boy, answer me."

"He might be upstairs in his room," Connery added, while heading for the second floor of the house. "Wentworth, quit messing around."

"Come see this," Mabrey yelled out in panic, causing his brothers to race back to the den.

"What?" Harper asked.

The ball game had been interrupted because of special coverage from the news media. Around the globe, citizens were reporting mysterious disappearances of loved ones, friends, and coworkers, and catastrophes plagued the earth.

Fill-ins and other news crews worked frantically from their headquarters after their star reporters, Rosie Miller, Gwen Muex, Mahlona Thomas, and Sandra Cervantes-Jones disappeared, and journalists aired from different locations around the globe. Myers Anderson, who happened to be with Juitton Hardge in South Dakota on a medical conference before she vanished, raced to Mount Rushmore to cover a jetliner carrying 246 passengers that had slammed into the side of the mountain. Judging from the bloody body parts and wreckage that spread out for miles, all passengers were presumed to be dead. Simultaneously in Moscow, a monorail plowed into a four-story building and then exploded. The black, dense smoke, falling debris, and the horrible cries of hundreds stirred fear in scores of nearby onlookers. The New Madrid Fault Line and the San Andreas Fault Line shifted, producing earthquakes that were felt around the globe. In the Pacific, tsunamis dispersed waves of displaced water onto shorelines, massive mudslides ravished Australia as well as Central America, floodwater invaded Europe and the Middle East; and Mount Pinatubo, Mount Rainier, and Kilauea spewed out volcanic ash, gases, and hot magma.

Reporter Dallas Maloney, who filled in after Rosie Miller disappeared, suffered a sprained ankle after leaping out of the way of an oncoming motorcycle with no driver. Although in major discomfort, he listened as pedestrians reported seeing unmanned vehicles slam into other vehicles, fixed structures, and sadly, innocent bystanders. Millions of accidents, many fatal, were being reported.

Pandemonium ran rampant as police agencies around the world worked frantically to investigate millions of missing person reports after the public turned to them for answers. Most were ineffective due to the disappearances of their own families and lack of manpower. Large mobs formed in front of the police stations after parents, who demanded to know the whereabouts of their underage children, received no answers. Scratching their heads, the police were clueless.

Militia groups from all over placed blame on their governments as well as foreign governments and occult groups. Tension climaxed among high-ranking officials when countries pointed fingers at each other.

"We need to find Wentworth," Harper stated, opening the front door. He watched in horror while neighbors ran frantically about, crying out for their children. Crashes were heard from blocks away, and clouds of dense, black smoke invaded the sky.

"There's no need, Harper. Close the door," Connery replied, watching his brothers fall apart.

"Wentworth is missing. What the hell are you talking about? What do you mean, 'there is no need?' He's your damn brother, too!"

"He's not missing, Harper. He's not missing. He's with Mama," Connery replied in a calm and convincing voice. "He's with Mama."

"What the hell are you talking about, Connery?" he yelled. "Mama is dead."

"The Rapture, Harper. Wentworth was caught up in the Rapture. It's in the Bible. God removed His people out of the world before perilous times exploded."

"I remember Mama talking about something like that," Mabrey admitted, turning to Harper. "I remember something like that."

Harper, now paralyzed with fear, walked back onto the front porch, accompanied by his brothers. Police cars raced back and forth, their emergency sirens blaring and their rooftop lights activated.

"I remember, Connery," Harper stuttered nervously. "The Great Tribulation has begun."

Connery spent the following hours informing his brothers of the events that were about to unfold. His knowledge of current events and his strength eased their nerves. They were elated, knowing that Wentworth had made it to the other side, but they feared what was in store for them.

For weeks, the brothers sat glued to their television, monitoring the world's chaotic state. Disappearances remained a mystery, and suicides escalated to an all-time high in order to escape uncertain times. Corpses remained piled on public streets due to overpopulated cemeteries and a lack of burial sites. The smell of death and decaying flesh loomed over poverty-stricken islands such as Barbados and Costa Rica, and animals, feeding off dead flesh, scattered half-eaten organs across the ground. In Africa, bodies were taken far out into the water and dumped, further polluting already contaminated drinking water.

When the media focused on international world events, the world caught a glimpse of an unknown political figure originating out of Europe. He had just become a household figure after orchestrating one of the most difficult treaties ever attempted.

He appeared to be middle-aged, tall, and thin in stature, with dark, straight, silky-looking hair. The clean-cut and well-dressed individual had a mysterious aura about himself. Introducing himself as Drexter Luciphon, he was well educated and fluent in several foreign languages. Above all, he took great care to show himself as a peaceful and highly religious man of God.

In a broadcast directly from Israel, he sat between two world leaders: those of Israel and Palestine. After years of violent history, millions of casualties, many failed attempts at peace-seeking, and constant threats of total destruction, the two nations, under the leadership of Drexter, had finally reached a peace agreement. The world watched as the two leaders shook hands as a token of good faith.

Political figures from all over the world stood in awe of the politician's brilliance. Patiently, they waited in line to shake hands and align themselves with the figure they deemed to be a future controlling force.

"So it begins. There sits the answer to the one question that the world has always wondered about," Connery mumbled to himself while staring defiantly at the television. "Finally, he's come out of hiding and revealed himself."

An eerie feeling formed inside Connery as he examined Drexter's hands, fingernails, and forehead for physical signs. Never before had any man's appearance instilled uneasiness in him until now.

His thoughts turned to his mother and Wentworth. When he imagined the two of them together with the rest of his kin, he smiled. In his heart, he longed to see them again. At that moment, an electrifying vibration went through his body. "Mama must be praying for us down here," he mumbled to himself.

⤙══ ══⤚

When the Messiah neared the Pearly Gates, they swung open, and the angels prepared to receive their latest residents. After Jesus and the Army of God entered, the heirs to the throne followed.

They were escorted by angels to a humongous valley filled with flowers. In the heart of it were twelve straight passageways made of stone that stretched for miles ahead and were all lined with white lilies. At the very end of the passageways sat the Hill of Life. On the hill and aligned in a single row, were twelve white thrones accented with jewels. Directly centered above the thrones was the Master's Seat. It was massive in size, pearly white in color, luminous, and accented in pure gold.

When the heirs entered the valley, they observed the twelve disciples: Simon-Peter and his brother Andrew; James, the son of Zebedee, and his brother John; Philip; Bartholomew; Thomas; Matthew (Levi); James, the son of Alphaeus; Thaddeus; Simon; and Matthias, who took Judas's place. They were sitting on the thrones and were all dressed in white garbs and barefoot. Seated royally above them and surrounded by angels whose beauty was unsurpassed was the Messiah, who was passionately looking down and out toward the heirs.

Hundreds of angels flew back and forth, carrying two thick, solid-gold manuscripts, which they handed to the disciples. One by one, the heirs nervously forced their stiff feet to step one in front of the other, near the thrones where they were read aloud their life stories while on earth. Engraved on the cover were the words "Evil Deeds" and the individual's name. Inside, the contents listed every sin the individual had ever committed. As the disciples read it aloud, their eyes watered, their heads sank, and they sobbed uncontrollably. Falling to their knees, they repented and begged for forgiveness. Wails sounded throughout the lines. They looked to each other for comfort while awaiting their turn. Every now and then, a remorseful eye made a quick second contact with the Messiah's, hoping that their facial expressions and demeanor would gain His sympathy.

The Messiah watched as redeemed murderers and serial killers were read aloud the facts of their horrendous crimes and were once again brought face-to-face with their victims. But instead of anger, hatred, and retaliation, they were embraced with forgiveness, hugs, and kisses while they all wept. Redeemed rapists and others who were once deemed violent offenders on earth also stood and faced their past and were forgiven by their victims. Children who had fallen victim to abortion were brought before and introduced to their guilt-ridden mothers. Upon seeing their children and being called Mama, they held them in their arms and begged Jesus for mercy.

Also listed in the book were the number of times that they had turned away the poor, refused to feed the hungry, used God's name in vain, bore false witness against their neighbors, lied, stole, committed adultery, dishonored their mother and father, and every other sin imaginable.

The Messiah also shed tears. At one point, one of His children yelled out, "Thank You, Lord, for the shedding of Your blood so that I can stand here before You today." He smiled and then gently stroked the holes in His palms.

After the reading of the first book concluded, the disciples were then handed the second book. Engraved on the cover were the words "Righteous Deeds" and the individual's name. It listed all the good deeds that the heirs had done: fed the poor, visited the imprisoned and sick, spread the Gospel of Christ, and every other righteous deed. Still guilt-ridden, they listened attentively. Afterward, their rewards were made known. Their heavy hearts were soon filled with gladness as they rejoiced and shouted.

Upon conclusion, angels standing by proceeded to settle them in. Ellen watched as they were washed and clothed with new garbs just as she had been. There were so many that she could hardly keep track as to where they were ushered off to. At once, she commenced her search for her boys, and as she did so, she witnessed families reuniting and exchanging hugs and kisses. Her heart melted but soon sank when she was unable to locate any of her own family.

After the heirs were made ready, they followed Jesus to His Father's temple where they filled the Holy structure. Inside and out, God's children kneeled down and gave praise to the Creator. "Blessed be Your name. Praises to the Lord, for He is good and worthy to be praised. Hallelujah! Hallelujah! Praises be unto the Lord."

Old spiritual hymns filled Paradise when everyone lifted up their voices to give thanks to God Almighty, and holy dancing took place in the streets and gardens. The heirs followed Christ to a humongous palace.

While en route, angels flew past with baskets of food in preparation for the feast of feasts. Upon entering the palace, the heirs observed tables adorned in fancy cloths, beautiful bouquets, expensive cutlery, and elegant crystal. From the sculptured ceilings hung the most exquisite chandeliers their eyes had ever seen. At the front of the palace sat an elongated table prepared for a king.

"Mama," a familiar voice shouted from one of the tables when Ellen made her way inside. To her right, she saw Wentworth sitting with her mother, father, and the rest of her beloved family.

"Wentworth, my baby," she yelled. Tears instantly streamed down her face.

She held him in her arms as she had done when he was younger. He kissed her on the cheeks and embraced her. "I made it, Mama. I really made it. I don't know how, but I made it," he cried joyfully.

"By the grace of God, baby. By the grace of God and His sweet, tender mercy," she advised him.

"Woman, behold your son. Son, behold your mother," Jacob approached them and whispered after he observed them embracing. "Jesus sure is wonderful, isn't He?"

"Yes! He sure is, Jacob. He's a prayer answerer," Ellen responded. "He's marvelous."

When Jesus entered the Palace, she raced over to Him with arms wide open. "I praise Your sweet name, Lord. Even in Heaven, You still answer Your children's prayers. I love You, Master," she cried and tenderly kissed His hands.

After He kissed her forehead, she returned to her family, and He approached the head table. Silence fell over the Palace when He stood with the twelve disciples beside Him. After looking around the room, He addressed the assembly. "For so long, I have desired to eat this feast with you here in My Father's Kingdom. The will of My Father be done."

At Jesus' command, all heads bowed down with gratitude, and all hands interlocked from table to table while the Solid Rock blessed the plentiful spread that awaited them. Giving all praises to His Father, He quoted an intimate prayer of thanksgiving. At the end came a loud and sincere "Amen" as the multitude lifted up their eyes to meet Jesus.

Without further ado, He sat down, and at the first breaking of a piece of bread, the heavenly feast began. It consisted of manna to symbolize how God provided for the Israelites, wine to celebrate Jesus' blood given for all, and lamb to symbolize the ultimate sacrifice.

Ice sculptures decorated every table and maintained their form. The wine flowed freely for all. Little children ran around laughing and playing while nibbling on lamb shanks, and adults fellowshipped while sipping on wine. Jesus made His way around the palace, serving His flock with the angels.

After the feast, the gala took to the streets of Heaven. The heirs spread out to every corner, singing and dancing. Heaven was filled with laughter and joy. Jesus took His seat on the throne at the right hand of God and watched over His flock.

Chapter 5

IT HAD BEEN one year since the mysterious occurrence of the Rapture, and those on earth were no closer to finding answers as they struggled to put the pieces of their life back together. Some speculated that the disappeared had been abducted by aliens, while others incorporated the services of soothsayers, tarot-card readers, and witchcraft. Some turned to false prophets and worshiped idols for answers. But some, fearing a dark and grim future ahead, turned to the Holy Bible for answers and in doing so, turned their hearts to God and repented of their sins.

Many began to look to Drexter in hopes that he might have the answers they needed. No one knew much about the political figure except that he had become very famous and powerful over the last year. His intellect was unsurpassed, and his quiet demeanor and peaceful manner led the vast majority to believe that he was truly a man after God and had only their best interest in mind. No one knew much about his background, and he was very reluctant when it came to answering questions. Some found it odd that he never talked about, nor was ever seen with family members, and when asked, he somehow always seemed to avoid the subject by switching to politics. Basic questions as to his parent's identity, where he grew up, his date of birth, and other known information about public figures remained a mystery.

World leaders from across the globe flocked to hear him speak, as he often headlined world summits. He traveled the world extensively, establishing personal relationships with the heads of all nations, studying their social systems, economic standings, and their military forces.

His rapid rise to fame and power, combined with his political influence, afforded him a top position on the panel of the United Nations. With the exception of very few diplomats, no one dared or cared to question his political agenda, and those who did were ostracized or faced harsh retaliation from their peers.

One thing was certain: he was very methodical when it came to his political tactics. He aligned himself with key political figures, gained their confidence, and then used their influence to gain and persuade added supporters. He seemed to have a natural gift for inspiring others, and he knew the correct things to say and do and the exact timing in which to do it.

After orchestrating the most talked-about treaty ever signed by two nations, he took responsibility in monitoring their progress. At his discretion, the two leaders continuously engaged in supervised peace talks to maintain order. All violence ceased after both nations laid down their arms, ceased the production of weapons of mass destruction, and citizens traveled freely within each other's borders.

At the start of the second year and upon the advice of Drexter, Israel finalized their greatest accomplishment. The erection of the Holy Temple was completed, and the world watched as they meticulously decorated the stone-and-marble structure with only the finest furnishings. It was considered by many to be the most sacred and exquisite temple in the world, one that was truly designed for a king.

Its main attraction, the Mercy Seat, was erected to resemble God's throne and was the symbol of their dedication to Him. It was erected on a high platform with replicas of brass angels encircling it, and it was surrounded by Holy Water, except for a narrow strip that led up to the front for sinners of the world to kneel down, pray, and be redeemed. It was secured in a private sector of the temple behind unyielding glass where no man was permitted but could only view, unless a dire emergency or until the arrival of the Messiah.

To commemorate the defining moment, all Israeli citizens agreed to put aside their biases and reside as one nation, but they agreed to continue to embrace their cultural and religious beliefs. An open invitation to the dedication ceremony was extended internationally. The Jewish nation donned its finest attire and flocked to the temple to give praise to the Sovereign God above. Due to other important obligations on that day, Drexter couldn't attend but sent word of his intentional future visit.

Instead, he organized a conference at United Nations Headquarters and requested that all world leaders attend. Considering Drexter's conference a priority, political heads, with the exception of Israel, opted out of the temple ceremony and flocked to New York. Anticipation ran high as the audience waited patiently to hear what the leader had in store for them. When the cunning, clean-cut figure, who was dressed totally in black, walked out onto the stage with a clergyman at his side, he received a standing ovation. After greeting the audience with a grin, he made his way to the podium, carrying an oversized portfolio.

"I thank you for taking time out of your busy schedules to hear my address. This past year I have traveled extensively, visiting your nations and studying your cultures and your political and social standings. I have spoken with you in depth about your needs and goals for your countries, and you have given me invaluable insight on the needs of this world."

He paused to take a quick breather and to take notice of the engrossed looks on their faces; this boosted his confidence. In the same masculine and distinctive vocal tone, he gripped the podium and then continued on. "My reason for asking you here tonight is simple, my fellow constituents. I stand before you to offer you and the entire world the same thing that was offered to the Palestinian and Jewish nations—a world of peace and tranquility. I offer you the prospects of a stronger, more systemized, take-charge political government."

"Ooh!" the audience responded and then rose to their feet and followed up with vigorous applause, which lasted for well over a minute. It wasn't until Drexter waved his arms that the clapping ceased, and the diplomats regained their seats.

"I campaign here tonight for a unified, universal political power. You have the authority to terminate the so-called superpowers of the world and their invasion on less fortunate countries. I extend to you, tonight, a resolution to war, and that resolution exists in a one world government that will regulate fairness and equality for all nations regardless of size and strength."

Silence overtook the auditorium. Diplomats surveyed each other's facial expression. Before they could respond, Drexter quickly continued on.

"Now, before you reject the idea, I ask that you please hear me out with open minds and open hearts. The sole purpose of this united government is to better serve all nations. Imagine a world government with the capability and the capacity to better respond to world emergencies. Countries rattled by earthquakes will benefit because of faster response times, dispersing much-needed food, water, and medical supplies where it is so desperately desired. People stranded and displaced by tsunamis and other uncontrollable natural disasters will be promptly administered to, whether it be more organized evacuations, faster emergency rescues, or the rebuilding of homes and communities lost in the devastation. They will reap the benefits of returning briskly to their normal, daily, and productive lives in society.

"Less fortunate countries will no longer suffer due to famine and disease while more prosperous countries stand by and turn a blind eye to their suffering and misery. Smaller countries will no longer have to fear larger ones that resort to military violence. With a united World Militia, all can enjoy the peace of world protection."

Rising to their feet, the audience showed their support by applauding and then turned to each other to show their compliance by shaking hands. Once again, the congregation was hushed by the waving of Drexter's hands.

"My fellow diplomats, I attempt my final plea to you for diligence in finalizing this matter. A delay in progress could mean the demise of desperate individuals." Seeing that he had successfully solicited the support of almost every member in the congregation, he confidently approached them as he always did and thanked them personally for their undying support.

Within months and with virtually no resistance, he orchestrated a united world government and army. All nations, even the superpowers, transferred all their power and armed forces over to Drexter, rendering them powerless. It was an army assembled for total domination.

Citizens weren't made aware of the change until well after their leaders had finalized all agreements and then disclosed it in a televised event, leaving them totally defenseless to harm at Drexter's discretion, and those who rejected his political tactics were helpless when confronting their lawmakers. Sensing that their elected officials had made a grave mistake, they braced themselves for an uncertain future. More people turned their hearts to God, repented of their sins, asked for his protection, and began to study their Bibles.

Still, the vast majority continued to open their hearts to Drexter and to cling to his every word. After the event was aired, they showed their support by taking to the streets and rallying in his name. Across the world, large masses of followers displayed signs deeming him the savior and commending his political excellence.

The Sutton brothers sat glued to their television and watched as world leaders all met in Europe. As they were interviewed one by one, they voiced their approval of the United World Armed Forces Protection Agreement.

"How can our world leaders be so damn stupid?" Harper asked as he watched in disbelief. "You can see deception written all over that son-of-a-biscuit's face," he added. "Un-freaking-believable."

"It isn't over, brother. You just mark my words. It isn't over yet. I don't know exactly what's going to happen, but it's a long way from being over," Connery warned, studying the mysterious political figure smiling in front of the camera. "They don't know it, but they've just signed over our lives and our freedom to a stranger, and there isn't a damn thing any of us can do about it."

He was hushed by the airing of the prime minister of Israel who publicly scoffed at Drexter's blatant disrespect for the Jewish nation. Prime Minister Charlton Zebulon expressed his displeasure concerning Drexter's decision to hold the conference on the same day of the dedication ceremony because Drexter knew that he wouldn't miss the event. He also accused Drexter of purposely excluding him from the summit because he wouldn't have agreed to a one world government and followed up by saying that he would not allow the Israeli Armed Forces to be disarmed and leave the Israeli nation powerless. Nor would he participate in sending any Israeli fighters to unite with the United World Armed Forces.

Continuing his attack, he called the other world leaders foolish and followers and not true leaders. He rebuked them for hastily rushing into an agreement that could prove to have devastating results and accused them of sacrificing their own people to further their own secret political agendas for monetary gain and power. In concluding his interview, he stood steadfast on his decision and declined to speak to Drexter or any of the other world leaders at that moment. He stated that he would act in what he believed to be the best interest of the Israeli people.

Drexter denied the accusations and further stated that he would seek to maintain peace by speaking with Prime Minister Zebulon personally at a later date and time. In his usual calm and peaceful manner, he stated that Prime Minister Zebulon was overreacting due to a lack of information.

Other world leaders took the opportunity to rebuke him for his public scoffing of Drexter and referred to his behavior as embarrassing. Russian Ambassador Mikhal Ivor pointed out that his accusations were not only false and lacked merit, they were also fueled by unwarranted jealously. He and other leaders from around the world, ranging from China, Japan, Romania, Germany, New Zealand, Canada, and the United States, denied having hidden agendas and scoffed at his claims of any personal financial gain. Some of them even went as far as calling for his immediate resignation and demanded that the nation comply with rules and regulations established by the United World Armed Forces Protection Agreement or face harsh consequences.

Prime Minister Zebulon responded by saying that the Israeli nation didn't play any part in its drafting; therefore, its rules and regulations didn't apply to it. He further urged that the Israeli people would not hesitate to defend themselves from outside interference if need be.

Drexter publically made a solemn vow to the Israeli people that there would be no repercussions, assured a peaceful resolution to the matter, and urged world leaders to also seek peace. Shortly afterward, he flew to Israel where he and Prime Minister Zebulon met for a private discussion. During the first meeting, Drexter went into exclusive detail outlining the basis and the benefits of the agreement.

Prime Minister Zebulon countered by adamantly standing his ground. Referring to the agreement as nothing more than a cover-up, he expressed his insecurities of leaving the Israeli people defenseless and advised Drexter that he and the Israeli people would defend their nation and their decision, even if it meant the drawing of blood.

After discovering that Drexter would lead the united government, Prime Minister Zebulon was outraged, labeled him a dictator, accused him of harvesting ulterior motives, and abruptly ended the meeting. Highly disturbed by Zebulon's accusations, Drexter left peacefully and immediately flew back to his headquarters in Mount BoeYourne, Rome.

The following months resulted in additional meetings where both leaders adamantly expressed their viewpoints. During Drexter's visits to Israel, the nation rejected his political standings by taking to the streets in protest upon his arrival. Signs referring to him as the devil were displayed for his viewing when he attempted to greet them. Not only did they refuse to disarm themselves, but they demanded that the agreement be withdrawn. On each visit, Drexter's requests to view the Holy Temple were rejected when the citizens used their bodies as human shields to secure the entrances. After stones were tossed at him, with one barely missing his mouth, he bade them a peaceful farewell and left the country.

Deeply troubled by the events that had taken place, Prime Minister Zebulon took to his study to reflect on the future of his nation. Having accomplished nothing, he feared that the controversy could only end one way: war. It was a war that he wanted desperately to avoid.

But the shedding of blood was something that he had gotten used to over the years while living in Israel. After losing many dear friends and loved ones to violence with Palestine, death had become a way of life.

He leaned back in his antique chair and stared at a photo of him and his brother, Oded, that had been taken in happier times. He cradled it in his hands and gently caressed it with his thumb. Kicking off his footwear, he eased down in the uncomfortable chair that had been given to him by his father as a gift upon becoming prime minister, and he recalled the dreadful day that his brother was executed by Palestinian soldiers. Once a peaceful man of God, he had abandoned his faith and had been transformed into a savage animal.

He examined his violent past that was filled with carnage. It often returned to haunt and torment him when he thought of the horror and violence that had been carried out by his filthy hands. During a period in his life, he was proud of the violence he had executed in the name of Israel. In the eyes of many, his unseen face was more famous than a martyr. He remembered every explosive device that he had ever assembled and every location that had suffered the devastating aftermath. Time and time again, he had sat and watched in satisfaction as the horrendous cries of his enemies and the innocent casualties of war produced a smug grin on his face. He vividly recalled the sound of high-powered rifles exploding amid panic-stricken and fleeing crowds and the sound of fatally-injured bodies crashing to the pavement. Sweat poured down his frozen face onto his mustache and dripped onto his dark, long, silky hair. To this day, his past life remained a haunting secret.

How he came back to faith after the Rapture was still somewhat of a mystery to him. It took nothing less than a miracle for Christ to melt away the cold and evil from his heart and replace it with love and compassion. Because of his defiance to Drexter and other nations, he feared that the carnage and violence he witnessed might repeat itself.

"What have I done? What price shall this nation pay?" he questioned Christ. "What cause could You possibly have that could involve a savage beast such as me? What purpose could I serve in any divine and master plan of Yours? I'm just a man, Lord. I am nobody. What is it that You will of me, Lord? What power do I possess that can resist the evil that will violently come upon this nation? What manner of voice do I possess to speak that may cause man's heart to hearken to Your commands? Please help us."

He cried out to Jesus as he allowed his body to fall face-first onto his desk. With the Israeli nation's future hanging in the balance, he humbled himself unto the Almighty God.

After failing to reach the Israeli people, Drexter reached out to the races where he was warmly accepted. They gathered just to obtain a glance of him and hoped that they would be blessed by his presence. Churches and auditoriums were overcrowded with followers wanting to hear him speak. Upon visiting hospitals, he laid hands on the sick and critically ill and healed them for the world to see. To show alms, he provided meals for the poor and hungry and showered the homeless with clothes and personal items.

More powerful and renowned than the pope or any president, everywhere he walked, palms were placed down in front of him. Tears of joy flooded the eyes of most who encountered him, and praises were bestowed upon him by the masses as they reached out to touch a piece of his garment or his hand. Many saw him as a prophet and looked to him for hope. His religious stance and his message of love and peace comforted them.

By the start of the third year of the Tribulation Period, he had summoned all world leaders back to United Nations Headquarters for another world conference. Arriving in droves, they curiously rushed to be the first to fill the rows in an effort to show their endless support.

Drexter's entrance onto the platform garnered a standing ovation from his audience, and it pleased him. The sight of hundreds of admiring faces boosted his ego to unimaginable levels. Dressed in an Italian, navy-blue suit with coordinating tie and handkerchief and expensive Italian loafers, he took to the podium with vigor and energy.

Accompanying him onstage again was Priest Alexander Batteast, who was dressed in a black *collarino* with a white-cloth insert and a cassock. He took a spot in a dimly-lit corner at one end of the stage. Many perceived him to be Drexter's spiritual advisor; however, much like Drexter, his background also remained a mystery.

Addressing the crowd with enthusiasm and liveliness, Drexter extended a hearty and warm welcome. "I've never seen any of you more jovial than I have today," he joked with a flashy smile, which showed his perfect, pearly-white teeth.

The auditorium exploded with a roaring applause. Sensing the vibrancy and energy in them, Drexter wasted no time and focused on the topic at hand. "Your past support has been essential in our effort toward making this planet a better, more organized, more economical, and more efficient united earth. You have displayed your dominating strength in numbers. Your desire to aid your fellow man and your undying determination were key in establishing the world's united government, and I thank each and every one of you here tonight. Please, give yourselves a round of applause."

Boosting their own egos, the audience displayed smug grins of satisfaction on their faces while they congratulated each other with handshakes.

"Thank you! Thank you!" Drexter replied while nodding his head up and down.

The applause continued while Drexter scanned the room. Out of the corner of his eye, he observed Prime Minister Zebulon sitting in his usual seat reserved for the nation of Israel. After noticing his refusal to applaud, Drexter sighed, and his grin slowly faded, but he quickly regrouped when their eyes made contact. He flashed Prime Minister Zebulon a smile. Prime Minister Zebulon acknowledged him with the nodding of his head and a blank stare on his face. Still discontent with the results of their meeting, Prime Minister Zebulon sat patiently in his seat and waited for the conference to resume. Allowing his mind to wander, he assumed the worst and braced himself for uncertainty. When the clapping finally settled, Drexter continued.

"I almost forgot what I was about to say. For a minute there, I became so wrapped up in the ovation," he laughed while reorganizing his documents.

The audience joined in on the laughter, and they became more and more anxious to hear his forthcoming agenda.

"Oh yeah! We must not allow our past success to cause us to become lax and content in our future endeavors toward change for the better good of our society. We must continue to strive for global economic achievement, focusing on methods that would prove advantageous to all nations."

Before he could finish, the audience was nodding in approval. Seeing that he was on the right track, he smiled.

A chill ran up and down Prime Minister Zebulon's spine. He anticipated the worst. After evaluating Drexter's confident facial expression and after sizing up the response from other diplomats, any glimmer of hope that he had left vanished.

"My fellow leaders, I offer to you tonight a solution to economic conflict."

"Ah!" the audience responded with enthusiasm.

"I afford you stable, constant, and prosperous stock markets that will forever stamp out crashes and financial meltdowns that bring into existence periods of great depression as in 1929. We can black-out historical dates, such as Monday, October 19, 1987, otherwise known as Black Monday, when stock markets plummeted around the globe, causing worldwide hardship."

The diplomats rallied on their feet with an applause that almost rattled the structure. Drexter, drawing added momentum from the vigor of his audience, raised his right hand in an attempt to bring a hush over the crowd. After doing so, he continued. "Thirty-five pesos will no longer be the equivalent of one American dollar, or twenty-two pesos will no longer be the equivalent of one British pound. One American dollar will no longer be the equivalent of eighty-eight Jamaican dollars. All nations can benefit from one level economic plateau. Diverse world currencies, such as the Netherlands Antillean florin, Japanese yen, Indian rupee, US dollar, and the Danish kroner will be absorbed into a common, one-world currency. I propose to you tonight to make preparations in enacting the euro as the only valid currency of the globe."

"And who, may I ask, will have the responsibility of monitoring this merger of monetary systems?" Prime Minister Zebulon blurted out, not giving the audience another chance to applaud.

"The European Union, since the euro is their official currency," he replied.

"With all due respect, Mr. Luciphon, you already oversee all matters concerning the European Union."

Drexter stood silent at the podium while the other constituents peered at Prime Minister Zebulon with contempt. Refusing to be swayed by their looks, he continued on with his examination.

"So literally speaking, it is you who will oversee the world monetary system as you already do the government? Am I correct in assuming this, Mr. Luciphon?"

"There will be other world leaders who shall take part in implementing capital rules and regulations and the allocation of world funds."

"And those world leaders, I assume they are present here tonight?" Prime Minister Zebulon took a deep sigh, shook his head in disbelief, and then continued before Drexter could answer.

"Sir, with all due respect, the shekel dates back to the beginning of time. It has also been the official coin of Israel since 1980, and I'm sure you are well aware of its importance."

After standing on his feet, Prime Minister Zebulon reached into his pocket, produced a silver shekel, and waved it around the room for all to see. Acting out of anger, he addressed the assembly in a commanding tone. "It was thirty pieces of these that persuaded Judas Iscariot to betray innocent blood. It was thirty pieces of these that sent an innocent man, the Messiah, to the cross on Calvary. The Israeli people will never part with it."

Turning back to Drexter, he gritted his teeth and said, "Your quest for world power and total domination has been fulfilled due to the ignorance of these men. How will you execute your power? What will you accomplish with it? Your underlying motives remain evasive. Whatever your desire, I fear the worst."

Turning back to the assembly, he warned, "The ignorance that you gentlemen have demonstrated here tonight can only result in total destruction.

Complete power in the hands of one man shall prove disastrous. History has proven this time and time again. Have you learned nothing? Do you not remember Hitler and his quest for world power? Thank you! Because of you feeble-minded individuals, we are all doomed."

He paused for a moment to scan the room at the pathetic assembly that surrounded him. Gathering his documents, he bellowed out without giving one thought to his words, "I cast my fears on the Almighty God and Sovereign Lord above who will defend the Israeli Nation." Looking back at Drexter he avowed, "You will be defeated in your evil endeavors. By the grace of God, Israel will stand as you crumble."

He stormed out of the conference, gravely disturbed by the ignorance of his fellow diplomats. Upon reaching his vehicle, he tore his garment and cried out to the Mighty Lord above. Extremely distressed, he clutched his Bible to his chest and quoted a prayer of protection for the nation of Israel.

Once back in Israel, he silently entered the Holy Temple where he made his way past the secured area to the Mercy Seat. Kneeling on his hands and knees and with his face toward the ground, he cried out to God for mercy. There, before the throne of God, he quoted an intimate prayer of protection for the nation of Israel. Afterward, he denied any further invitations or meetings with Drexter and other world leaders.

Over the next six months, he faced extreme criticism from fellow constituents after his outburst was televised by news outlets across the world. Not only was the tiny nation ostracized by the world, but it was called names and endured constant threats of sanctions.

Drexter remained silent, neither condemning nor defending the Israeli people. Instead, he focused on the task at hand. Whenever he was in the public eye, he took care to present himself as a man of peace and commented only on the transformation.

Within the next six months, the world had made the smooth transition of converting over to the euro. Drexter and a few personally-handpicked diplomats oversaw the affair by editing monetary systems, enacting fresh policies, and allocating funds across the globe.

The Israeli people, refusing to part with their shekel, stood steadfast on their decision. They rejected rules and regulations created by Drexter and as a result were restricted to bartering and buying within their own nation. They were expected to succumb under the pressure of having to rely on their own resources for survival; however, the tiny nation stood stronger and more united than ever. After publically relying on God to supply all their needs, they showed no signs of weakening.

⋆⟶⟫ ⟪⟵⋆

It was now three-and–a-half years since the Rapture, and the heirs of Heaven had settled into their new home and assignments. Earl went about his daily activities, preaching and teaching the word of God to the heirs. That was one of his many rewards from the Redeemer, and he was thrilled to hear it when Simon-Peter informed him. From that very moment, he hit the ground running. For him, preaching and teaching came easy. After all, God had prepared him well for his duties while on earth.

He took his duties as seriously as he had on earth. He continued to study the word of God and meditated for hours without interruption. With the creation of every new sermon, his heart went pitter-patter, and his toes curled. He couldn't wait to stand before the masses in one of the temples and spread the good news, and as always, he gave God all the glory and praise.

Equally fulfilling were his teaching duties. After learning the number of people who rarely took the time to open their Bibles while on earth and those who thirsted for a deeper understanding of God's word, he developed in-depth lesson plans, beginning with Genesis and ending with Revelation. But he never judged any of them. In fact, it motivated him more. The way he saw it, the Messiah entrusted him to teach His flock, and he was determined to do just that. He even welcomed the moans and groans after assigning them lengthy homework assignments, but they dared not show up without it, because none of them wanted to face Michael, the Archangel.

Ellen was also keeping busy. After being rewarded the duties of overseeing the young who had been separated from their parents during the Rapture, she settled into her daily duties, tending to their needs. The way she saw it, the Messiah had blessed her with millions of kids, and she couldn't have been happier. Being a born nurturer, her hours were spent mostly in the gardens along with three angels, Shepherd, Israel, and Grace. She took joy in teaching the children their alphabets, numbers, and reading them Bible stories.

It also warmed her heart to see Wentworth progressing in his faith. Once in a while, when the tots were sleeping, she would sneak away to the temple, stand outside the window, and listen to him speak on the Bible. Looking at him made her think of her four other sons. No matter how she tried to be content, she wanted all of them with her. She constantly prayed for their safety as well as their salvation, and she hoped that one day they would make it to Paradise.

--->|==⊕ ⊕==|<---

Ellen, Shepherd, Israel, and Grace sat on the bench and took full advantage of nap time after countless hours of running after restless little ones. Getting the last of them to close their defiant, little eyes proved to be quite a challenge, and an occasional rollover from one or two of the children was enough to send them into panic. She and the angels sat back for their usual chat, and per the norm, their conversations ranged from Paradise to earthly events. As the first half of the Tribulation Period came to an end, much time was spent talking about the second half and the imminent return of the King, Jesus Christ. Angels kept meticulous watch on earthly events and then reported them to Gabriel and Michael, who in turn reported it to the Messiah. Jesus could often be seen with them alone in the gardens, engaged in what appeared to be serious conversation. From time to time, the saints also looked down on earth from above.

"Why is it that the children go straight to sleep for Jesus? He makes it seem so easy," Ellen stated.

"Our Lord has that special touch," Shepherd replied.

"Well, hello there," Earl hollered from afar while leisurely walking down the golden pathway toward them.

"Shh! Please, don't wake them. They'll never go back to sleep," Ellen and the angels replied laughing.

"I'm sorry," Earl whispered, tiptoed over to the bench, and sat down.

"Class is over early today. Did you give them a break?" Ellen asked.

"Not a break but another lengthy homework assignment."

"What is it on?" Israel inquired.

"It's on current earthly events. Since the second half of the Great Tribulation is at hand, they need to know what's to come. I want them to know how caring and loving our Lord is, and how He spared us from those perilous times that are to come upon the earth. Once they understand that, they can begin to understand the true goodness of God."

"That time has come, hasn't it?" Ellen asked as she got more into the conversation.

"Yes, Mary Ellen, the time of darkness and great sorrow is at hand, and the Son of Perdition shall illustrate himself," Shepherd responded. "The second period shall bring about such times as never were before nor shall ever be again. All will have to make a choice, and many shall be destroyed because of their choices."

"My prayers go out to all of them who must suffer through that spiritual warfare," Ellen sighed. Her thoughts fell upon her boys. "God is still in control, though," she asserted in an attempt to ease her mind.

"He always has been in control and will always be," Earl assured. "He can do all things." Having shared many intimate talks with Ellen, he sensed worry in her voice; therefore, he changed the subject in hopes of boosting her spirits. "Just imagine a new Heaven on earth when Jesus returns. Can you say Hallelujah?"

"Hallelujah," they yelled out in harmony.

"Where is Jesus, by the way?" Ellen asked, looking around.

"He was walking toward the temple talking with Enoch and Elijah," Grace responded.

"I see," she replied.

Earl nodded his head up and down and then looked at Grace, but he decided against verbally responding. His knowledge of end-time events allowed him to piece together what was about to take place.

"To God be all the glory. His word is infallible, faithful, and true. His love, grace, and mercy are endless." Earl rejoiced as he thought about the new millennium. "Well, I must be on my way. I must meet with Daniel." He leaped to his feet as if he was a twenty-year-old. With an echo of good-bye, he darted down the street, leaving a fire trail behind him. Ellen and the angels waved as they watched him take off.

"I'm going to check on Wentworth," she stated.

"May I walk with you?" Shepherd asked.

"That would be wonderful."

The scenic view never ceased to take her breath away, and every stroll opened her eyes to something new.

During their journey, she observed a colossal angel sitting near one of the fountains. To her recollection, she had never observed him in the past. After seeing that his height towered over that of the archangels, she became a bit intimidated.

"Shepherd, I don't believe I've seen that angel before. Who is he?"

"That is the Angel of Death."

Her eyes widened. "Oh my," she replied. "You mean as in Egypt and Pharaoh from the book of Exodus?"

"That's correct—that Angel of Death."

"Where has he been all this time?"

"Waiting," Shepherd replied.

"What do you mean?" she asked.

"Mary Ellen, our Lord's mercy on man is endless. Our Lord is slow to anger, quick to be merciful, and slow to judge. But when man's heart has hardened and he refuses to turn from his wicked ways, our Lord intervenes. It's not often that the Angel of Death is summoned, but when he is, nations shall be destroyed, and death shall linger long after. They shall lie in ruins. Their weeping shall be heard throughout all the lands."

When they passed by the angel, Ellen grinned. Shepherd, sensing her intimidation, took her hand and led her toward the angel.

"Doest not be afraid," he instructed. "He's also a son of our Lord. Like us, he's also loving and kind."

"Hello!" she greeted in a near whisper. She wrapped her hands around him as far as they would reach and gave him a warm hug.

"Hello, Mary Ellen," the monstrous voice sounded. He wrapped one of his large arms around her frame. Immediately, her intimidation subsided when she observed the beautiful and comforting smile on his face.

"Your name doesn't quite fit your serene nature," she joked and then kissed him on the cheek.

He laughed. "Every once in a while, I live up to my reputation."

"Yes, you do," Shepherd replied as he and the Angel of Death greeted each other. "We're on our way to the temple. I wanted Mary Ellen to meet you."

"Would you like to join us?" she asked.

"I must wait here for our Master."

"The time draws near," Shepherd stated.

"The day of the Lord is upon the earth," he responded. "I've been summoned."

They bade him farewell and then continued on their way while the Angel of Death waited patiently for Christ.

Chapter 6

BY THE START of the second half of the Tribulation Period, Drexter had achieved all of his political goals. With a unified world government and world economy all under his control, loyal political figures overseeing day-to-day global operations, and Priest Batteast keeping him abreast from his heavily-guarded abode at Mount BoeYourne, he found the time to travel the globe.

Six months into his travels, he was forced to put a halt to his visit in the United States and rushed back to Rome upon word that Priest Batteast was bedridden. Drexter was kept abreast of his condition via air phone from his private jet. Upon speaking with Priest Batteast and not being able to decipher his words, Drexter realized the severity of his illness and ordered the pilot to push the jet engines to record speed. Hours later, he touched down in Rome where his private limousine awaited. Bishop Caesar was there to greet and update him on the priest's condition.

"How is he?" Drexter asked in a concerned tone.

Bishop Caesar didn't answer; instead, he looked away and stared at the dark, tinted windows. After a deep sigh, he reclined his head back on the headrest. A dead silence loomed over the vehicle as the chauffeur was ordered to hurry. When Drexter reached for his car phone, Bishop Caesar grabbed his hand. Nodding his head in dismay, his eyes drooped.

"I know how close the two of you were," Bishop Caesar finally found the strength to say.

"Is he dead?" Drexter commanded to know.

After a brief pause, he reluctantly responded, "Officials at Mount BoeYourne will take care of all the arrangements."

"That won't be necessary. Stop the vehicle," he yelled to the chauffeur.

On the side of a dark road in the middle of nowhere with no visible structures or lighting, Drexter exited the vehicle. After violently slamming the door shut, he walked several feet into the night. From within the limousine, Bishop Caesar heard two voices speaking in Latin, one of which he recognized as Drexter's, but the other strange and menacing voice disturbed him. He peered out of the window, but the dark shade combined with the blackness of the night prevented him from seeing. Puzzled as to whom Drexter was speaking to, he cautiously opened the door. As he was about to step one foot out, the door slammed shut with tremendous force. Stricken with fear, Bishop Caesar leaped to the other side of the vehicle.

"Drexter," he stuttered. With a rapid heartbeat and escalated breathing, he sat trembling, listening to the voices.

"Drexter," he yelled a second time, assuming that was who had slammed the door.

Terror ripped through him when the limousine started to shake with monstrous force, followed by intense and rapid rocking that lifted the vehicle three feet off the ground. Unable to brace himself, his body shuffled from one side of the vehicle to the other, fiercely colliding with the interior. Catching hold of the seatbelts, he held on for dear life and yelled out to the chauffeur from the passenger side of the partition. Seconds later, the tires crashed to the ground where it came to a standstill. His beaten-up body landed face down on the footrest. Highly traumatized, he inventoried the contents of the vehicle; nothing was disturbed. Sweat poured from his panic-stricken face. Banging on the partition, he yelled for the chauffeur but received no answer. Climbing back into his seat, he inspected the windows for cracks; they, too, were intact.

Minutes later, the menacing voice stopped, and Drexter calmly stepped in. Fastening his seatbelt, he smiled at Bishop Caesar as if he hadn't noticed his petrified state.

"Call ahead to Mount BoeYourne. Have them dress and display the body for public viewing, please, and tell them not to embalm it," he instructed Bishop Caesar, handing him his personal phone.

Bishop Caesar sat comatose in his seat. Severely disturbed, he was unable to move a muscle. His eyes pierced Drexter; his heart raced.

"I'll do it," Drexter stated with a sigh. "To Mount BoeYourne, please," he yelled to the chauffeur, all in the same breath.

Silently, Bishop Caesar stared straight ahead the remainder of the journey, trying to reasonably justify the events that had just taken place.

Upon reaching Mount BoeYourne, Drexter quickly got out of the vehicle and without saying a word, abruptly excused himself from the frantic crowd. Bishop Caesar remained inside until he was out of sight. Only then did he clutch his crucifix in his hands.

Drexter secluded himself in his oversized private chamber and refused to entertain visitors or the media. There, he prepped himself in a black, ankle-length, hooded robe that was held in place by a white, knotted sash. He rolled away the floor covering that meticulously concealed a five-point pentagram centered on the face of a large, horned goat. After placing lighted candles around it, he kneeled down and bowed his head. With his hands out to his sides, he quoted sections of the Satanic Bible and then called out to his Father in the Latin tongue.

By noon the next day, news of the clergyman's death had spread like wildfire. The world watched as the corpse was clothed in religious attire and placed for all to see. Questions of Drexter's whereabouts surfaced as well as rumors of his odd behavior.

With media coverage spanning the globe, Drexter finally made his presence known. Departing from his chamber in a chipper mood and dressed in his usual business attire, he proceeded to view the clergyman's remains. Other members of the clergy, with the exception of Bishop Caesar who had mysteriously disappeared, gathered to watch Drexter pay his respects to the middle-aged, salt-and-pepper-haired priest. Leaning over the black-and-solid-gold-trimmed casket, he placed his palm on the priest's forehead.

"Wake," he ordered, peering down into the casket.

Priest Batteast's heart jump-started. Blood once again circulated through his veins. His pale skin was rejuvenated, his cold, chapped lips trembled, and his rigid eyes batted rapidly from the beaming sun.

Per Drexter's orders, cameras were positioned directly on the casket for all to witness the event. All around the world, people watched in awe as the dead corpse came back to life.

"Rise," Drexter commanded with a shout.

When the priest placed both hands on the edge of the casket, his stiff bones cracked from rigor mortis. Sitting straight up, he inhaled a deep breath. Drexter wasted no time helping him out of the casket and over to the cameras for the entire world to bear witness.

From among the crowd came a host of praises and cheers that traveled throughout the streets of Rome. Taking full advantage of the moment, Drexter relished the praises, which sounded like a beautiful tune to his ears. Stepping forward to center stage, he stood godlike before the media to address the world.

"I hold the power of life and death within my hands," he proclaimed as he held out his hands to the world. "I am a way to eternity."

"Yeah! Yeah! Yeah!" The crowd gathered momentum. Many reached out in an attempt to touch his hands. Guarded by soldiers of the militia, he continued his address. "Follow me, for I'm everlasting. Exalt my name, and I shall be your Savior. I shall sit on the throne of Israel and rule. You shall be my people and shall serve me forever."

"Savior! Savior! Savior!" the crowd rallied.

The televised event was met with mixed views from around the globe. Many embraced him as their Messiah and publically praised his name, but some didn't know what to believe. Some voiced their doubt about his claims and summed up the event as a mere hoax, while others accepted his claims out of fear. But those who had come to know the Lord rebuked him and labeled him a liar and a deceiver. They vowed never to worship him, only the true God above.

⋆⇒ ⇐⋆

Prime Minister Zebulon sat in his study and watched the televised event. Drexter's words sent shock waves through his body, and Drexter's deceit of the masses saddened him. After turning off the television, he rested his head in his hands. He knew that he couldn't fight the powerful politician and that the tiny nation of Israel was no match against Drexter's army. But most disturbing was hearing Drexter promise to sit on the sacred throne of God. After assessing the powerful force that he was up against and realizing that dark days lay ahead, he began to question God's word. His faith began to falter.

"My blood shall spill in the streets first," he yelled out in anger and desperation.

Immediately, the voice of his mother and her teachings began to fill his ears. After his brother's death, she had told him that at one time or another, everybody questions their faith in God. But instead of running away from God, it's then that you should run to Him. She had always instructed him to just open up and tell God when he didn't trust His word and ask God to show him.

"How can I trust You when this nation is up against a power so forceful? How can I not question your authority? I feel as if I'm standing on sinking sand," he yelled out to God in anger. "This nation stands alone. I need You to speak, please. Please, speak to me. Please, show me."

Greatly distressed, he grabbed his Bible. Rambling through the pages, he found himself in the book of Psalms. Skimming through it, the 44th Psalm grabbed him. He read aloud, "We have heard with our ears, O God, our fathers have told us, what work Thou didst in their days, in the times of old. How Thou didst drive out the heathen with Thy hand, and plantedst them; how Thou didst afflict the people, and cast them out… Thou art my King, O God… Through Thee will we push down our enemies; through Thy name will we tread them under that rise up against us.

"But they are many, and we are few. How, Lord?" Shaking his head in disbelief, he forced himself to continue reading aloud. "Through Thy name will we tread them under that rise up against us. For I will not trust in my bow, neither shall my sword save me. But Thou has saved us from our enemies and hast put them to shame that hated us. In God we boast all the day long, and praise Thy name forever. Selah…"

The word of God began to console him. He skimmed over to the next page. There, the 46th Psalm called out to him. "God is our refuge and strength, a very present help in trouble. Therefore, we will not fear,…though the mountains be carried into the midst of the sea; though the waters thereof roar and be troubled, though the mountains shake with the swelling thereof… The Lord of hosts is with us; the God of Jacob is our refuge…"

He found himself in the 56th and the 57th Psalms. From there, he read aloud the 64th Psalm. A breath of fresh air came over him. Looking up toward the sky as if he could visibly see the Lord, a slight grin adorned his face. Turning the pages of his Bible backward, he glimpsed at the 43rd Psalm and read aloud: "Judge me, O God, and plead my cause against an ungodly nation: O deliver me from the deceitful and unjust man. For Thou art the God of my strength…"

Skimming over to the 37th Psalm, he continued to read aloud, and as he did so, his faith was again renewed in Christ, and his fears diminished. That indescribable peace that he had experienced many times before had once again taken hold of him.

"Forgive me, Lord, for doubting You and Your word. Thank You for showing me what I needed so desperately to see. Thank You for speaking to me. I know that You're the Solid Rock on which I stand and cast all my fears. I offer You my highest praise. Please, find it acceptable in Your sight."

As he sat there in the presence of the Lord and meditated on the book of Psalms, his thoughts turned back to his mother. Grateful that he had taken her advice, he closed his Bible.

"You were right," he said aloud, as if she was sitting next to him. "You were right."

⋅→▅◉ ◉▅←⋅

The media continued their coverage of the public's view from across the globe. It wasn't long before they set their sights on Israel. Prime Minister Zebulon took to the airways where he rebuked Drexter's address and labeled him an antichrist and a deceiver. After dispelling his claim to be the Messiah, he and other Israeli delegates, along with the Israeli nation, took to the streets for a prayer vigil to the Almighty God above. The world watched as they publically pleaded to the Lord for His protection.

Drexter monitored the interviews closely. Choosing to overlook the billions of people who had already deemed him their Messiah, he could only concentrate on the nonbelievers. Their mocking enraged him, and his failure to conquer them was haunting. Being the lone heir to the earth's throne, which had been given to him by his father, he had all intentions of ruling from it. His father obtained it when he fell from his original dwelling place and had long groomed him to take over. He demanded everything in it—its wealth and resources—but most of all, its occupants, and he would not be shortchanged by one of them. His satisfaction wouldn't climax until the entire world was on its hands and knees and had their faces bowed down to the earth in front of him, crying out praises.

After summoning several members of the militia, he commanded them to obtain a solid-gold calf and deliver it to the ruins of the Roman Coliseum. With the media standing by and Priest Batteast by his side, they started on their way.

When they pulled up in front of the massive structure, he was taken back in time to AD 80 when it was first completed. He tried to depict his father's description of the original Flavian Amphitheater. A chuckle escaped from him when he realized just how old his father really was, and he envied his father's longevity on the earth. He remembered his father's vivid account of the many different performances with gladiators, mock naval battles, and animals.

As they walked toward the coliseum, he paused to take a look at his future kingdom that would choose to bow before him after his pending show of supremacy. He had every intention of ruling it just as his father had—through lies and deception.

"Thank You," he looked up at the Heavens and stated with a devious smile planted on his smug face. "Thank You for giving Your precious creations the freedom to choose for themselves."

He thought back to his younger days when his father accounted how he had conquered so many souls. One tactic used was the power of deception. It was a tool almost as powerful as love. After all, his father hadn't only invented it; he mastered it.

He envisioned all the deceived and devastated souls suffering in his father's kingdom. There were millions of partygoers, club-hoppers and bar-holics who had been deceived by Satan into thinking that Hell was one big party after another, with all the free liquor they could possibly slurp. They were told that it was equipped with more dance floors, clubs, bars, and DJs than one could imagine, and that "Party All Night" was the number one song on the music charts. As a child, he watched millions go down into his father's kingdom expecting a party but quickly discovered that the party turned out to be an endless, living nightmare. Instead of "Party All Night," the number one song was "Disco Inferno." The oversized dance floors turned out to be five-by-seven and were surrounded by bars with no escape. They found themselves isolated from all the other dancers, and their surroundings consisted of filth, darkness, a nasty stench, and flesh-eating worms.

"Gotcha," he shouted out loud.

His thoughts turned to the rich, famous, and greedy. His father had taught him early on that these were the easiest to deceive, and that the best way to conquer their souls was through temptation of worldly things. That, too, was another powerful tool.

"No matter how much man obtains in life, it's never enough. He'll always want more. 'As his friendship with the world grows stronger, he becomes an enemy of Jehovah,'" he cited his father's words verbally. "That's what you taught me, father. See, I haven't forgotten."

As his father provided them with more and more, they chose to abandon all things eternal and set their sights on all things worldly. They were promised that they could even bring it to Hell when they died. Many went down into Hell looking for their mansions, cars, and fortunes; instead, they only found empty promises.

"From riches to rags," he giggled to himself. "Enjoy."

His thoughts turned from the rich and famous to his father's many worshipers. As a young boy, he had often helped the demons count the numerous souls that had been sold in exchange for power. They believed Satan's idle promises that they would be placed in positions of power when they entered his kingdom. How distraught they were when they were tortured, beaten, and terrorized equally as the other lost souls. They all sought Jesus then.

"Ah! That's another one of your deceptive tools, father," Drexter said aloud.

He was also taught early on that man was considered nothing unless he had power. The more powerful he became, the more respected he was. He was taught to build human beings up and make them think that they were invincible.

"I still remember the tri-deadly combination you taught me: jealousy, ungodliness, and devastation. Man's jealousy produces an ungodly heart, but without power he's frail. With power he does as he wishes and never considers the damage he institutes. See, I didn't forget that either, father."

It wasn't until he felt the touch of Priest Batteast's fingertips on his back that he remembered his reason for coming to the Coliseum. "Thank you, old friend," he stated. "For a minute there, I was lost in childhood memories. It's been a long time since I've been home. Maybe it's time for another visit."

"Maybe," Priest Batteast agreed. "They're waiting," he advised, pointing at the Coliseum.

"Then let's go," he smiled at his friend.

As they made their way to the gold idol, Drexter shot a quick glance at the media standing nearby that he also controlled. Using them as his primary means to communicate his message to the world, he proceeded to the microphone and spoke eagerly. "I am the light of this world. I offer to you truth and a way—a way that leads to a world eternal. I offer salvation to all who will follow me." He paused to look out at the world via the cameras. His eyes appeared caring. He stared on without one blink. "Come unto me, and I'll give you eternal life. I hold the power of life in my hands. I'll be your king, and you will be my people. For the nonbelievers, I show you signs of my power. I show you that I'm all-powerful so that all of your doubts are cast down. Then you'll know for sure that I am the Messiah."

He looked at Priest Batteast who stepped toward the idol, placed one hand under its chin and the other on its ears.

"Speak," Drexter commanded.

Life entered the golden statue. It raised its head up toward Drexter, its eyes turned fiery red, and it trotted to him as if Drexter was his master.

Cries of amazement filled the arena as it once had in the Roman Ages. Members of the militia fell to their knees and bowed their heads to Drexter, while the media closed in to get an enhanced shot of the idol whose mouth opened to deceive the world. "You offer eternity to all who follow you. You are the light of this world."

It kneeled down to Drexter and lowered its head. Seconds later, it stood upright and again took up its original form.

Certain that trickery was involved, one of the journalists jumped onto the stage, nudged the idol, and then lunged backward where he waited for it to charge. After receiving no response, he nudged the idol a second time but held his position. Sensing its hard, cold texture, he rested his hand against its side. Convinced that what he had just witnessed was not a façade, he faced Drexter, dropped to his knees, and kissed his shoes.

Drexter stood, looking honorable with a look of contentment painted on his face, as the young, professional, white male at his feet praised his name. He figured that it wouldn't be long before his vision of sitting on the throne became a reality. He and his father would rule with a mighty hand, and no one would rebuke his authority, not even the nation of Israel.

He stared defiantly into the cameras, knowing that the entire world was watching. Bending down toward the journalist at his feet, who now had tears streaming down his cheeks, he kindly helped him upright.

Without another word, he motioned at Priest Batteast who had taken his place alongside the media in order to give Drexter center stage.

"Let's go home. I want to see my father," he stated, walking out of the Coliseum and entering their vehicle.

Later that evening, they excused themselves from Mount BoeYourne. Refusing the services of his private chauffeur, Drexter adjusted the driver's seat of his luxury vehicle for the long drive ahead. The conversation was a pleasant one. They cheerfully critiqued the day's event. Satisfied with the end results, they were anxiously anticipating the world's response. After driving for hours, they observed no signs of human or vegetation life in sight. Finally, they arrived at a remote, gloomy, and dead-looking piece of land that Drexter had previously purchased.

After treading six miles into the still night, they came upon a small hole partially concealed by branches. When Drexter kneeled down and touched the ground with his fingertips, it dilated, and the earth gave way to reveal a portal. An awful smell of death and decaying flesh filled the air, and smoke rose above it. When Drexter took in a deep breath, the familiar smell of home stimulated his nostrils. Closing his eyes for a second, he enjoyed the sweet aroma. The portal opened up to reveal a large crater, which was one of many gateways connecting earth and Hell. A dense, black smoke escaped, and the fiery flames from the pits of Hell illuminated the night.

Their bodies drifted effortlessly to the center of the crater where they stood suspended in air. Like little children, they giggled and grinned and then descended into their home—deep down into the dark depths of Hell. Thousands of demons and evil spirits eagerly ascended out of the portal and onto the earth to carry out their assignments of wreaking havoc on the races.

"Raise hell," Drexter yelled out to them with a grin. They bowed to him in passing.

The feel of home soothed Drexter as it had in his younger days. He savored the stench of rotting, worm-eaten flesh, mixed with the foul odor of filth and muck. The feel of maggots squishing and the murky mush sent tingles through his body. But what he loved most was the black eclipse of his home. The human eye couldn't see one-sixteenth of an inch in front of it, but to Drexter and Priest Batteast, the darkness seemed as bright as the sun.

"Home," he delightfully shouted to Priest Batteast. "Let's take the scenic route through the corridors, shall we?"

The long, winding corridor was filled with hair, blood, body parts, and half-eaten flesh. It was infested with rodents that squealed when they were smashed under Drexter and Priest Batteast's footsteps. Moaning and groaning could be clearly heard when they neared the end, which opened up to the sector reserved for false prophets. Like severely abused animals, some were unable to stand, and others were curled over on their hands and knees. They were dragged from secured cages by demonic carnivores, and their already ravaged bodies were ripped apart. Thorn-covered demons with flaming eyes sank their razor-sharp teeth into the flesh of the unrepentant and viciously ripped it from their bodies. Evil entities without eyes transformed into spirit form and then entered them. The unrepentant screamed in terror as they were being tormented mentally, and then a small shimmer appeared in their eyes that ignited into flames and quickly consumed their bodies. The evil entities fled from within them and again took up their original form while the unrepentant were torched. Demons laughed and were delighted at the tormenting sounds of their prey.

Drexter and Priest Batteast watched gleefully while the unrepentant pleaded for mercy. Their pain and agony sounded like a symphony in their ears, and the sight of never-ending torment thrilled them.

"Just as I remembered it," Priest Batteast laughed.

After becoming bored with the false prophets, they proceeded down another corridor that opened up to a sector reserved for unrepentant murderers. Demons were gouging out their eyes with huge, pointed objects. In excruciating pain, the unrepentant cried out for relief, but their pleas were mocked. Evil entities that appeared to be centuries old were carving the initial *S* into the foreheads of the damned with their razor-sharp fingers that flamed like fire.

"Satan!" they cheered. "You are the eternal property of our master. Do you know what that means?" Their husky voices echoed when they laughed. "I can do whatever I want to you."

When the evil entities waved their fingers like wands, hundreds of deep gashes ripped across the bodies of the unrepentant; instead of blood oozing from their wounds, the flames of Hell erupted. Pitiful cries bellowed out across the huge sector mixed with delightful cheers.

"Please help me," their heartrending cries blared out over and over, but relief came not.

"I guess they know how their victims felt," Drexter joked with the priest and then passed on to the next sector.

"I'm sure they must," he responded with a chuckle and a look of evil delight on his face.

Upon entering the next sector reserved for the proud, demons with the mixed physical form of many creatures subdued their victims with chains. As the victims lay helplessly in the muck, demons viciously beat and tortured them mercilessly with heavy chains until their mutilated forms were unrecognizable. Legs, arms, and other body parts, as well as internal organs, were strewn about.

"Help me, Jesus," one of the unrepentant cried out as her intestine was ripped from her abdominal area.

Demons roared out in laughter. They listened to the horrid cries of the tormented as they begged for death. But death never came, only never-ending torture.

"You won't find Jesus down here," the demon, Hysteria, responded jovially in a rasping tone. "He can't help you now."

"Please kill me," she responded. "I've had enough. Please, give me death. Relieve me from this torment." Her faint voice could hardly be heard over the horrid outburst of the others.

Drexter and Priest Batteast continued their tour of home. They passed through hundreds of chambers and witnessed billions being tortured. Upon reaching the sector reserved for fornicators, they were taken aback at how crowded it had become. Drexter noticed the demons Sinister, Misery, Devour, Sorrow, Reaper, and Pandemic ushering in two hundred newly condemned, unrepentant beings.

"Young master, it's been awhile," Pandemic stated, bowing down to Drexter. "High Priest," he acknowledged Priest Batteast with a smile.

"Somehow, I don't remember it being this congested," Priest Batteast responded.

"The world continues to evolve into a sexual one. Man insists on living in a sinful state of sexual lust, immorality, and impurity. His flesh is weak."

"Good."

Out of the corner of his eye, Drexter observed an unrepentant male who was slouched down with his chest to his knees and with the partial remains of his facial structure resting in the muck. Maggots feasted on his ravaged body, which had turned as black as the filth that surrounded him. Drexter neared the suffering individual.

"I remember you from my childhood. You were a rich Texas oil-man," he said. "You had the entire world at your fingertips."

"I've been here for what seems an eternity," his weary voice responded.

A throbbing pain stopped him from continuing. A frown formed on his partially eaten face when a serpent slithered out of his chest cavity.

Barely lifting up what was left of his arm, he stretched it out to Drexter. "I beg you. Please, just destroy me."

Another serpent escaped his chest cavity, slithered down his side, and reentered a cavity in his thigh. He struggled to form more words. "I can't endure this torment any longer. Tell Jesus I understand now what He meant when He said, 'What shall it profit a man if he gain the whole world and lose his own soul.' Tell Jesus that I know now. Tell Him I repent of my sins. Ask Him if I could have just one more chance. Ask Him to set me free, please."

"When I see Him, I shall surely ask Him," Drexter replied in a condescending tone and with a wicked grin plastered on his face. Laughing, he and Priest Batteast moved on toward the core of Hell.

Directly in the center was a dark hole that the demons referred to as Forbidden Way. When Drexter and Priest Batteast descended into it, they went deeper into Hell. They passed the forbidden chambers that were off-limits to all descendants of Hell, including Satan himself. The chambers were huge in size and secured by flaming swords that turned in every direction. Inside were gorgeous angels that were once sons of God. Unlike Satan's demons, the angels were bound in chains and forbidden by God to roam free on earth. They weren't part of the legions that sided with Satan and rebelled against God. They were angels, who after being tempted by Lucifer with the beauty of daughters of earthly men, abandoned Heaven and took up residence on earth. There, they mated with the daughters of evil men, producing a mixed breed of species with the spiritual intellect of Heaven and the corrupt, wicked, and evil heart of the worldly man. For their sins, they were condemned to the darkness of Hell until judgment day. They never spoke, not even to one another, and the residents of Hell were barred from having any contact with them.

Drexter, as he had in his childhood days, stood at a distance and watched the caged angels who looked terrified and resentful. They had been confined there since the days of Noah, long before he was born. Their appearance remained exactly as Drexter remembered.

Drexter's thoughts traveled back in time. He remembered his father saying how he thought he had the battle won when these angels sinned and when the bloodline of Seth mixed with the bloodline of Cain. He remembered anger swelling up in his father when he told the story of how God brought forward the great flood that thwarted his scheme to prevent redemption by reserving the sacred bloodline through Noah and his clan. His father had told him that tricking Eve into eating the fruit and her persuasion of Adam to do likewise was easy, because all he had to do was twist God's words.

But Noah—that Noah couldn't be conquered because his faith couldn't be shaken. His father had tried everything to tempt Noah until he and his family entered the ark. But after God sealed it, his father had again failed because evil couldn't permeate anything that was sealed by God. And so, until the water receded, he and his demons returned to Hell where they regrouped and waited for mankind to replenish.

No matter how hard his father tried, he could never prevail over God, and the thought infuriated Drexter. God always received all the glory. Drexter's hatred for the Father and the Son intensified. But he would accomplish what his father couldn't—defeat Christ. Then, his father would sit on the throne and rule eternally, and he would sit at his left side.

Drexter and Priest Batteast proceeded to the master chamber. There, Drexter observed his father's huge, filthy throne. Standing guard was one of the head demons, Macabre.

"Young Master," he blurted out with a deep, menacing voice and then bowed down on his knees. "It's been awhile since I last saw you," he continued, acknowledging Priest Batteast with a nod of his head.

"So it has, Macabre. Where's my father?"

"He's not here, Young Master. He's up roaming the earth."

"I didn't see him leave with the other servants."

Just as Macabre was about to answer, Hell quaked from the sound of heavy footsteps. Drexter smiled at the familiar sound. A light filled the chamber after the heavy, iron doors flew open. Drexter didn't turn around; instead, he waited until his father had taken his seat on his throne.

"My son." The scary voice sounded like an earthquake, shaking Hell. "Why doest thou come here? Is it not thy time to rule?"

"It is, father, but I desire your counsel."

Sensing that his son strongly required his leadership, Satan motioned at Priest Batteast and Macabre to leave his chamber. Only after they had done so did Drexter sit down at his father's throne and engage in intimate conversation. Hours later, he reunited with Priest Batteast and the two departed Hell.

The drive back to Mount BoeYourne started out on a quiet note. Priest Batteast observed Drexter to be deep in thought. At first, he assumed that Drexter had become homesick, but an inkling within advised him that there might be more.

"May I be of any assistance?" he asked Drexter.

"No."

"What counsel did you require of your father?"

Drexter paused before responding, "The nonbelievers."

Chapter 7

MABREY SAT ON the front porch of his residence as he found himself doing most mornings after the Rapture. He wanted to enjoy the peace and quiet before the rest of the world woke up and to inhale the cool, fresh, morning air before the sun assumed its regular position in the sky. It was his private time to meditate on his mother and brother. He often wondered what they were doing. Were they sitting and talking with Jesus? Were they just running around Heaven at their leisure, having fun? Were they looking down on earth from Heaven? Could they see him and his brothers? Did they still remember them, or were their memories wiped clean? His pleasant thoughts were interrupted by the presence of Connery and Stanton who had also come outside to enjoy the fresh morning air.

"Where's Harper?" he asked.

"He's still asleep," Stanton replied as Connery handed Mabrey a hot cup of coffee and then claimed his own spot on the porch steps.

"I hope there's enough sugar in it for you," Connery said.

Mabrey, after smelling the aroma of the steaming coffee, sipped a small bit. The smooth, sweet taste combined with fresh pet milk sent a warm sensation through his insides. "It tastes almost as good as Mom's," he admitted before taking another sip.

"Almost as good, did you say? I'll have you know that Mom loved my coffee more than she liked her own," Connery replied in a boasting tone.

"Did she really? Let's see. How hard is it to make coffee? Well—" Mabrey was about to continue but was cut off by his brother.

"Here we go. Here we go."

Laughter erupted until Mabrey jumped up and yelled, causing a silence to fall over the porch. After licking his hands, Connery and Stanton realized that he had spilled hot coffee all over him.

"Would you like a napkin, or would you like to continue licking your hand like a dog?" Stanton asked.

"Would you like to...and you can fill in the rest of that blank?" Mabrey replied jokingly. "It was pleasant before the two of you came out here."

"We thought that you needed company. You looked lonely," Connery joked.

"Looks are deceiving, aren't they?" he replied, shaking his head up and down.

"If we hadn't come out here, what would you be doing?" Stanton asked.

"Let me see. I'd be enjoying the peace and quiet, soaking up the cool air, and thinking."

"Thinking about what?"

Mabrey paused for a second. He didn't want to lower his brother's spirits by bringing up the Rapture. Deep down he knew that his brothers missed their mother and Wentworth just as much as he did and struggled with their absence. But he often wondered about them, and if anybody had the answers to his questions, it was Connery.

"Are you OK?" Connery asked.

"Let me ask you a question, Connery."

"What?"

"What do you think Mom and Wentworth are doing in Heaven?"

Connery paused for a minute to take a deep breath. "I don't know. I'm sure they're OK, though."

"Do you think that they can see us?"

"I don't know, Mabrey. I don't know if they're permitted to look down on earth. Maybe they can," he guessed.

"Do you think that they remember us?" he further questioned.

"I believe they do. I think they still possess their memories and think of us just as we think of them."

"I'm just curious. What about the folks in Hell? Do they still remember their loved ones on earth?" he further inquired.

"I'm sure they do also. If the people in Heaven can remember, I'm sure that the people in Hell can, too," Connery assumed.

"You know something; all those predictions in the Bible are coming true just as Mama used to talk about," Stanton added.

"They're prophecies, Stanton, not predictions. Nostradamus predicted; that's why he was sometimes wrong—because he guessed. Prophecies are not guesses. They're visions given by God to specific people of events that will take place," he explained.

"I have another question for you. For you to know so much about the Bible, how come you're still here?" Stanton teased, giving Mabrey a high five.

"Because Heaven didn't need any more heroes, and who else is going to take care of you degenerates?" he quickly shot back. "I'll be back. I need another cup of coffee."

As Connery made his way inside their residence, Stanton demanded, "Cook some bacon and eggs and grits while you're in there."

"I've got your bacon and eggs and grits," he replied. Passing by the den, he observed Harper sitting in his drawers, watching the morning news.

"What are they talking about?" Connery asked, pausing for a second to view the screen.

"That punk politician or magician from Rome—whatever he calls himself," he replied in his usual scratchy, morning voice.

"What are they saying?"

"Something about that statue talking." He shrugged his shoulders.

As media stations across the globe continued to broadcast the event, the public again weighed in with their views. The vast majority still deemed Drexter their savior while others stood steadfast and unmovable in Christ.

"I don't believe he's the Savior," an elderly, white female acknowledged from Mobile, Alabama. "He can claim to be what he wants, but I know what he isn't, and he is not the Messiah."

"If he's the Messiah, I'm the Easter Bunny," a male stated from Atlanta, Georgia. "We all wish and dream."

"He needs to get a life," another weighed in from Rio de Janeiro, Brazil.

"He sucks," came another opinion from Punta Cana, Dominican Republic.

"I have come to know who Christ really is. Unfortunately, it took a long time for me to realize it. I know that many false prophets have arisen in this world, and one of them resides at Mount BoeYourne. I'll only worship the true God in Heaven, and I shall have no other God but Him," another female in India proclaimed.

"I'm a believer of Christ Jesus and only Jesus," aired another statement from Africa.

Harper found the statements to be amusing. With every rebuttal, he let out a hearty chuckle, but Connery failed to find humor in the public's comments. Not wanting to miss one negative mention, he tuned in to the television without blinking an eye. Sitting patiently in his seat, he waited for the media to interview Drexter, but it was reported that he couldn't be reached for comment. That eerie feeling that always seemed to come over him at the mention of Drexter's name or the showing of his image had resurfaced. He figured that the negative remarks in regards to his display of power wouldn't go unanswered. Something inside alerted him that the public's pessimistic comments would somehow bring about unsympathetic and cruel consequences that would cause them to deeply regret their slips of the tongue and that they wouldn't have to wait long before that rage was vented.

Connery made his way to the kitchen where he poured himself another cup of coffee. Surveying the refrigerator, he realized that they desperately needed to visit the grocery store. He wasn't one to cater to his brother's every demand, but for whatever reason that morning, he felt the need to meet Stanton's demands. Pulling two of his mother's old, cast-iron skillets from the bottom cabinet, he placed them on the stove and filled them with what was left of the country, hickory-smoked bacon and maple-syrup-flavored, linked sausages. Learned from whom he considered to be the best chef in the world, his mother, he placed two cups of water into a pan and placed it on the stove to boil. After taking another sip of coffee, he retrieved a large mixing bowl to scramble the eggs.

As the aroma of bacon and sausage frying made its way through the house, he heard the stampede of his brothers' footsteps heading toward the kitchen. Without being distracted, he added three cups of grits and salt to the hot, boiling water. After taking another sip of coffee and tending to the bacon and sausage, he cracked eggs into the mixing bowl.

"Do you need some help?" Stanton asked, making his way over to the kitchen table.

"Nope," Connery replied as he continued to show off his remarkable skills. "I got it."

His brothers stood back and watched while Connery showcased his talent. For a split second, he resembled their mother and how she use to prepare their daily meals. Never breaking a sweat, Connery eased around the kitchen, making sure everything was prepared just right.

"I'll tell you what you can do. You can make out a grocery list of everything we need. I'll pick it up later today," Connery advised.

"All right," Stanton replied. After obtaining an old flyer from the kitchen drawer and an ink pen, he surveyed the contents of the refrigerator and then scribbled on the back of the paper. "I'll pick up groceries tonight. I've got to go out anyway."

"Sounds good to me. You know where the money is," Connery replied, adding milk, butter, and sugar to the grits.

Connery finally made his way over to the china. While setting the table for four, he added the eggs to a large skillet of melted cheese. After spreading butter on the toasted wheat bread, he turned and smiled at his brothers. Without a word, they took their places at the kitchen table.

<hr />

Meanwhile, the heirs of Heaven, along with the angels, were busy erecting a stage on the grass in the Valley of Harmony. Another celebration was under way, one that included singing, dancing, delicious food, plenty of love, laughter, joy, and good times. Messenger, an angel in Heaven, had informed Jesus' children that Jesus had never learned to dance while on earth. With this in mind, they set out to teach Him all the latest dance moves and the older ones—the fun and respectable dances, of course.

An oversized stage equipped with pyrotechnics was erected for all who had been musicians while on earth. Thousands prepared to show off their musical talents that had been given unto them by the Good Lord. Miles of grassy area in front of the stage served as the dance floor, and multicolored, rotating lights were created in the sky. Instead of tables, they chose to place blankets on the lawn to create a picnic-style celebration. Suddenly, amid all the planning and preparation, Heaven stood still.

"Hooray! Thank You, Lord. We praise Your Holy name." They rejoiced over another soul on earth coming to Christ.

Once again, expectations ran high as Heaven's occupants continued to make haste. Jesus walked nervously around, observing their cunning smiles when they passed Him by.

"Hi, Lord!" they greeted Him with loving smiles and vivid imaginations of what was to come.

He didn't answer; instead, He lifted His head up high and let out a hearty laugh. At every turn, His children bombarded Him with greetings and secretive grins.

"Are You ready, Lord?" they questioned, jumping for joy.

No way could He talk Himself out of this one. Knowing already what awaited Him and knowing that His children were looking forward to the event, He would never disappoint the ones who loved Him dearly.

Soon the stage was set, and Michael led a shy and reluctant Messiah to the front of the stage. When the Gospel music started, His children twisted and jumped, and He laughed and watched.

"Jesus, do this," a male heir yelled and then performed the hustle.

Everybody joined in, even the angels. Jesus closely eyed the movement. Reluctantly, He began moving His legs back and forth but quickly stopped when they laughed.

"Try it again, Jesus. Try it again," they encouraged.

"Jesus, try this," someone else yelled out and then performed the Texas two-step.

"Oh yeah!" the heirs shouted with excitement and then joined in.

Jesus' pearly-white teeth sparkled as He emitted a smile so beautiful. After watching for a couple of minutes and receiving step-by-step instructions on how to execute the move, He slowly moved His feet. A wrong twist of His body brought about another mighty roar; He stopped. The elders seated on the blankets fell backward and laughed at the Messiah.

"Try it again, Jesus," they encouraged.

"OK," He agreed in His normal, soft, calming voice. Once again, He attempted the move, and another awkward twist sent His children falling to the grass with laughter. He, Himself, let out a mighty roar as He struggled to learn the dance.

"Don't give up, Lord. Keep going, Lord."

"I can't do it," He laughed.

"How about this one?" With the changing of the tune, they started to do the tango.

"Yeah!" they yelled.

The elders got up and joined in. Jesus tried, but He couldn't execute the dance.

"Don't give up," they yelled. Even the youngest heirs of Heaven joined in and attempted to ape their elders.

"Jesus, break-dance," they yelled when the music changed to Gospel rap.

"No! This is where I draw the line," He shook His head adamantly when His children started to break-dance. "I refuse," He laughed.

"Watch us, Lord. Just watch us first." They again showcased their talents, and He fell to His knees laughing.

"Go Jesus! Go Jesus! Go Jesus! Go Jesus! We love You. We love You. We love You. We love You."

"No!" He again refused, after surveying the different moves.

"Go Jesus! Go Jesus! Go Jesus! Go Jesus!"

"Only because I love thee dearly, I will try this once," Jesus laughed and then shook his head.

After a deep sigh and against His judgment, He attempted to break-dance. His efforts once again caused a roar among His children. Out of nowhere, Heaven trembled from a thunderous laugh that drowned out the music and brought a hush over the gala. The heirs turned to Jesus for answers.

"Father!" Jesus stated with a smile after realizing that His Father was laughing at Him.

"Father! Creator!" the heirs repeated. "You scared us," they yelled.

The music resumed, and Jesus, willing to do almost anything to make them happy, put forth another effort. Another failed attempt caused Gabriel to turn in the opposite direction and cover his face to hide his laughter.

"I see you, Gabriel," Jesus laughed.

"Lord, if You'd like, I will try this one on for size," the angel, Dove, stated with a smile on his face.

After Jesus motioned for him to proceed, he was led center stage by the heirs and shown several techniques. With a nodding of his head, he was ready to give it a try.

"I do believe I've got it," he stated. "Here goes nothing."

He started off moving at a snail's pace while executing the robot, and then rotated his head from side to side. The heirs jumped for joy.

"Go Dove! Go Dove! Go Dove! Go Dove!" they shouted when he ascended off the grass.

"You've got it, Dove! You've got it!"

Seeing His children enjoying Paradise, fellowshipping with one another, exchanging hugs and kisses and dancing brought so much joy to Jesus' heart. He didn't mind not being able to dance or the laughs that came with it. There was nothing that He wouldn't do for them, and they knew it. For a moment, He thought back to the cross and to all the torture, pain, and agony that He had endured to make the moment possible. Just to have them with Him forever, He would, without doubt, do it all over again if He had to, He thought. He had longed to be with them for so long, and it crushed Him to be away from them when He went back to Paradise to prepare a place. But He had promised that He would come again someday to receive them, and so they were with Him now.

"Go Jesus! Go Jesus! Go Jesus! Go Jesus!" He was brought back to the present by the roaring voices that waited anxiously for Him to give it another try.

"OK," He stated calmly, and without a moment's hesitation, attempted to execute the move once more.

It was a joyous event that continued for hours and hours. But as the heirs continued to enjoy all the goodness of Christ and Paradise, night had fallen on the occupants of earth, and the moon cast its light down half as radiantly as the sun.

⋆⇢▬◉ ◉▬⇠⋆

Connery, Harper, and Mabrey sat at the kitchen table playing Spades while they awaited Stanton's return. After calculating their scores, Mabrey found that he had taken a considerable lead over his brothers. Nearing game point, he prematurely took advantage of his bragging rights.

"I'm four books away from winning, by the way."

"Your calculations must be wrong. How did you get that far ahead?" Harper asked.

"I've had a bunch of good hands, plus I set you back on a couple, remember?"

"Let me see the paper," he demanded.

"You can take a look at it if you like. It's added right," Mabrey insisted, handing Harper the score sheet.

When Harper scanned the paper up and down and computed the figures, something out of the ordinary caught his eye. A grin materialized on his face that indicated to Mabrey that his calculations were incorrect.

"What's wrong?" Mabrey asked.

"Mabrey, how much is two hundred and thirty-six plus fifty-four?"

Mabrey paused for a minute to examine the score sheet. "What do I have written on the paper?"

"What is two hundred and thirty-six plus fifty-four, sucker?" Harper asked again.

"It's two hundred and ninety. Why? That's what I have written on the paper."

Harper paused for a minute to reexamine the score sheet. After rechecking the figures, he realized that Mabrey's calculations were correct.

"OK, that's correct," he admitted. "I guess you're right."

"I am right, fool. Elementary math isn't that hard. Maybe you should try and learn it sometimes. *Hooked on Phonics* is available for old folks, too," Mabrey joked.

"Deal the cards," Connery demanded, slamming the deck down in front of Harper. "It's your turn."

Looking down at his watch, Connery noticed that it was nearing ten o'clock. He wondered if Stanton had made it to the grocery store. Since Stanton didn't have a mobile phone, Connery couldn't call him. He figured that Stanton had stopped off to get a drink and had one too many. After contemplating going out to look for him, he quickly dismissed the thought after realizing that Stanton had taken the car and that he could be at any one of his usual drinking places. With the grocery store sort of within walking distance, Connery figured that it wouldn't take him long to walk up there and hopefully spot him.

Harper was about to deal the cards when the kitchen lights blinked out. Slamming the deck on the table, he felt his way over to the doorway where he finally found the light switch. After flipping it up and down several times, he figured that the circuit breaker had failed until it dawned on him that all the lights in the house were out. Their only source of light came from the moon and stars above.

"It must be a blackout. The lights are out everywhere," Connery stated, peering out the back-door window.

"Get some candles," Harper ordered, rummaging blindly through the kitchen drawers for matches.

Mabrey felt his way through the dark hallway and into the den where he attempted to find candles. He knew that his mother kept some around the house somewhere; he just didn't know where. Feeling his way into the bathroom, he managed to find two long candles laying on the window sill. Grabbing them both, he slowly felt his way back into the kitchen where Harper was waiting with a lighter that Connery had given him.

"Come look at this," Connery yelled in disbelief for them to join him on the back porch.

The dim light in the kitchen, cast by the moon, seemed to be fading away. When they stepped onto the porch, they panicked.

"What in the hell is going on?" Harper asked as his eyes became fixated on the sky.

"I'm not sure," Mabrey replied in sheer awe.

Connery didn't answer; instead, he and his brothers watched intensely as, one by one, the stars disappeared from the sky. Millions of streaks of light painted the sky like fireworks as stars descended with the sounds of missiles. The further they fell, the smaller the streaks became until they disappeared in midair. Soon, all that was left was the full, milky-colored moon.

"We need to get back inside," Connery advised, backing up.

Mabrey and Harper followed suit. Just as Mabrey was about to close the kitchen door, he was taken aback when the moon started to change shades. Its white hue took on a light, pinkish color but gradually turned darker. As it did so, its texture evolved into a runny, fluid-like structure that eventually turned red—blood red.

"I knew it would start sooner or later," Connery admitted.

His brothers dared to ask him what he meant. Judging by the events that had taken place within the last three and a half years, they figured that it couldn't be good. Out of the corner of his eye, Mabrey caught sight of the moon. It shifted. His heart nearly stopped beating, and his mouth gaped open when the bottom portion of the moon divided and then dripped blood. As it did so, its form changed to mirror the image of both man and a large, horned animal and then rapidly faded before they could clearly make it out. They could hear the screams of their neighbors who had by now come outside to witness the terrifying event.

"I need to find Stanton. The two of you stay here," Connery ordered, making a dash for the porch steps.

"You can't go out there. What are you doing?" Harper yelled, grabbing Connery by his arm and pulling him back. "Look at that." He pointed toward the moon. "What the hell?" he stuttered in complete shock.

Within seconds, a thick, black, fog-like substance gradually overtook the moon like an eclipse and then began its descent upon the earth. It was a darkness that prevented the human eye from seeing one inch ahead. With the exception of Mount BoeYourne, the entire globe was submerged. Connery, Harper, and Mabrey wandered blindly into the kitchen.

"I've got to get to Stanton," Connery said, brushing his fingers through his hair. "We don't know if he's OK or not. I have got to find a way to get to him."

"You don't even know where he is," Mabrey replied. Mabrey turned in the direction of his voice. "How are you going to get to him? You can't even see where you're going."

"Mama said to stick together," Connery shouted back.

"I know what Mama said. Believe me, we love Stanton just as much as you, but use common sense. There's no way you, me, or anybody else can get to him right now. If you go out there, you might as well be committing suicide. You will die trying." The sound of a car crashing into a nearby building interrupted Mabrey, causing him to almost jump out of one shoe. "What the hell was that?"

"Who knows what that was," Harper replied, turning in the direction of Mabrey's voice. "Do you know how many people are trapped out there in that darkness?"

"Where are the candles?" Connery asked.

"In my pocket," Mabrey replied. "Say something so I can locate you."

"Give it to me. I'm over here," Harper responded. "Reach out and try to locate my hands," he advised, waving them about until he finally made contact with Mabrey.

"Where is the lighter?" Connery asked.

"You gave it to me. I have it in my hand," Harper replied.

With two flicks of the lighter, Harper managed to strike a flame that dimly illuminated the kitchen. Nervously, he lit the first candle, passed it to Connery, and then lit the second candle in Mabrey's hand.

Connery gazed around the kitchen. "Find as many candles as you can and bring them to the kitchen. Let's place everything we need on the table so we'll know where it is when we need it."

Another loud bang sent the brothers jumping, followed by another and then another immediately after.

"What's going on out there?" Mabrey asked. His thoughts quickly turned to Stanton. "I hope Stanton isn't trying to drive home. Wherever he is, I hope that he stays put."

Connery chose not to respond; instead, he thought back on the promise that was made to their mother. Guilt set in as he worried about his younger brother. Being the eldest and the toughest of the bunch, he felt responsible for his brothers' safety. Had he just gone to the grocery store in the first place, Stanton would be home and out of harm's way, he thought. He made every attempt to disguise his facial expression from his brothers because he didn't want them to panic any more than they already were, and seeing him in a state of fear would only make matters worse.

After taking another long, hard look out the kitchen window, he calculated his odds of surviving if he ventured out with nothing more than a candle. He tried to determine how long the candles would burn and how many it would take. Where was Stanton? What if he wasn't at the grocery store? Then what? What if something awful happened to him in the process? What would happen to his brothers? Deciding against his heart and using his better judgment, he came to the conclusion that the risk of going out would be too costly.

Dominion Angels, Omega and Anointed, gracefully lured Michael away from the gala. After being placed under Michael's command, they were assigned the task of overseeing all incidents concerning the second half of the Tribulation Period. With this information, they kept Michael abreast, who in turn recorded the information to maintain accuracy. After all information had been thoroughly checked, Michael subtly motioned to the Lord. With so many dance moves to execute and bands waiting to be heard, His children didn't notice Him quietly slip away from the gala.

Jesus and Michael sat quietly in one of the temples while Michael reported the facts. After the conclusion of the meeting, Jesus reported to the front gate of Heaven where He looked down on the universe. Although overtaken by pure darkness, being capable of all things, He saw clearly.

The perilous times that He had warned of had now come upon the earth. Tears escaped His eyes while He watched the universe tremble with fear. He listened to the cries of the faint at heart and the fearful, and He took note of the evil-hearted as they swore out loud at Him. He listened attentively to the prayers that were ascending to Heaven from the ones who had come to know Him. Jesus' deepest desire was for them to be with Him in Paradise, but they knowingly made the decision to disobey His commandments and because of their choices, had to suffer through the tribulation. As He stared down, He thought about the imminence of His return.

He zeroed in on Israel. They sat guarded for whatever attacks the darkness might conceal. Millions of prayers were being delivered to Him by the angels, and His heart sympathized with the nation from which He would one day rule from His throne. Summoning Michael to His side, Jesus instructed him to send an angel to descend over the chosen land.

Making haste, Michael immediately summoned the Dominion Angel, Immaculate. He was a tall, slender angel and like the others had an aura of radiance about himself, but more intense. His body sparkled and glistened mightier than the sun. Upon receiving his instructions, he departed Heaven and began his journey to Israel. There, he hovered above the tiny nation like a hawk stalking its prey and peered down on the land that his Lord found much favor in. With his body erect and his wings fully extended out at his side, he mimicked the image of the cross. Lifting his head to Heaven, rays of light beamed down on Jerusalem and then spanned across all of Israel. The darkness subsided.

Immaculate's unmovable form hovered in the sky as a symbol, not only to Israel but to all, that God's grace was still raining down on man. Regardless of their choices, He hadn't let go of them but held them tightly within His grasp. He sent Immaculate as a symbol of His sovereignty, unlimited power, undying love, and never-ending protection, and as a reminder that He was watching and waiting from above. God's light, which shined amid total darkness, was a symbol of just how great "I AM" really was.

The whole population of Israel immediately took to the streets to witness the miraculous event. They fell on their hands and knees with their faces to the ground and offered up their highest praises to the almighty Savior above for answering their prayers. With their eyes filled with tears of happiness and their hearts overflowing with unyielding joy, they cried out the name of Jesus. If only the rest of the world would be able to do the same.

→==◎ ◎==←

Ellen sat in the grass by the younger heirs. A few of the dances she mastered, but some were a bit too complicated. Without warning, an uneasy feeling came over her. Trying with all her might to shake it off but being unable to do so, her thoughts quickly turned to her boys. As worry swelled up in her, she dismissed herself from the gala and wandered down the streets of Paradise. She wasn't able to pinpoint exactly what the problem was, but something deep inside told her that her boys were the cause. Briefly, she paused to inhale a deep breath and then quickly resumed her journey so that Wentworth wouldn't see her.

After several turns, she stumbled upon the Garden of Calvary where Mary was tending to roses, lilies, and lilacs. On the hill stood three crosses made of ivory, and at the bottom of the middle cross was a beautiful pillar. "Destroy this temple, and in three days I shall raise it up" was inscribed on it. Ellen observed how serene Mary appeared to be while she sat quietly, meticulously maintaining the garden.

After deciding that she didn't want to disturb Mary, Ellen quietly tiptoed by, but Mary caught sight of her. They had talked many times in the past and had come to know each other quite well. After observing Ellen's facial expression and sensing that something wasn't right, Mary pulled off her bonnet and put aside her flower basket.

"What's wrong, Mary Ellen?" she asked.

Struggling to grin, she shook her head from side to side. Evading the question, she commented on the garden. "The garden is beautiful as usual. You always seem so tranquil and joyful when you're maintaining it."

"And why aren't you tranquil and joyful?" Sensing that Ellen was trying to avoid the question, she waited momentarily for an answer, and after receiving no response, motioned for Ellen to come sit down beside her.

Ellen remained silent. She made her way inside the garden where she planted herself on the grass, curled her knees to her chest, and rested her head. She could no longer fight back the tears that were now streaming down her face. Mary lovingly embraced her by wrapping her arm around Ellen's shoulders and then leaned her head next to Ellen's where they rocked from side to side.

"I don't want to burden you," Ellen stated.

"I'm your sister. If you can't burden me, who can you burden?" Mary paused for a quick second before continuing on. "What's wrong with your boys?"

Ellen stared at her in amazement. "How did you know it was my boys?"

"We're mothers. Mothers know these things, don't we?"

"You're right," she smiled. "You are the most famous mother that ever lived, aren't you?"

"No!" Mary shook her head. "I'm not a famous mom, Ellen. I'm a mom. I'm just an ordinary mother who gave birth to the most extraordinary man who ever walked the earth—to a man who bore the sins of the world so that we might live forever."

"Yes, He did. You must be proud of Him?"

Mary paused, took a deep breath, and then thought on Ellen's question. "Proud? Looking back now, yes, I am. But at the time I was a total wreck."

"Tell me about it," Ellen replied.

Mary curled her legs under her and then reminisced on the painful memories. She seized Ellen's hand. "I'll never forget what they did to my son. Forgive them, I have. I had to. But I'll never forget. They hurt my baby, Mary Ellen. I sensed that something was terribly wrong when he was in the Garden of Gethsemane. I knew not what had happened until later."

She paused for a moment as if it was happening all over again. She had to prepare herself in order to form the words. Her tear-filled eyes alerted Ellen that the tragic event still caused as much pain today as it had then.

"You don't have to talk about it. It's OK," Ellen assured.

Mary paused briefly before she spoke. "They hurt my son. They hurt Him, Mary Ellen. They beat my son. They tore the flesh from His back. They mocked Him and spat on Him," she cried. "I saw my baby's badly beaten body and Him struggling to carry a wooden cross on His back. There was nothing I could do. I'm His mother, and I couldn't protect Him. Yes, He is the Savior, the Messiah, but He is also my baby. If I could have, I would've given anything to take His place on the cross and spare Him the pain and agony He suffered. I would have gladly given my life to spare His, but God's will be done." Mary paused for a second. An image of Jesus hanging on the cross displayed vividly in her mind. "They murdered my baby, Mary Ellen. They beat, tortured, and murdered my baby. They killed my baby. He died for the same world that despised and killed Him." She paused for awhile. "But, it's OK now. They thought that they had ended everything, but little did they know that in three days the temple was rebuilt."

"What kind of child was Jesus?" Ellen wanted to know.

"Oh! He was perfect," she admitted, bursting into laughter while wiping the tears from her eyes. "He was absolutely perfect. He never did anything wrong. He spent most of His time in the temples and the rest learning carpentry from Joseph. As a child, He possessed more wisdom and understanding than all the world combined. Did you know that as a child, He entertained the wisest of men?"

"How amazing it is."

"They were astonished at His understanding. There were so many things He said as a child that I had no understanding of. I know now, but then I had not a clue. His wisdom increased as time went on. He prayed daily, even multiple times. Looking back now, I can see so clearly."

"You keep this garden so beautiful," Ellen stated.

"It's where eternal life began. The cross is the symbol of all hope, and without the shedding of His blood, there could be no salvation. It was on the cross that Jesus bridged the gap between God and man. Looking at it from that perspective, Mary Ellen, His death is a lot easier to accept. What I didn't know is that when He died, He descended into Hell to preach the gospel to the souls in prison. It's truly amazing, isn't it?"

"Yes, it is," Ellen agreed.

"I want you to do something for me," Mary instructed. "I want you to go back to the gala and have a joyous time. Don't worry about your sons, OK? Jesus will make everything OK. Just lay down your troubles on Him, and then be still while He works. He already knows your troubles, Mary Ellen."

"Huh!" she nodded in agreement.

"Do you remember what He said? Where two or more are gathered together in my name, there am I in the midst of them," Mary reminded her.

"He does already know, doesn't He? I almost forgot."

"Now go back to the gala and have fun," Mary encouraged.

Ellen hugged her for what seemed an eternity. Their conversation had been so uplifting and comforting that the uneasy feeling inside her subsided. She kissed Mary on the cheek and then bade her a sincere and heartfelt departure.

"Thank you, Mary. I love you."

"What are sisters for?"

Ellen began her journey back to the gala, and Mary wasted no time locating the Messiah. She found Him standing outside the gates looking down on the universe. Already aware of Mary's concern, Jesus' sweet, warm smile greeted her.

"I know You already know, son," Mary admitted.

"I already know, Mom," He replied.

Just as Mary had said, Jesus had quietly appeared over them in the Garden of Calvary while they sat and fellowshipped in His name. He shared their laughter as well as their tears and pain and had listened attentively as His earthly mother shared the intimate details of His thirty-three years on the earth. It was a story that she enjoyed sharing with all the heirs of Heaven.

"Thank You, Lord."

Mary gently kissed His cheek and then sped toward the gala. She found Ellen singing along with the music, and in no time, they were up dancing and giving the younger heirs a run for their money.

Jesus had already commanded Michael to disperse angels to earth to aid Stanton. Dominion Angels, Passover and Eden, were summoned and upon receiving their assignments, immediately exited Paradise.

⋅→═◉ ◉═←⋅

Stanton sat nervously in his mom's old sedan. Every now and then the sound of groceries shifting in the bags caused him to panic. He regretted arriving at the market at the last minute but was fortunate enough to obtain what he needed. While loading groceries into the car, the stars began falling from the sky. Stricken with fear, he remained parked on the lot. How he wished that he had run back inside the market with the workers; then he wouldn't be alone. Before the darkness evolved, he could see them peering out the window. Their presence was a glimmer of comfort to him, but as their images faded in the dark, so did his courage. He contemplated feeling his way up to the building, but the fear of taking a wrong turn overshadowed the thought. Bottom line, he deemed it safer to stay put. At least inside the vehicle, he was somewhat sheltered from the unknown.

After struggling to find the control button, he finally managed to recline the driver's seat. He figured if it was going to be a long wait, he was going to make it as comfortable as possible. Positioning his head on the headrest and closing his eyes, he thought of his brothers. He figured that they must be concerned over his whereabouts and safety. Had he gone to the market earlier that day and not procrastinated as usual, he'd probably be secure in his home right now, he thought.

After pondering the fate that awaited him amid the darkness, he figured whatever was going to happen was inevitable. With nowhere to run or hide, he was a sitting duck with no fighting chance. After remembering the bottles of cheap wine in the back seat of the car, he figured if death was imminent, then at least he wouldn't feel it. Allowing his hands to be his guide, he reached in the back seat and felt through the contents in the plastic bag until a ray of light appeared in front of the car.

"Ahhh!" he yelled out and then felt to make sure that the door locks were secure. With his heart racing and his hands trembling, he frantically searched for his car keys hidden in his pocket. After pulling out coins and other foreign objects, he finally retrieved them, hurriedly slid a key into the ignition, and with a stroke of luck, the engine started.

Passover and Eden didn't speak; instead, they stared at him with grins gracing their angelic faces. When Stanton attempted to switch gears, Passover simultaneously placed his hand on the hood, wedging the gear in park. Stanton slammed on the gas, revving the engine. Eden held out his hand, but Stanton, now panic-stricken and drenched in sweat, slammed on the gas a second time. With all his might, he jerked on the gearshift. When Eden placed his hand on the hood, the engine jerked and then shut down. Stanton fiercely stroked the gas pedal and forcefully turned the key but got no response.

"Be not afraid," Eden finally said as his body glided over the hood of the car. "Our Lord, Jesus Christ, has sent us. Fear not, for we are not here to harm you but to protect you. We were sent to be your light in the dark. Take your foot off the pedal and your hands off the steering wheel."

Stanton hesitantly obeyed. "Mama must be praying for me up there," he thought out loud. "Thank you, Mama."

Eden didn't respond; instead, he placed his foot on the lukewarm hood of the car, and it lifted off the ground. With the angels leading the way, the old sedan glided out of the parking lot.

As they proceeded down the boulevard, the radiance shining from the angels revealed the horrors that the darkness concealed.

Vehicular collisions lined the streets like parked cars. Stanton rolled down his window and stuck his head out in order to get a closer look. His heart ached when they passed an unrecognizable body lying in a puddle of its own blood on the hood of a mangled vehicle. It had collided with a brick wall, and the driver was ejected through the windshield. At the end of the same block, the severed corpse of a once-beautiful, teenage girl stood crushed between two blazing vehicles. It was the beginning of many tragic scenes that his eyes bore witness to.

"Why me?" he said out loud after realizing that he could have been one of the less fortunate victims. "Why me? Why me, Jesus?"

His thoughts quickly turned to his brothers. He wondered if they would believe his story. Connery maybe, but Mabrey and Harper wouldn't buy it for a minute. But how else could he explain his arrival home in such chaos? Anticipation swelled inside him until his body jerked due to an abrupt halt in their travel. Sounding from within the darkness was heavy breathing and an intense snarl that caused his fear to resurface. He eyed Passover and Eden, who were staring straight ahead. Curious as to why the standstill, he leaned over the steering wheel in time to see a figure forming out of the darkness. The lower body resembled the shape of a bull, the upper torso a man, the neck a dragon, and the head a bat; the hands were as large talons, the eye was that of a Cyclops, and the teeth were as snake fangs. The demonic figure towered over the angels easily and breathed down on them a thick, black film from its mouth.

Even though they sensed that they were not equally matched in power against Slaughter, a general over Satan's army, the angels showed no sign of fear. The two Sons of God stood steadfast and unmovable and spoke bravely with authority. "By the authority of our Lord, Jesus Christ, out of the way, Prince of Darkness," Passover commanded as he and Eden stood shoulder to shoulder.

Slaughter's breathing intensified. He leered at the angels. "Your Lord, doest thou say?" His husky voice snarled. "Who is Your Lord that commands this?" Smoke protruded from his nostrils and oral cavity.

"Our Lord, Jesus Christ, the righteous King of Kings," Passover replied. "By His authority, we shall pass."

Slaughter paused to examine the two Sons of God standing before him and then laughed. "Ye shall not pass; for I am many spirits in one." His face took on the appearance of multiple creatures and evil spirits, and the screams and torment of Hell sounded from his mouth. "I know not thy Lord. Thy journey tonight shall end in destruction." With his razor-sharp talons spread apart in a striking pose, he leaned his neck over the two angels.

"We shall not fear. By the power of our Lord, Jesus Christ, thou shall be moved from our path," Passover commanded and then rebuked him.

Slaughter's rage and wickedness intensified. His dominating size and power ensured him an easy and swift victory; his strike would be sudden and deadly.

Stanton sat panic-stricken and unable to move a muscle. Slaughter's size, his appalling appearance, authoritative voice, and the dimensions of his talons assured him that death was imminent. He wished that he had drunk the bottles of cheap wine in the back seat; at least then his demise wouldn't be so horrifying. The thought of not seeing his brothers again and the fear of what awaited him after death caused tears to swell in his eyes. Where would he end up eternally?

"Jesus!" he yelled out loud. "Jesus, please!"

After releasing a howl that made the pavement tremor, Slaughter mounted on his hind legs with his front legs spread apart and his fangs fully exposed. Stanton threw his hands in front of his face and prepared to die, but Passover and Eden stood courageous. As the demonic figure swooped down on them, his attack was thwarted by a light mightier than the angels. Temporarily blinded, he withdrew.

Directly in front of the two angels and more superior in size than Slaughter, appeared another Son of God. His long, snow-white tresses protruded from under his helmet and fell down his back, partially covering his body armor. With his sword strategically elevated in both hands, his posture poised for battle, and his fierce eyes fixated on Slaughter, he commanded, "By the power and authority of our Lord, Jesus Christ, I command thee back."

Slaughter snarled; he prepared to do battle.

Passover and Eden retreated and forfeited the battle to the archangel who had been sent from above to clear their passage.

Another growl escaped Slaughter. He circled the angel in search of the ideal moment to strike. With every movement of his body, the pavement shook. Like lightning, he charged at the archangel with a forceful thrust of his front legs. His talons landed within inches of the archangel's face, and his razor-sharp teeth barely missed his chest cavity. After maneuvering out of the path of Slaughter's attack, the angel retaliated with a swift strike of the sword, wounding his adversary's side. Instead of blood, slime oozed down his side, and the air reeked with a foul odor. The powerful blow sent Slaughter tumbling to the pavement with his talons strapping the deep gash. The archangel regrouped and prepared to deliver another life-threatening blow. Slaughter recovered and charged a second time, but the agonizing pain caused him to partially cave forward after two steps. With the flames of Hell protruding from his nostrils, inch by inch, he retreated.

"Thou hast no dominion over my Lord, Jesus Christ. By His power and authority, I command thee back, Prince of Darkness."

"You still choose to serve Your Lord, my brethren," Slaughter mumbled with scorn.

Refusing to be pulled into Slaughter's verbal snare, the angels didn't answer; instead, they rebuked him and remained focused on carrying out their assignments.

Slaughter's eyes displayed pure and immense contempt that his heart harbored. His evil quest for destruction, ordered by the authority of Hell, had been thwarted by the goodness above. After realizing that he, too, was subject to the power and authority of Jesus Christ, he retreated into the darkness, leaving behind the smolder of Hades to dissolve into the night.

After ascertaining that the demonic entity had fled, the archangel stepped aside and relinquished the passageway back to Passover and Eden. With a nod of their heads, they proceeded on with Stanton in tow.

Traumatized by the ordeal, Stanton didn't know whether to remain silent or speak. Deciding on the latter, he yelled out the window at the two angels. "Exactly who were they, and who are you?"

Passover and Eden halted their journey once more, and after deeming it safe to exit the vehicle, Stanton jumped out.

"I am Passover."

"I am Eden."

"And who was that big angel?"

"That was Ariel, the archangel," Eden responded. "He was sent by our Lord, Jesus Christ, to aid us on our journey."

"Where did he go?"

"His assignment is complete. He's returning to Heaven."

"And that thing I saw?"

Eden paused for a second before responding. "At one time he was our brother, Appollyus. He was assigned under Satan and was apart of the one-third of the angels who decided to rebel against our Creator for the throne. After they were driven out of their original dwelling place, he became Slaughter."

Stanton paused momentarily to try and absorb everything that had just happened. "This spiritual warfare between Heaven and Hell that my mother talked about, it's true?"

The angels stared on in silence.

"It really is true. There really is a battle for souls being fought behind the scene of what we see in this world. Thank you," he said in an authentic tone.

"Do not thank us. We're not worthy of praise. All praise and glory be to our Lord, Jesus Christ," Eden advised. "It was our Lord who sent us to protect you."

"Is it possible to take a look at what's really happening behind what we see in this world?"

"The human mind is not strong enough to comprehend what the eyes shall behold; your spirit will grieve for the longest while," Eden responded.

Stanton didn't respond; instead, he stared away and thought about all the things that his mother had preached about. Leaning against the vehicle with his head down, he became overwhelmed with emotion. "I'm sorry," he whispered.

"It's OK," Eden assured him. "We must be about our journey now."

Stanton climbed back into the vehicle and shut the door. The remainder of the journey proved to be a quiet one as he put into perspective the past years of his life that had led up to that moment. After analyzing all the low points and failures that had caused him to fall short of the glory of God, and knowing he still had God's unconditional love poured out on him, he figured that a change in his life had to come about.

Turning his thoughts to his mother and Wentworth, he longed to be with them and desperately wanted to speak spiritually with her once more.

"Our journey has ended," Eden informed him when they came to a stop in front of the Sutton residence. "Follow us."

Stanton gathered up as many bags of groceries that he could and then trailed the angels up the walkway to the front porch. With one touch of Eden's hand, the bolted door creaked open. Stanton turned to take one last look at his guardian angels.

"May I touch you?" he asked.

"Thou may."

He was caught off guard by the lack of physical matter. His facial expression prompted Eden to laugh.

"We are not physical beings but spiritual ones; however, we possess the power to take on human form, and at times we do. You must go in now."

With a nod of his head, Stanton turned and simultaneously entered the dwelling while the angels disappeared into the night.

With candles lighting their path, Connery, Harper, and Mabrey flocked to the foyer and were speechless to find Stanton standing there. It had been well over five hours since the darkness developed, and they knew that there was no possible way that Stanton could have found his way home.

"How did you get here?" a relieved Mabrey asked.

Stanton took a deep sigh before finally answering. "Angels."

"What?" Mabrey asked.

"I know you don't believe me but by the grace of God—I think. That's what Mama would say. I really think we need to start taking this Jesus more seriously."

Chapter 8

DREXTER STOOD POISED on the well-lit steps of Mount BoeYourne. The darkness, the sound of fear, and the smell of death gave him a natural high. He felt right at home surrounded by the grim, dark universe. After all, it closely resembled his childhood environment and contained all the elements that he had come to love: death, darkness, hate, fear, and destruction. Still, a part of him felt shortchanged by Immaculate's presence in the sky. Even after Priest Batteast called upon the powers of Hell by performing several demonic destruction rituals in an attempt to banish him, God's angel could not be moved. When his attempts failed, Drexter's rage swelled against Israel. The thought of them being under God's protection provoked hatred in him he never knew existed. The fact that the tiny but independent nation was able to produce everything they needed to survive without his or the rest of the world's aid haunted him. The thought of conquering God's people became unbearable. He would rule Israel. He would sit royally on the Mercy Seat in Jerusalem, or there would be no Israel.

⊷▶◉ ◉◀⊶

For three days the darkness of Hell loomed over the earth. Civilization came to a standstill, halting all normal and daily activity that had until then been taken for granted. When the darkness subsided, it left behind devastation and destruction that caused a great cry to be heard throughout the lands. For three days, the foul odor of death filled the air like smog, decaying bodies once again lay scattered about homes and businesses, and structures lay in ruins.

When the public tuned in to the media, they were addressed by Drexter with harsh words and a clear and present warning. "Your ignorance and your arrogance have caused great pain and sorrow to befall you, and your taunting has brought upon you immense suffering that no nation shall evade. Because you reject my truth, you shall now endure my wrath. And Israel, even you shall experience my fury." At the touch of his finger in a glass of water, it turned red. "For six days every nation shall drink of my blood."

Like a plague, blood spread out across every body of water: from the Nile River of Africa, the Caribbean Sea, the 365 rivers of Dominica, the Amazon River of South America, the Baltic and Mediterranean Seas, the Mississippi River of the United States, Lake Superior, the Timor Sea of Australia, the Yellow Sea of China, Lake Victoria of Tanzania, Lake Vanern of Sweden, Great Bear Lake of Antarctic, the Red Sea of Asia, to the Sea of Japan.

From one corner of the globe to the other, pandemonium of epic proportion spread. From every household, business, religious site, and public facility, blood flowed within the walls. The everglades of Florida emptied when reptiles and other animals sought refuge on land, and the surfaces of rivers, oceans, and seas became congested with the lifeless, floating bodies of its inhabitants. Raw sewage, mixed with blood, overflowed in dwellings, bringing forth sickness and disease.

Widespread violence erupted after the hearts of men ran cold when confronted with the question of survival. Businesses were ransacked for their stock, neighbor rose up against neighbor, friend against friend, and family against family as provisions became scarce. Reserves were concealed and consumed with caution, and many went days without to ensure survival in such uncertain times. Cries for mercy sounded around the globe as desperation set in. Many faltered and humbled themselves on their hands and knees and begged Drexter for mercy, while others maintained their faith in Jesus Christ and endured. At the end of the sixth day, a very desperate plea went out to Mount BoeYourne that fell on deaf ears.

But under the protection of Christ, the nation of Israel continued to strive. Though the Mediterranean and Red Seas streamed blood as did canals and other surrounding bodies of water, Israel's wells, fountains, and homes flowed pure water. Israel watched with heavy hearts and teary eyes as the rest of the world slowly succumbed to Drexter's wishes. They opened not only their hearts but also their gates to anyone who could make it to the Promised Land.

Drexter took pleasure in seeing the world fall humbly on their hands and knees to him. Finally, the praises that he felt he rightfully deserved and longed for were coming due. But it wasn't enough. The rejection, taunting, and disbelief of some still played well in his memory, and God's church still held on to its faith. But most of all, Israel's defiance and prosperity were a non-healing wound that plagued him.

"What will you do now?" Priest Batteast asked Drexter bluntly while sitting over tea and hors d'oeuvres.

"Enjoy," he responded in a matter-of-fact tone while savoring the taste of brie on wheat crackers.

"Will you restore the water?"

"Why would I?" he replied in a whisper and with a flashy, sly grin. His demeanor alerted Priest Batteast that he enjoyed the state of panic more than his hors d'oeuvres. "Let them suffer."

"And for how long shall they suffer? They won't last very long without water."

"They're the least of my worries."

"Is this what you and your father discussed?" Priest Batteast asked curiously.

Drexter paused for a second and thought fondly back to their father-and-son talk. "Yes."

"What's next?"

"Israel." Drexter frowned. The word painfully escaped his lips.

"What about Israel?"

"It's time for Israel's compliance with world order," he frowned again. "No longer will the world stand by while their insubordination is tolerated. They shall be governed the same as all other nations. I want an order of compliance issued to the nation immediately, and make certain that it's addressed to Prime Minister Zebulon. Advise him that Israel will convert to the euro immediately, and I don't give a damn what their currency means to them or how significant a role it played in history. Furthermore, advise him that their nation's rules and regulations are hereby obsolete, and starting immediately they will adhere to new laws and bylaws enacted by the world government and none other. Make certain that they are issued a copy, even the minutest ones. Also, they will surrender their armed forces over to the One World Army immediately, and I don't give a damn how defenseless they deem themselves to be. Their source of protection will now be provided by this government.

"Also, they will not unbolt their gates for anyone. Make it public that foreigners in Israel will have to have written consent by me personally, and anyone caught fleeing there will be executed for public showing. Last, inform Prime Minister Zebulon that his letter of resignation will be typed, signed, and delivered to me immediately with my approval already in place. I will, at a later date, assign his replacement and one to my satisfaction, of course. And make it clear to all of Israel that refusal to obey any orders that have been issued here today will be met with harsh repercussions. I would like the order sent out immediately."

"Very good." Priest Batteast leaned back in his chair with a smile of satisfaction. "Your father's traits are well entrenched in you." He was about to continue but was interrupted by a knock at the door. "Are you expecting anyone?"

"No," Drexter replied, answering the door.

Standing in full military uniform with an assault rifle strapped to his body and a machete at his waist was one of his soldiers. After saluting Drexter, he stared straight ahead and waited authorization to speak.

"What is it?" Drexter asked in a disturbed tone.

"You have visitors, sir."

"Am I forgetting something?" he asked Priest Batteast for reassurance. "You know my schedule better than I do." He grinned. "Am I to meet with someone today?"

"Not that I can recall."

"Who is awaiting my presence?" Drexter questioned the soldier.

"There are two foreign dignitaries, sir. They stated that it's urgent they meet with you."

"Send them in," he ordered. "What could this be about?" he thought out loud, taking a seat in his executive chair.

Minutes later, Ambassadors Mikhail Ivor from Russia and Trace Jerich from Canada were led into the office. The poised and well-dressed men eyed Drexter sternly; their unreceptive facial expressions alerted Drexter that their visit wasn't a social one. Ambassador Ivor only acknowledged Drexter with a nod of his head. His eyes examined the politician with whom he had once found immeasurable favor.

"Gentlemen, I don't believe we have an appointment," Drexter stated.

His words were a bit staggered. After briefly studying their stern facial expressions and almost hostile demeanor, and after realizing that they hadn't formally greeted him, Drexter continued. "I assume this matter is a serious one and couldn't have been postponed, seeing that I wasn't informed prior to your arrival."

"On behalf of our nations and other nations as well, we were elected by world leaders to pay you this visit."

"You were elected," Drexter started to say but was rudely cut off by Ambassador Ivor who paused only to inhale.

"As I'm sure you are aware, existing world conditions have caused quite an alarm globally. World leaders are requesting your presence at an emergency summit to discuss such matters."

"I'm pleased to know that world leaders are making decisions without my knowledge or my authorization for that matter." Drexter flashed Priest Batteast a swift glance. "Let me start by saying that I understand your concerns, and that I'd be more than willing to meet with you at a later date and time. At the moment, I must address other matters that cannot be delayed."

"And I'm sure those matters can be postponed, given the present global state." Ambassador Ivor leaned forward on Drexter's desk with his fingertips pressed tightly against it. "I think you'll agree that it takes precedence over all other matters at this time."

"I understand your concerns." Drexter sighed. "I assure you gentlemen that I'll address them almost immediately. You do understand that overseeing daily global operations demands a lot of my time."

"And so do the people who allowed you to obtain it," Ambassador Jerich snapped.

"Allowed me?" Drexter repeated. "Know that it had already been given to me. I would have obtained it with or without your support." The words dragged out of Drexter's mouth in a murmur. His matter-of-fact tone sparked anger in Ambassador Ivor. Drexter stood up and peered at the two ambassadors without blinking an eye.

Drexter's arrogance infuriated Ambassador Ivor now that his hidden agenda had become a lot clearer. The man who had once presented himself as a calm, peaceful, and caring political leader of the people had begun to show his true colors. Ambassador Ivor, once an avid advocate of Drexter and his ambitions, who had been appointed by him to oversee financial operations in Russia, now perceived the arrogant dictator standing before him as nothing more than a con artist.

His memory flashed back to past summits and conferences; only now the truth painted a more accurate portrait. He visualized Drexter standing behind the podium hiding his real agenda behind a cunning smile and carefully structured, idle words. Drexter's once inspiring speeches were now nothing more than idle promises. He became angry with himself for falling blindly into Drexter's political trap and for not questioning his motives or investigating why he had to have control over global finances and the militia. Feelings of betrayal rushed him; he struggled to maintain professionalism.

Prime Minister Zebulon's words of warning, which he had once perceived as being jealous accusations, blared in his ears. He realized that only one man possessed the wisdom to understand what the end results would be. He recalled Prime Minister Zebulon standing alone before the assembly with his shekel in his hand, fighting not only for his nation, but also for the lives of those that had opposed and ostracized him. Now, standing before him stood the offspring of that warning: a man with ungoverned power whose core was comprised of greed, deceit, and destruction.

"Mr. Luciphon, I speak on behalf of all world leaders when I say this: have your monkey ass in Switzerland on Thursday," Ambassador Ivor stated in a commanding tone and pointed his finger in Drexter's face. "We expect to see you there. Good day, Mr. Luciphon." He straightened his coat jacket and then fixed his tie. "No need to see us out. We're more than capable of finding our way."

Ambassador Ivor cut his eyes at Ambassador Jerich, signaling his intended departure. After one last glance at Drexter, they boldly walked out, talking to each other. "I'm afraid that Prime Minister Zebulon was right," Ambassador Ivor stated. "Our ignorance has created a problem that threatens the well-being of this world, and it demands our immediate attention and prompt action. Upon returning to our hotel, we're to start making calls to fellow constituents. If we're to correct this problem, we'll need the aid of all diplomats. I'm sure convincing them won't be a problem after hearing what we've witnessed here today. In the coming weeks, we may find it benefitting to pay Prime Minister Zebulon a visit."

Drexter stood outside his chambers and listened as the two ambassadors conversed but only managed to take in part of their discussion. He was somewhat stunned by the ambassadors' show of power and their display of arrogance. But more so, it was their blatant act of disrespect that perturbed him. He stared at Priest Batteast as if in a trance and then replanted himself back in his chair.

"Where were we on Israel? Oh yeah! As I was saying, make certain that Israel is on track with world compliance. Also, have someone make travel arrangements for us for the summit in Geneva on Thursday, and after that, put a freeze on all global monetary systems. Until I say otherwise, no country shall receive aid of any type, whether it be currency, food, clothing, or what have you. Order the militia on standby in case my orders need enforcing, please. Anyone who disobeys them shall be harshly dealt with. If they can make decisions on their own without my knowledge, they can fend for themselves. If you'll excuse me, old friend, I find myself a bit preoccupied."

"Very well." Priest Batteast, sensing that Drexter was gravely disturbed by the ambassadors' visit, gathered up his notes and made his way toward the door. "I'll see to your demands." As he walked out into the corridor, he was turned around by Drexter's voice.

"By the way, happy birthday. Just how old are you, anyway?" Drexter laughed jokingly.

"Almost as old as your father," he responded with a grin and then closed the door behind him.

Priest Batteast wasted no time overseeing the completion of his friend's commands. He personally edited the orders to ensure that all was to Drexter's specifications. By the end of daylight, an order of compliance was personally signed by Drexter himself and then delivered to Israel.

Upon making a few phone calls, monetary systems were shut down immediately, and all dignitaries who had been placed over banking and other financial operations were barred from their positions without notice and replaced by the militia. Frustrations filtered across the world as political leaders' requests for aid were redirected to Mount BoeYourne for Drexter's authorization, where they were denied without explanation.

Two days later, Priest Batteast and Drexter boarded a private jet en route to Switzerland. Drexter was his usual calm and cunning self.

→▶■◉ ◉■◀←

Prime Minister Zebulon signed for the package addressed to him from Mount BoeYourne. The bold, red letters stamped URGENT on the front jumped out at him. Instantly, his thoughts were pessimistic as he figured nothing good could possibly come out of Rome in such times. After returning from touring his nation, he decided to return to his office early Thursday morning instead of taking the weekend off.

After settling into his desk, he scanned through hundreds of written messages that awaited his response. Oddly, most were from diplomats whom he hadn't had any contact with since his outburst at the summit, and several were from Ambassador Ivor who requested his urgent response. Assuming that the messages were somehow linked to the package, he flung them to the side.

After realizing that he couldn't put off the inevitable, he cautiously tore open the package. On top was a letter that outlined new laws that were soon to govern Israel. His mood soured. The remainder of the memorandum spelled out his intended resignation, preparations to appoint his replacement, and the rest of Drexter's policies. After scanning through hundreds of pages of rules and regulations, he called an urgent assembly of Israel's ambassadors, foreign and defense ministers, and other political heads. By midday, they had all united to discuss the future of their nation.

"Upon my return, I found this material awaiting me. Let me begin by saying that it has always been my primary duty to act in the best interest of this nation. I place the welfare of the Israeli people and this nation before my own. Know that whatever decisions that are made here at this assembly, I will abide by them.

"We all understand that it has been Drexter's underlying mission to have me removed from power. Only now he has expressed, explicitly, such in writing. Know that I have no intention of backing down unless I'm forced to do so by this administration. I feel that I've been the strong, effective leader that Israel needed to lead them through these uncertain times."

"We agree," the assembly blurted out.

"Thank you," Prime Minister Zebulon replied. "It's my belief that if Israel should adhere to world government laws, it would surely bring about our swift destruction as intended by Drexter. Israel would not have a leg to stand on if we surrender them our military forces."

"Prime Minister Zebulon, I certainly understand and agree with your outlook, but what other choice do we have?" Defense Minister Meers asked after reading the memorandum.

"We fight," an ambassador asserted.

"How?" Defense Minister Meers asked. "Israeli forces are no match for the World Militia. Have you forgotten that they outnumber our forces by a million to one? We can't possibly overpower the world's forces, and to even try would spell destruction for this nation." He shook his head in frustration while continuing to scan through the laws. "We have no other recourse to fall on."

"Of course we do," Prime Minister Zebulon interjected.

"Who?" Defense Minister Meers leaned forward in his seat. "Who shall we rely on? All of our allies have turned against us because we oppose Drexter's laws. The treaty with Palestine is void, and even our longtime ally, the United States, has abandoned us. Tell me what country would dare go against a man so powerful to aid this nation?"

"Israel shall rely on the same recourse that they've always relied on since time began. The same power that delivered the children of Israel in the Old Testament and the same power that reunited us again as a nation shall also deliver us in the end."

Prime Minister Zebulon stood strongly on his faith and boldly confessed God's protection while exerting a look of complete confidence.

"I understand, but how do we stop the World Militia from a savage invasion on this nation any time they desire?" Defense Minister Meers threw his hands in the air in disgust. "Our nation would not last a minute against their arsenal of weapons."

The mention of weapons sent fear through the hearts of the assembly, causing many to shuffle in their seats. They whispered among themselves, and others dropped their heads, signaling defeat.

"No weapon formed against Israel shall prosper." Prime Minister Zebulon placed his hands to his lips and formed them in a praying position. He paused and then lowered his head. "No weapon formed against Israel shall prosper."

"It already has," Defense Minister Meers pleaded.

"No, it hasn't. Mr. Defense Minister, God didn't say that the weapon wouldn't form; He said that it wouldn't prosper. Whatever calamity Drexter Luciphon has in store for this nation, it shall not prosper. God will intervene on Israel's behalf, and we shall be delivered. In the end, Israel shall stand."

The assembly weighed in on Prime Minister Zebulon's testimonial. "And how is it that you can reassure us of this?" Foreign Minister Ashalon inquired.

"Has He not already reassured us of this? When darkness invaded the earth, did not His light shine down on all of Israel? Was not His promise of protection clearly visible in the sky for us to see? Does not your water still run pure while the rest of the world scavenges? Where is your faith? Where is Israel's faith? If our faith fails us, then know that this nation is surely doomed. It's all that we have now, and surely it is all that we need."

—═◎ ◎═—

From his private jet, Drexter called ahead to the Palace of Nations and alerted them of his tardiness. After a sincere apology, he requested that all dignitaries be present and prepared to start upon his arrival. Due to time restrictions with his schedule and prior obligations pending, he would need to respond immediately back to Mount BoeYourne. Upon arriving at the airport in Geneva, he phoned ahead to inform them of his estimated arrival time and was reassured that world leaders were present and anxiously awaiting his arrival. Heavily guarded by the militia, his motorcade was escorted to the Palace of Nations.

Soldiers lined the driveway that led up to the front of the Palace. Inside, the well-structured building seemed vacant except for the soldiers that guarded the corridor. Drexter was his usual jovial and confident self entering the conference room but was stunned by the number of dignitaries. Sitting room had been created to accommodate the higher than usual number of attendees in the assembly, and standing room only had been filled by dignitaries who lined the walls in rows.

Drexter's presence was met by dead silence when he walked onto the platform. After checking their timepieces, the dignitaries stared at him with disdain. The silence and cold looks irritated Drexter. He had become accustomed to the standing ovations, cheers, and praises that his presence once commanded. Out of the corner of his eye, he observed whispering among them, and this, too, annoyed him.

"I wasn't expecting such a warm welcome as this," Drexter joked in an attempt to break the ice; he received stares of contempt and disgust.

"Excuse us if we no longer find your humor amusing. I'm sure everyone will agree that now is hardly the time for your antics. Instead, why don't we get to the gist of why we summoned you here?" Ambassador Ivor spoke bravely.

A murmur echoed throughout the crowd. Drexter peered at the politician who had twice flexed his muscle without any repercussions. Also disturbing was the popularity that he seemed to have garnered with the assembly.

"And the gist of it is?" Drexter paused briefly. "Um," he sighed. His anger was beginning to surface.

The attention of the assembly was undivided as Drexter and the defiant ambassador from Russia, who wouldn't be intimidated by power or status, stood at odds.

"When we put you in power—" Ambassador Ivor started to say.

"Pardon my unpreparedness, but I seem to have left documentation for this conference in the vehicle. I want to ascertain that the information conveyed to you is concrete."

Drexter grinned at the congregation and then politely excused himself. The beauty of Parc de Nations jumped out at him: the well-manicured yard, the sculptures, and the lake all soothed him as he calmly proceeded down the stairs. "Ugh," he griped in disgust, throwing up his left hand.

The main entrance doors of the palace bolted with force, inner entrances shut and locked, and glass rattled with every window that slammed and fastened. Panic consumed the assembly after a brief minute of shock. Constituents scrambled to escape the deadly entrapment.

Casually, Drexter strolled down the walkway, passing the arrangement of national flags; they burst into flames on their poles.

At the end of the driveway awaited Priest Batteast in their black limousine. Drexter stopped to view the soundly built structure one last time before ordering his motorcade to depart. He felt the rumble of the earth's core beneath his vehicle. The palace shook, forming large cracks in its foundation. Glass shattered from the pressure of the collapsing structure. The havoc within was overshadowed by the earth's rumble. Diplomats trampled each other in a desperate attempt to elude hefty falling debris. Columns supporting the structure snapped and then gave way.

With all his might, Drexter tried to resist the temptation of gloating, but it was much too powerful even for him; therefore, the motorcade halted. He enjoyed the catastrophe as it unfolded. A small number of dignitaries clung to their last breath after being pinned under tons of rubbish, and others lay crushed. A handful of diplomats were able to hold on to each other for what little comfort it offered. Like an atomic explosion, dirt and rubbish ascended from the ground and expanded outward, swallowing up the ruins. In the aftermath of the catastrophe sat a crater commemorating the site of world peace. The look of triumph on Drexter's face evoked laughter from Priest Batteast.

"This sort of reminds me of a scene my father described long ago," Drexter started out by saying.

"Jericho, do you speak of? The walls of Jericho?" Priest Batteast finished the statement.

Drexter stared at his friend in amazement. "How did you know?"

"You keep forgetting, Young Master, that I'm almost as old as your father."

Kicking off his shoes and removing his coat jacket, Drexter eased back in his seat. His thoughts turned to Ambassador Ivor and the blatant disrespect he demonstrated that ultimately cost him his life. Retribution felt invigorating to him.

He anxiously anticipated his return to Mount BoeYourne to resume daily operations, but above all, looked forward to Israel's compliance with his orders and Prime Minister Zebulon's resignation.

⟶▰ ▰⟵

Unexpected pounding on the conference-room door, followed by an abrupt entrance by his aide, caused Prime Minister Zebulon to temporarily halt discussions by Israeli dignitaries. Frantically, his aide informed them of the frightening event that was unfolding. In horror, the world watched as the Swiss locals scrambled to paste together the pieces of the catastrophe. As information became available, it was made clear that a conference among world dignitaries had been scheduled for that day.

Prime Minister Zebulon frantically rushed back to his chambers to retrieve the pile of messages in his desk drawer. His hands trembled as he dialed call-back numbers, and the horrified voices on the other end of the phone confirmed his worst fears.

As more information became available, it was later confirmed that the structure was indeed occupied with world leaders when it collapsed, and that all inside were believed to have perished. As the victims were identified individually, Ambassador Mikhail Ivor's name was mentioned.

Prime Minister Zebulon remembered that the ambassador had made several attempts to contact him in the days leading up to the disaster. He deeply regretted not responding, and he wondered what the ambassador had attempted to tell him. Or had he attempted to warn him?

Graphic photos told the horrifying tale of the diplomat's last minutes. The structure had sunk deep within the earth's soil—so deep that it made the removal of ruins and the retrieval of dead bodies virtually impossible.

Once back at Mount BoeYourne, Drexter wasted no time ordering the World Militia into place so as to enforce his forthcoming orders. Soldiers closed and secured the doors of all markets, food banks, and hospitals. Per his orders, bartering was outlawed; no one was permitted to buy or sell goods of any sort without his authorization. And anyone caught in violation was to be beheaded on the spot.

Six long days had passed since blood began flowing across the earth's waters. As reserves were depleted, the struggle for daily survival became virtually impossible. The races were faced with the dilemma of ingesting blood or perishing. For some, the mere thought of it was inconceivable, and their perseverance ended in death due to dehydration. The lifeless and precious bodies of infants born after the Rapture and of children were found cuddled beneath the corpses of their caregivers. Their tiny hands remained clinging to their parents' garments, and the agony of those parents' last days remained forever frozen on their faces.

Those whose spirits had been broken succumbed to the demands of their weakened flesh and tasted blood. The nauseating taste sickened their stomachs, and the foul, offensive odor made even the strongest of them regurgitate. Their immune system's inability to fight off germs and bacteria caused an outbreak of sickness and disease that spread like the Black Death.

As food supplies dwindled down to nothing and the struggle for survival increased, the human population turned to the earth's resources. Animals, insects, worms, rodents, vegetation, and even family pets were sacrificed for food.

No one stood exempt from Drexter's orders, not even the wealthy. Hollywood's rich and elite who had stored up their treasures on earth and placed faith in their riches for survival were distressed after finding that their millions and billions were of no value when it came to bargaining with Drexter. The famous found that their notoriety, prominence, and celebrity status carried no weight. They, too, were alarmed to find that their arrogance, self-importance, and oversized egos didn't ensure their survival.

Sheiks and princes of the Middle East were astonished to find that their oil was without value, and that they, too, were subject to Drexter's tyranny. After failing to build their lives, hopes, and dreams on God, and having relied on false hopes and dreams for so long, the rich and the elite found themselves totally astray. Unable to function under such adverse conditions, they turned to suicide as an easy escape.

Chapter 9

"THE MEASUREMENTS ARE slightly off. It shall have to be redone. I'll tell you what, put this one aside. We may be able to use it later, but this piece is cut perfectly. Good job, young ones, good job."

Noah patted the male heirs on their shoulders before hauling away the piece of gopher wood and fetching another. Before reentering the Pearly Gates to be about His business, the Good Shepherd stood and watched His sheep flock together to accomplish their goals. The sound of laughter and an occasional foot race that turned into a foot chase warmed His heart. His children had asked if they could erect arks as Noah had in his days and if He would bring forth the rain upon completion. Wanting to give them all the desires of their heart, Jesus agreed. Immediately, they made haste and, with the help of some of the angels, worked diligently directly outside the Pearly Gates.

Noah and his three sons, Shem, Ham, and Japheth, were appointed by Jesus, who by trade was a carpenter, to oversee the project. When they briefed the heirs on all the material they would need to complete the project, many became discouraged upon hearing gopher wood and pitch. From where would they obtain such material? They hadn't seen any in Paradise. The angels and Bible greats all laughed at how quickly they became discouraged and at how amazing it was when an ample amount of gopher wood and other materials formed right before their very eyes.

"Thank You, Lord. Thank You, Jesus," they shouted out at the top of their lungs.

"Where is your faith, young ones? Where is your faith? Did our Lord not supply all of your needs while on earth? Surely then will He do the same in Paradise." Noah sighed and then shook his head and smiled. "Remember, faith is the substance of things hoped for and the evidence of things not seen."

"What happened here?" Shem laughed, inspecting a piece of wood that had been cut by the women. Let's see if we can find something else for you females to work on. I think building may be more suitable for men."

"Isn't it pretty?" they laughed, caressing the rugged edges and crooked form.

"It's a good thing we have plenty of wood because it looks as if we're going to need it. Why don't we throw this one away with the other seven pieces you've destroyed," Shem kidded.

The sound of saws blaring and joyous conversations filled the atmosphere. Noah was well pleased with the determination of the heirs in their endeavors. He sat back to watch for a moment; memories of his history flooded his mind. He envisioned his family working tirelessly to fulfill God's command. He remembered the taunting, jeering, and name-calling he endured when wicked men walked past. But he would not be deterred because his walk with God was more important than the perception the world had of him.

He laughed at how his wife and he chased after chickens and hens for the longest time in order to secure them in the ark. He could still sense the elephant's trunks caressing his cheek and the lion's mighty paws when they reached out to greet them.

He could still hear God's authoritative voice in his ears telling him that it was time to enter the ark. At the ripe age of six hundred, he gathered his family and without hesitation entered their new home. He could still feel the force of the door slamming shut and the distinctive hum that echoed off the walls when God sealed the entranceway. He wiped the tears from his eyes. He had walked with God throughout his entire life and never regretted one moment.

"Noah, are you OK?" the heirs asked while hugging him.

"Oh yeah! I'm just reliving my years again, and God has seen me through every last one of them. Thank You, Lord. I am a living testimony."

"What happened the day you entered the ark, Noah?" Some of the female heirs who had come to comfort him wanted to know. After making a seat on the ground around him, they waited patiently to hear his life story. "What was it like on that day?"

"When our Creator sealed the door, we never looked out again until after it stopped raining. I can still hear the laughing and the jeering from outside. For days they kept asking where the rain was. We were busy getting the animals settled in. Then, seven days after we entered, I heard the first raindrop strike the roof. It was louder than a ton of giant hail falling at once. The jeering stopped abruptly. I think your generation calls it the calm before the storm."

He sighed and stared off into Heaven. More female heirs came and sat down around him while the male heirs continued erecting the arks. They always found stories from biblical times inspiring and fascinating. Noah didn't notice the crowd he had drawn. His face was still focused toward the sky.

"The rain came crashing down at once. We couldn't see it, but we felt the force of it against the ark. The animals became a bit agitated. They sensed it, too. It rained as it never had before and never would again. I can still hear the yelling, screaming, pleading, and crying. I still feel the pounding on the ark as they begged to enter. Young heirs, our Creator sealed the entranceway, and when God seals something, only He can open it—only God, Himself, can open it."

He finally looked down and was caught off guard to see how his audience had expanded. "Where did all of you come from?"

They laughed and then begged him to continue.

"Thank you," he kissed his earthly wife after receiving a cup of cool water. After taking several small sips, he continued. "Not long after, the yelling stopped." He nodded his head up and down. "I knew then." He sighed. "I knew then. All evil had been removed from God's world just as He said He would. I still believe today that the rain was God's tears falling down."

"Why do you say that, Noah?" one of the heirs asked for clarification.

"I believe our Creator mourned when He destroyed the very thing that He loves and cherishes the most. I believe His heart ached as He cleansed the earth. Anyhow, it rained, young heirs, it really rained. For forty days and forty nights, it poured. It was awhile before the ark began to sway, maybe days I believe, but I didn't keep count. I remember that the rain kept pouring." He sighed.

"Anyhow, eight lives were spared. Out of a world of people, only eight of us, my family, lived our lives in God's favor. An entire world was abolished because they made the choice to live their lives sinfully and outside of God's favor. But the wages of sin are death." He sighed.

"Giants they were—evil, wicked, and corrupt. All in all, it was Satan's attempt to corrupt the entire race in order to prevent our Lord's arrival to redeem man. But our Creator wouldn't allow His blood-line to be cut off, and so it was preserved." He chuckled. "It was preserved through the bloodline of Seth. From him came Enos, Cainan, Mahalaleel, Jared, Enoch, Methuselah, and then my father, Lamech. Anyhow, when it stopped raining, we finally looked out. There was nothing there. Everything as we knew it had vanished: trees, mountains, animals, and sadly, life. There we were. It was just us and water—and the Good Lord, of course." He smiled.

"One day the ark stopped moving. It had rocked for so long, it scared me when it ceased. My wife and I looked at each other. We had come to rest on a mountain top; Ararat was its name. The waters were still visible on the earth but had greatly receded. I'll never forget it. What a joyous sight. Then one day the face of the earth showed itself, and it was time to come out. I think we spent a year in the ark or something close to it. Anyhow, we were commanded to go forth, multiply, and replenish the earth, and we did just that. We replenished the earth.

But sadly I say, young heirs, that history has repeated itself. You would think that man would have learned from our mistakes. With all the things that our Creator has given man to aid him—the prophets, the Bible, and our Lord, Jesus Christ—you would think that he would heed God's warning. But once again, those giants from my days have resurfaced, and their hearts are more corrupt, and their deeds more wicked than ever."

He looked out at his audience and then at the male heirs busy at work. He smiled at the generations of races all mixed together just as God had intended and the love that each of them harvested and bestowed upon one another.

"Look around, young heirs. This is what our Creator intended for us on earth: love, peace, happiness, and alms."

"Why is it, Noah, that man's heart is filled with evil?" a gentle voice sounded from the audience. "Why?"

"They no longer fear God, young heirs. They no longer fear Him. The fear of God is the acknowledgement of His presence, Deity, and power in our lives that restrains us. When that fear no longer exists, man is unguarded from evil, and he's totally defenseless to Satan's attacks." He paused momentarily and then gently whispered, "They no longer fear Him, but they will. Before it is all over on earth, they will. I tell you, all eyes shall behold Him, and they shall weep. Some shall weep out of joy, but others…" He paused again. "Our Lord, Jesus Christ, have mercy on their souls."

"Noah, why does God love us so much?" another voice asked.

"I'll be honest with you. In all my years, young heirs, and they are many, I still don't have the answer to that question. I, too, still wonder why. I just know that He does. His love is incomprehensible. He said that before He formed us in the womb, He knew and loved us. Young heirs, His love is beyond the perimeters of our understanding, as are His peace, grace and mercy, blessings, and miracles."

"Noah, where did God come from?" an adolescent asked.

"Young heir, I don't know. Nobody knows, and we'll never know. It's something we need not know, and neither is it important. Young heirs, just know this one thing: Our Lord is, and our Lord was. Before time began and before the earth was formed, God was."

"Noah, what happened to your boat?" another juvenile asked.

"It's still there, is it not? Doest it not still sit on Mount Ararat?"

"It wasn't destroyed over time, Noah?"

"Young heirs, anything that our Lord builds shall stand the test of time. It'll stand forever. Our Lord created it, and only our Lord can destroy it."

"Man has never been able to find it, Noah."

"And it is because they know not where to search." He sniggered. "But I tell you, it still sits on Mount Ararat, untouched and unmarred."

"Will man ever find it, Noah?"

"Perhaps they will. Perhaps they won't." He giggled. "Our Lord's will be done."

"But Noah, because of the lack of evidence, they attempt to discredit God," an older female replied.

"Young heirs, when you dwelled on earth, you never saw our Lord; yet, you still believed. How else could you have gotten here, except you walked by faith. Young heirs, the ark is embedded in the hearts of God's children; therefore, it shall sit on Mount Ararat forever. The worldly man will never find it, but God's children need not look very far to find it. It is our faith that tells us that our Lord did everything He said He would. Man must also learn to walk by faith and not by sight. He must walk by faith and faith alone. In the end, it is man's choice what he chooses to believe, but God's children walk by faith. Well, isn't that a blast from the past."

The ark slowly started to take form. The heirs marveled over their accomplishment.

"Can we name it, Noah?" the female heirs asked.

"I suppose we can. What did you have in mind?"

"The Jehovah-Shammah," they yelled, clapped, and then jumped for joy.

"The Lord is there." He nodded his head up and down. "The Lord is there. I think that would be a perfect name for the ark. His presence is always abiding with His people, isn't it? OK, I'm sure He would love that written on the front."

When the heirs ran to find Jesus to ask for paint for the dedication title, Noah took advantage of the quiet moment to raise his hands to God. "Father, it was Your will that I walked the earth for nine hundred and fifty years, and every one of those years was surrounded by Your presence. You said that You would never leave me, and You never did. You never have, and I thank You, Lord. I pray for those on earth. Father, please intervene on their behalf. Strengthen them and their faith in You. Make Your presence known. Touch the heart of man that he may come to know and walk with You. Deliver them from evil, gracious Lord."

Noah cried. Lifting up his voice, he offered up a song of praise to God Almighty. His rugged, husky voice disclosed his age. Like the wind, his praise travelled across Paradise from one perimeter to the other for all to hear. Soon, Heaven transformed into a symphonic orchestra of praise. Heads nodded, bodies swayed, and feet stamped to the melody. Noah's voice surpassed Heaven's choir as he poured out his heart and soul into the hymn.

⇥━◉ ◉━⇤

"How much longer shall they be made to suffer?" Priest Batteast questioned Drexter. As the media broadcast alarming images of the world's suffering, he questioned their odds of surviving. "Without basic necessities, they shall surely perish if that be your wish."

His words landed lightly in one ear and exited directly out the other of a preoccupied Drexter, whose attention was focused on Israel's response. The carefully worded document clearly conveyed Israel's defiance toward world government and its laws, their strength as a nation united, and their willingness to challenge opposition, as well as their anticipated victory over him through Jesus Christ.

A part of Drexter envied Israel's resilience and perseverance to withstand opposition since reuniting as a nation in 1948. Despite their size, they emitted the confidence and might of a world superpower, but their defiance to world order would not be tolerated.

"Israel defied my orders. It shall not be tolerated," Drexter proclaimed. "Issue God's people one last ultimatum, and then assemble the World Militia for deployment. Station them in Greece, Turkey, Russia, Lebanon, Syria, Saudi Arabia, Iraq, Jordan, Egypt, Sinai, and Iran. Also, disperse military battleships into the Mediterranean as well as the Red Sea and any other channel of water nearby. See to it that they are geared and ready for battle upon my declaration."

"How many shall be deployed, Young Master?"

"Half the militia should suffice, wouldn't you say?"

"I concur. Consider it done. What about the races?"

Drexter didn't answer; instead, he stared at his friend in a dumbfounded manner.

"Have you not noticed?" Priest Batteast inquired. "You wanted praise; well, you have it. Take a look."

Drexter tuned in to the media. Weak, ravaged, diseased, and starving bodies of billions lay on their deathbeds, in streets, and in trenches, crying out his name for mercy and healing.

"You have them and their praise. How long shall it be before you restore the water? Without basic necessities, they shall surely die," Priest Batteast repeated. "You won't have praise if they're all dead, Young Master. When you sit on your throne, tell me who will be left to serve you if they've all perished?"

"You're right, old friend," he paused. "You are right. I guess I wasn't thinking. Summon the media at once," he ordered. "I shall finally consummate my flock with my sign. Order the militia to make preparations to reopen the markets and hospitals upon my command and under my strict orders."

⊷═◉ ◉═⊷

Harper wiped the sweat from Stanton's forehead and with the same rag, dabbed the oozing puss from his lesions. He smiled at Stanton as if to reassure him that everything was going to be OK.

"Try to get some rest," he said, pulling the covers further up on Stanton's shoulders, and then he left the room.

Mabrey and Harper found Connery standing on the front porch of their residence looking up at the sky with his hands folded. He seemed to be fixated on the heavens.

"It's funny how the sky displays such beauty: the beaming sun, puffy, white clouds, and the awesome blue background. But the earth displays such horror." Connery's eyes tracked a bluebird as it flew across his view.

"We need to get him help, Connery. Without medicine, he won't make it. His body isn't strong enough to fight off the infection," Mabrey pushed.

Connery hesitated. "Don't you think I know that?"

"We have no choice but to try and get past the militia and get into one of the hospitals. We can't allow him to die like that."

"I'm thinking. Give me a chance to think for a moment," Connery pleaded and then proceeded to walk down the steps and onto the sidewalk.

"Anything that you can give me, I'd appreciate it. I'm so hungry, sir."

The faint and unfamiliar voice startled Connery, causing him to spin around. He hadn't seen the scruffy-looking, Puerto Rican male, tattooed in scabs staggering behind him, and the sight of him alerted Connery that he, too, was on his last leg.

"I wish I could, sir. My brother is lying upstairs, dying right now." Connery paused to take a deep breath in order to bring himself to admit what was wounding him inside. "And I can't do a damn thing to help him."

"God help your brother," he replied in a sincere tone, momentarily forgetting about his woes.

"And you also, sir. Hang in there."

"Yeah, well, I didn't have to be in this predicament. Had I listened to the saints and chosen Christ, I wouldn't be here now." He looked down in sorrow. "But it was my choice."

"You're not alone," Connery sighed.

"God have mercy on us all." He shot Connery a quick but weak grin and then staggered down the avenue.

Connery redirected his attention toward Heaven and this time thought about the Creator. God's name was one that was mentioned on a regular basis since Stanton's encounter with the angels. It had inspired Stanton to take a long, hard look at his life and the surrounding circumstances, and give Jesus a try. Watching him stumble over his words while praying was a bit comical to Connery but also a bit refreshing. Even more bizarre was seeing the affect his change had on Mabrey and Harper. Out of nowhere, Connery found himself living with three redeemed believers in Jesus Christ. When they begged him to reconsider his stand on life, he declined the offer but encouraged them to follow whatever road in life they chose to travel. But what angered Connery was Stanton's current physical condition and why Jesus would allow such suffering to befall him, especially after his brother had turned his life over to Him.

"I hate You," Connery yelled out loud to the Messiah with passion in his voice. "I hate You for what you're doing to my brother. He doesn't deserve this. He turned his life over to You, and this is what he receive in return." That's why I depend on me, he thought to himself.

The sound of car doors slamming caught Connery's attention. The engine of the old sedan revved up. Mabrey and Harper quickly snapped their seat belts in gear.

"Wait a minute. Where are you going?" Connery yelled nervously.

"If we don't get medicine for Stanton soon, he's going to die," Mabrey affirmed.

"Wait a second, and let's figure this out for a moment," Connery begged.

"Stay here with Stanton. We'll be back."

The sedan started down the avenue with Connery in full pursuit on foot, yelling and screaming. After stopping in the middle of the street half out of breath, Connery watched as his brothers drove out of sight. An uneasy feeling overtook him. Reluctantly, he made his way back inside the residence to check on Stanton.

⊷═◉ ◉═⊷

"Everything has been completed according to your orders: Israel's final ultimatum went out this morning, half the World Militia has been briefed and is gearing up for immediate deployment, and the rest is on standby awaiting your command. All that is left is your address to the world, and the media is in place as you ordered."

After one last check, Priest Batteast neatly arranged his documents in his black portfolio and then placed it on the table.

"Thank you, old friend. Inform the media that I shall be with them shortly," Drexter advised.

"I shall."

Drexter confined himself to his private quarters. Opting against his usual expensive, Italian suits, he donned his black, hooded, silk robe and sash. From a secured compartment in his study, he retrieved his Satanic Bible and began quoting verses almost from memory. The walls glowed like fiery flames which brought his recital to a halt. Dense smoke ascended from the floor, the lights flickered and then dimmed, and room temperature repeatedly cycled from one hundred degrees Fahrenheit to an instant ten below zero. Immediately, his father's presence could be felt. He had come to witness his son's address to the world. As the familiar sound of his father's thunderous voice spoke out to him in Latin, Drexter eased back in his chair and warmly greeted his role model. Two hours later, an energized Drexter emerged to address his congregation.

"We have a visitor, Young Master." Priest Batteast smiled. He, too, sensed the presence of Satan nearby.

"Indeed we do."

Drexter's presence was met with pleas of mercy. The media aired in every nation around the globe. His once caring and sincere demeanor had now been exchanged for a more arrogant one.

"Your cries haven't fallen on deaf ears. I assure you that they've been heard. I see the pain, suffering, and affliction that have befallen my people, and I assure you, I have not turned a blind eye to your misfortune. Come unto me, and I'll give you comfort. I'll supply the needs of my people." Raising his hands and staring directly into the cameras, he commanded, "I restore the waters for my people."

Polluted bodies of water transformed back to their original state. Via the media, the world watched as the masses rushed into streams, lakes, and oceans to wash their wounds and to gulp up as much fresh water from the former two as their stomachs could store.

"My flock, denounce the Son of Man," he continued on. "I am the true Messiah. I heal the sick and strengthen the weak." With a nod of his head, he summoned the militia.

Several members emerged onto the platform with an ailing female who had to be supported in order to stand. She, too, was covered with lesions, her eyes dilated, her breathing escalated, and her scalp balding. When Drexter touched the kneeling woman's head, she sprang from the ground without assistance. Her skin was rejuvenated, and her health was fully restored. Kneeling before him once more, she kissed his hand and then offered up her appreciation and praise.

"On this day, I shall consummate my people with my sign."

Clenching her hand, he stared at each individual ridge pattern on her fingertip. His nail, which mimicked the hue of smoke, outlined her arches, loops, and whorls. With a taunting smirk on his face directed toward Heaven, he marveled with pride as he etched his mark, 666, into her palm. Victory seized him, causing his smirk to flourish into a full devilish smile. Overwhelmed with his accomplishment, he snickered at the sky. The thought of conquering God's beloved creation delighted him. He knew that all who accepted his mark would become the permanent property of his father's kingdom. Sensing the public's weakness and fear, he knew that they were easy prey and that the lure of vital necessities was all that was needed to seal their fate.

"For all who bear my symbol, food, water, medicine, clothing, and other vital necessities await you. I again open my markets for my people to freely barter, my hospitals for your healing, and my banks. My religion shall be your new faith. I shall soon rule from the temple of Israel and shall walk godlike among you. And for those who refuse my mark, death shall find you."

Reentering Mount BoeYourne, Drexter and Priest Batteast immediately confined themselves to Drexter's private quarters where they celebrated with Satan.

Upon direct orders from Drexter, the militia opened markets of all sorts. Around the globe, structures were flooded with long lines of desperate, frightened, and eager inhabitants in need of vital necessities. One by one, Drexter's eternal symbol was branded into the right palm and on the heads of the masses rendering them spiritually dead. Their souls were marked for eternal damnation in exchange for worldly goods.

→══◉ ◉══←

Harper and Mabrey stood impatiently in line. Every now and then, they stepped out to see how close they had gotten to the hospital checkpoints, which were heavily guarded by armed militia. Determined to save Stanton, their goal of obtaining medicine would not be thwarted by the long lines that slowed their race against time.

"What if we're too late? What if Stanton dies before we get him help?" Mabrey nervously questioned his brother.

"Why think like that? Just pray that he can hold on until we get back. Connery's with him. He's in good hands," Harper replied, attempting to remain positive.

Out of the corner of his eye, Harper observed soldiers moving from their work areas and toward the line.

"I don't want the sign, but my children are sick and need medicine. Please, help me."

Just ahead of them was a single female with three young children who were stricken with infection. She bowed her head and sobbed in desperation, and her hands shook violently while she wiped the tears from her eyes and cheeks. Mabrey and Harper listened as the soldiers refused her entry into the hospital unless she accepted the mark. She took a long look at the physical condition of her beloved children. Their innocent little eyes stared at her in desperation, which made her heart grieve further.

"I am now a child of the true, living God. I will not accept the sign of the beast, and neither shall my children bear it."

Distraught, she grabbed her babies and turned away but was grabbed from behind by one of the soldiers. Two soldiers grabbed her son, shoved his body to the pavement, and held him down by stepping on his back. With little strength in his ailing body, he struggled to break free. He reached out to his mother for protection.

"David!" she yelled.

Pleading and crying out in desperation, she struggled to gain freedom to try and protect him. A soldier with sergeant stripes on his uniform drew his machete and raised it above the youth's head, and with one mighty, downward blow, severed it. A splattered trail of blood streamed behind as it rolled within inches of his mother's feet.

"Jesus! Jesus! Jesus, help me," she pleaded.

After finally breaking free, she huddled at his side. Her trembling arms carefully lifted and cradled his lifeless, precious body. His blood stained her garment.

"My son!" she screamed and then paused. "Lord, why my son?" her voice mumbled in shock. Rocking his corpse back and forth, she dressed his wound with her hand to prohibit the flow of blood.

Her two daughters looked on in innocence. Observing her frantic state, they tenderly wrapped their little arms around her neck and squeezed with all their little might to comfort her. The display of love hardened the heart of the sergeant; he seized the two.

"Stop!" Harper and Mabrey yelled, rushing toward the militia.

Grabbing the two innocent victims, Harper thrust them out of harm's way and charged at the soldiers, knocking one to the pavement. From behind him came a sharp and agonizing pain that ended his attack. Helplessly, he plunged to the ground, gripping his lower back.

"Harper!" Mabrey screamed.

Being held at bay, Mabrey watched as two soldiers stood over a paralyzed Harper with machetes. The sound of his brother's screeching sent Mabrey helplessly to his knees. In horror, he watched while soldiers mercilessly pierced Harper repeatedly in the back. With every strike, his body responded with a jerk until a fatal blow caused his face to collide with the pavement. His unresponsive body lay in its own pool of blood.

Struggling wildly to break free, Mabrey's head was forced to the dirt while the militia cheered. His vision was blurred from tears and sweat, and he sobbed over the near-mutilated corpse of his brother. Within seconds, his skull rolled several inches on the concrete pavement until it came to a standstill upright.

Turning back to the woman and her daughters, the soldiers found her hovering over her young. "Where is your God? Where is your God?" the superior officer yelled in a commanding tone. Without mercy, he pulled his firearm, and three blasts echoed out. Maliciously, he gunned them down execution-style in the back of their heads.

"Will He save you?" he yelled over their dead bodies. "Will He save you? I think not." He turned to the masses and found them all huddled closely in gangs.

"Will you die for your Jesus?" soldiers ranted while brandishing their weapons before the crowd.

In an attempt to shield themselves from harm, they hid one behind another. Several in the crowd turned to flee and were shot down like dogs. Their bodies riddled with bullets, they mustered up what strength they had left to clutch the earth and slither to safety, but their attempts proved useless. At point-blank range, their lives were snatched from them as if they were useless animals.

"Will your Lord save you?" the militia yelled. Grabbing a middle-aged, Asian male from the line, they forced him to his knees and placed a machete at his throat. "Will you die for your Jesus?"

Fearing for his life, he refused to answer.

"Will you die for Him?"

"No! I don't know Him," he murmured in shame and then held out his quivering hand to willingly accept the mark of the beast.

"You denounce your Lord, do you?"

With perspiration dripping from his forehead, he reluctantly nodded his head up and down.

A slow, wicked grin materialized on the soldier's face. He shoved the trembling man to the ground in disgust.

A boisterous and boastful laugh escaped the militia. "How quickly you deny your Lord." Another round of laughter roared from the soldiers while they scanned the crowd. "Will you die for your Jesus?" Grabbing a black male by the back of his collar, they pointed a machete at his midsection.

After falling to his knees, he looked up to the sky and stated in fear, "Lord, You willingly died for me; so I willingly die for You." A sense of peace immediately came over him, and the Kingdom of God flashed in his mind.

"You willingly die for a God who leaves you defenseless?"

At peace with the horror he faced, he replied, "Jesus did not leave His children defenseless. He armed us with the most powerful weapon on earth: prayer."

"I have the power to take your life," the soldier barked.

"Mister, live or die, you have no power over my life. Remember this one thing: you cannot harm a child of God and expect to walk away clean. Touch not His anointed. Remember those words because you will hear them again someday. Maybe not today, but one day, you will have to answer to God for every murder committed here today. You can run and you can hide, but there is no escaping Him. In His own time and in His own way, God will right all the wrong in this world. I forgive you, and I pray for you. I pray that God Almighty has mercy on your soul, because when you stand before Him on judgment day, you will need it. You will need all the mercy God has to give." Closing his eyes, he silently prayed for his oppressor.

After searching for a response but coming up short, the soldier's heart hardened. Forcefully, he pierced his defenseless victim's belly button with the tip of his blade and then with a driving force, wedged it midway into his guts. With a grinding motion, he retracted only to follow up with a second attack, exposing his bowels. Wasting no time, he shoved the lifeless body to the ground, grabbed his next victim, and pushed her to the ground.

"Will you die for Him?"

"I have small children," she quickly offered up, shielding her body with her hands. "They have no one to care for them. Please!"

"Will you die for Him?" his angry voice echoed.

"No! No! I won't die for Him. Please, my children need me. They're sick. Please, allow me to go back to them. I'll gladly accept the sign."

Her trembling hands affectionately touched his leg. After lowering his weapon, she rose from the ground and ran to the checkpoint for branding.

"Will you die for Him?" He dragged his next victim from the crowd.

"Do you know who I am?" the elegantly dressed, diamond–clad, and well-made-over female celebrity bellowed in anger. "I'll have you know that I have starred in more than twenty-five films. I have won numerous awards, including two Oscars, and I am known throughout the world. I have millions of—"

Before she could finish, a single flash from the muzzle of the soldier's firearm silenced her forever. Particles of tooth enamel and bone from the projectile that penetrated her neck and shattered her vertebrae ricocheted into his forearm, puncturing his tanned skin. Her corpse fell forward within inches of him but was propelled backward with a thrust of his army boot.

"Enjoy them in Hell, witch."

Perilous times spanned the blood-stained lands after Drexter's order to destroy God's people and all who rejected his symbol was carried out. Across the globe, the temples of Christ lay about ruthlessly assassinated. Those who were fortunate enough to escape hid their existence.

⟶▭ ▭⟵

"Mom, can you tell me where in the Bible does God talk about the tongue? Reverend Earl assigned it for Bible study, and I can't find it anywhere. Is it in the Old or New Testament?" Wentworth swiftly fanned through the sixty-six books of the Bible. "I know I've seen it before, but I can't remember exactly where."

"Look in the New Testament in the book of James. You'll find something there to start with."

"In what chapter?"

"Try the second chapter."

"Mom, are you OK?" he asked after noting her nonchalant tone of voice. "You don't sound like your old self."

"I'm fine, sweetheart." Ellen managed to produce a fake smile. "Just a bit preoccupied, that's all."

"Are you thinking about Connery, Harper, Stanton, and Mabrey? Do you think that they're OK?"

"I hope so, Wentworth. Go ahead and prepare for Bible study. I'll check on you later."

Not wanting to upset him with her worries, she hurriedly made her way out of his presence. That uneasy feeling had overtaken her more intensely. Without verification, she knew it was because of her boys. Wandering aimlessly around Paradise, she struggled to keep it together.

Remembering her talk with Mary in the Garden of Calvary, she decided to rely on faith, but her heart desperately needed reassurance. Near the Pearly Gates, she observed the angels leading Jesus into the outer compound. The sound of amusement drew her in.

High-pitched screams, applause, feet running to and fro, and the highest praises to God echoed. The young heirs had completed their tasks, and the results were six remarkable replicas of Noah's ark. Each had been individually named and dedicated to the Father and the Son: the Jehovah-Jireh (Lord will provide), the Jehovah-Rapha (I am the Lord your healer), the Jehovah-Nissi (Lord is my banner), the Jehovah-Shalom (Lord is our peace), the Jehovah-Tsidkenu (Lord is our righteousness), and the Jehovah-Shammah (Lord is there).

As Jesus was led about by the angels, the titles were uncovered. Being somewhat tongue-tied at His children's love and affection for the Creator and Him, He shed tears of joy and happiness and gave out plenty of hugs and kisses. After a touching speech of gratitude, the heirs anxiously boarded the vessels. After all had claimed their places aboard, Jesus stood at the Pearly Gates with Ellen, the older heirs, and the angels. With one spoken word in the Hebrew tongue, it rained.

Excitement filled the atmosphere of Heaven. Arks swayed back and forth and creaked, while toddlers ran onto every level and compartment hiding from each other. Younger heirs seized raindrops with their hands and then proceeded to engage in water fights, while others used their mouths to guzzle down a refreshing drink. The Creator sat and delighted in His children. Angels flew about, entering and exiting Heaven. For a second, Ellen forgot about her worries until the image of a mother supporting her young triggered her emotions.

"Where is thy faith, Mary Ellen?" Jesus' soft, warm voice caught her off guard.

She stood speechless, not exactly sure how to respond. Her eyes remained glued on the Messiah. He tentatively watched His flock.

"Mary Ellen, where is thy faith?" He lovingly asked a second time.

"Lord, I thought that I had faith," she proclaimed like a little child. "I thought that I had faith. I'm trying not to worry."

He knew that her words were authentic and from a sincere heart, and when He turned to observe her frozen facial expression, His stare was enough to evoke tears. "Why doest thou cry, Mary Ellen?"

"Lord, I don't know. I thought that I had faith." She shrugged her shoulders. "Maybe I don't really know what it means to truly have faith." She wiped away the tears from her cheek. "After all this time, maybe I've never really grasped the concept of faith." Taking Jesus by the hand, she asked, "Lord, please, show me what it means to really have faith. Show me the faith that You speak of."

He led her to the outer compound. As they walked, she felt something rather abnormal, and a quick glance downward caught her off guard. Her feet hadn't sunk beneath the water. She froze.

"Walk with me, Mary Ellen," Jesus responded, scarcely breaking His stride.

"Lord, we're walking on water. I'm walking on water with You." She glanced down a second time and noticed that the bottom of their garments, which draped the surface, were dry. "Lord, I'm walking on water."

"Yes, Mary Ellen," Jesus softly responded with a chuckle and with His eyes fixated ahead of Him.

"Jesus!" Ellen shouted out in joy. "Lord, do You know we're walking on water?"

He laughed at her. Sidetracked, she had completely forgotten about their talk on faith and where she was being led. Her focus was on the water shifting underneath. She hadn't noticed that they had come to a stop in front of the Jehovah-Rapha, only the powerful impact on the water from the swaying of the boat. The waves had become more forceful but had no affect on her or the Messiah.

"Faith, Mary Ellen," Jesus stated, pointing at the top of the ark.

Blind to all others was a tot who had mysteriously made his way onto the top of the ark. Without a care in the world, he jumped and danced about, stopping momentarily to catch the cool raindrops with his tongue.

"Faith, Mary Ellen," Jesus repeated, never taking His eyes off the tot.

She watched as he danced unguarded and dangerously close to the perimeter of the moving ark, but he never displayed a hint of worry—even when he lost his balance. Understanding the lesson that Jesus was teaching her, she kneeled down on the surface of the water and bowed her head. "Thank You, Lord. I understand now. Thank You."

He smiled and kissed her. "Come," He commanded the tot.

They boy's small frame ascended into the atmosphere. Clapping and smiling, he extended his arms forward to the Messiah and drifted into His loving arms.

Seeing Ellen walk on water with the Messiah enticed the younger heirs to exit the ark. One by one, they cautiously stepped a foot on the water and then looked at Jesus.

"Come," He laughed and then shook His head at their apprehensiveness.

The Bible greats: Shem, Ham, Japheth, Sarah, Noah, Abraham, Moses, Joseph, Ruth, and the others, without hesitation, walked confidently onto the water toward Jesus. Seeing this, the younger heirs' panic diminished.

"Through Me, you can do all things," Jesus reassured them, kissed the tot in His arms, and then placed him on the water.

Instantly, the younger heirs went dashing about. From the sky, Jesus watched for miles as His flock ran on the waves.

Chapter 10

Prime Minister Zebulon stood outside the Holy Temple to take in a breath of fresh air. His weary body, suffering famine from fasting, hadn't slept for days due to monitoring world affairs. Via media coverage, he and the nation of Israel watched in horror as God's people, fearing for their lives, went into exile.

Ordered by Drexter to massacre anyone not bearing his sign, the World Militia went on a murderous rampage invading, ransacking, and destroying homes. Redeemed heirs to the throne were dragged into the street, viciously tortured, beaten, beheaded, burned alive, or otherwise slaughtered for the world to witness. Thousands who had willingly accepted the sign of the beast were also brutally sacrificed and publically displayed as a warning to all. Fighting against famine, sickness and disease, displacement, and certain death at the hands of the militia, survival became virtually impossible. The heirs sought refuge in tunnels, abandoned buildings, deserts, caves, mountains, sewers, and other places that afforded them concealment.

But for Israel, a very clear and more present danger brewed directly outside their borders. Via the media, Prime Minister Zebulon and other Israeli dignitaries became alert to the World Militia that had been deployed into surrounding regions, and via Israeli Armed Forces, they were kept abreast of their gradual but certain advance.

Fully clad in combat uniforms and heavily armed, the World Militia meticulously prepped their artillery. Their missiles were far more advanced than any that Israel had acquired or manufactured over the decades, and their explosives were capable of collapsing the tiny nation instantaneously. Their high-powered, .50-caliber sniper rifles were capable of taking out adversaries from distances far beyond the reach of Israel's weaponry, and the ground soldiers, equipped with 6.8 SPC (Special Purpose Cartridge) outfitted with .40-caliber grenade launchers, were armed for annihilation. Even more intimidating were the technically advanced and heavily manned battleships that appeared on the waters of the Mediterranean, strategically positioned from afar. Recruited, trained, deployed, and briefed for destruction, the World Militia awaited their authorization to attack.

Israeli forces were also assembled and prepped for battle. The undersized military geared up with weaponry that was average at best and appeared obsolete compared to the World Militia. Though outnumbered and outgunned, their commitment to defending their nation, however hopeless it seemed, made them more than willing to lay down their lives.

Sitting on the steps of the Holy Temple, Prime Minister Zebulon reevaluated the decisions that he had made that ultimately led up to this moment. Realizing that his defiance had triggered a war, he wondered if another route could have been taken. It was a war he wanted desperately to avoid but one he deemed inevitable.

Standing erect, he faced the Holy Temple. Its beauty moved him as it always had. Dressed in military attire, he entered the intricately designed structure and headed for the Mercy Seat.

"Prime Minister, come quickly. There's activity being initiated among the World Militia. We think they're preparing to launch."

The frantic voice of the Israeli soldier startled Prime Minister Zebulon. He watched his soldier hurriedly exit the temple to rejoin his comrades. Wasting no time, Prime Minister Zebulon hurried from the temple to assemble with his generals.

"Lord Jesus, I have no time for a long-winded prayer. I need You. Israel needs You," he begged, gasping for air and running full speed. "Lord, Israel needs You right now."

"Peace, are they still in the temple?" Ellen wanted to know.

"That's correct, Mary Ellen. They're receiving final instructions on their assignments from our Lord."

"Where is Meek?"

"He's talking with the younger heirs."

"Take care of them, Peace."

"Our Lord's will be done, Mary Ellen. Our Lord's will be done."

Heaven's occupants all gathered at the front of the Pearly Gates, awaiting the arrival of the two witnesses. Peace and Meek had received their final orders from Michael, as well, and were patiently waiting to begin their journey. The aura of Paradise had always been a never-ending celebration of joy, but on this particular day, a dark cloud draped above and rained on their parade. Sorrow filled the hearts of every heir and angel as they assembled, and tears had already begun to flow. Male heirs tried to put aside their grieving in order to console the females.

A hush fell over Heaven when Jesus appeared on the main walkway with Enoch on his right and Elijah on his left. Their hands were interlocked, and their demeanor and facial expressions displayed nothing less than pure, immeasurable joy. Their smiles were heartwarming and their laughter uplifting. Instead of their usual spotless, white garbs, they opted for sackcloth apparel and shabby sandals.

Slowly, they made their way down the pathway. An exchange of hugs and kisses and the wiping of one's tears were visible. Upon reaching the

Pearly Gates, Heaven's family all joined together for one big family hug, with Jesus and the witnesses sandwiched in the middle.

"Thou were waiting here for us in Paradise when we arrived," Moses intimately spoke to his Heavenly brothers. "Now, we steadfastly await thy return unto us."

He passed his beaten and somewhat eroded rod that had aided him through life's journey to Elijah, and Abraham simultaneously handed his staff off to Enoch.

"Through thy rods, may many wondrous works of our Almighty Father be done," Moses commanded.

With a nod of their heads and one final glance upon the face of the Messiah, Elijah and Enoch departed Paradise, escorted by Peace and Meek. With a slamming of the gate, they descended out of sight.

Mourning fell over Paradise. Jesus stood amid his children and inventoried their sobbing faces. His heart became burdened with their grief. "Let not your hearts be troubled, but rejoice with gladness," He encouraged.

Knowing that they could talk to Him about anything, they spoke without reservation. "Lord, how can we rejoice when we know what awaits Elijah and Enoch? We, too, feel their pain, suffering, and the torment that waits. Evil desires to destroy them, and the shadow of death diligently seeks their souls."

"I, thy Lord, conquered death on Cavalry—for it could not hold Me. And ye, being heirs to the throne, also through Me conquer death. Evil prevaileth not. Lay your burdens upon Me, and ye shall be comforted."

Without hesitation, they ran into His open arms sobbing, and in doing so found comfort.

"Rejoice and be glad, for the day of the Lord is at hand. Behold, a new Heaven and a new earth shall there be."

After a joyous and voluble journey, Peace and Meek bade Elijah and Enoch a sincere farewell at their destination of commencement. Briefly hovering about, they waited until the witnesses safely began their earthly journey and then proceeded back to Paradise to report to Michael.

The once-beautiful land of New Delhi and the rest of the world were again marred by blood and the stench of death. Drexter's malice for Christ and everything good was illustrated in the decomposed corpses that lay scattered about for the animals of the earth and the scavengers of the sky to feast on. No attempts were made to give the deceased a proper burial. The heirs of Christ deemed it too risky to expose themselves; therefore, they remained in hiding, only risking themselves at night for the sake of nourishment, and the heirs of Hell gloated at the horrendous sights. Bearing the sign of the beast afforded them necessities and bonuses in addition to freedom. They trekked around in arrogance, delighted in worldly things, and blew the whistle on God's heirs that were discovered in plain sight.

"Repent of your sins, for the day of the Lord is at hand. He is a just and merciful God. He offers salvation to any who shall call on His name."

With their rod and staff in hand, Enoch and Elijah unwaveringly went to work calling out to the residents of India. Spreading the Good News, they travelled the avenues, byways, hills, and mountains, administering to anyone who would listen. Their voices, thunderous and strong, could be heard from a distance. From New Delhi, they made their way to Mumbai and then Calcutta, shouting the Gospel.

Their presence and message were met with mixed sentiment. Stares of contempt surrounded them from the start. The heirs to Hell mocked and laughed at them, but Elijah and Enoch, being true men of God, maintained self-control and responded only with the word of God. Because they could not be provoked, the crowd became hostile. Humbly, they made their way from the mob and continued on their journey. Stumbling upon the ruins of what was once a place of worship, they sensed a strong presence. Surveying the structure, they noticed that they were being watched.

"Fret not because of evildoers—for they shall soon be cut down like the grass and wither like the green herb."

Seeking cover inside were a group of God's children. After hearing Enoch preach, they apprehensively gave up their concealment. In spite of burdened hearts, low spirits, malnourished bodies, and filthy clothing, they continued to give thanks and praise to God Almighty.

Elijah, touched by their unmoving faith, gripped his rod and tapped the ground. Upon the exact spot appeared a substantial pile of manna, followed by another close by and then another, until scores of food piled around them. Wasting no time, they helped themselves to the delectable victuals, stuffing their mouths until they were hardly able to chew. A second tap on the earth produced large jars of fresh water. Quenching their thirst, they drank as much as their stomachs could store.

"Thank you," they replied, briefly taking a moment to look up.

"All thanks be to the Lord; He is good and worthy of our praise."

After a heartfelt prayer and brief farewell, the two prophets proceeded onward. With their task complete in India, they touched pavement in St. Petersburg, Russia. Without a moment of leisure, they began their testimonial, travelling to Moscow and then on to Novosibirsk. From there, they touched ground in Asia. Expectedly, they were met with even greater hostility, spat on, and cursed.

Travelling on the Indian Ocean, they journeyed toward Australia, to Melbourne, Townsville, and then Sydney. Even though their presence failed to garner harsh or adverse reactions, the lost were unreceptive to their message. Ignored and regarded as foolish and madmen, they were laughed at.

Spotted treading the water of the mighty Atlantic, their arrival at Botswana, South Africa, immediately drew an audience for their testimony.

"It is a good thing to give thanks unto the Lord and to sing praises unto Thy name, most High. Show loving-kindness in the morning and thy faithfulness every night. The Lord has made me glad through Thy work. I will triumph in the works of Thy hands. Thou, Lord, art most high for evermore," Elijah shouted.

"Why should we give thanks to your Lord? He has done nothing for us." Revealing their palms, the crowd proudly displayed the mark of the beast. "Our Lord provides all our needs."

The witnesses responded with the word of God that profoundly angered the crowd. Yelling and blaspheming God's name, the crowd's hatred intensified, but the witnesses feared not. After being pushed by an angry female, Enoch plowed knee-first into the dirt. His staff was snatched, snapped in two pieces, and thrown at his head.

"Your clothes are worse than ours," they belittled. "And you give praise for that?"

An angry onlooker summoned a young boy to fetch nearby soldiers, and soon the prophets found themselves surrounded by four armed militia. Extending his hand to Enoch, one of the soldiers helped him to his feet, and in doing so, checked his palm for the mark. He then scanned Enoch's primitive, biblical-era, shabby garments.

"Who are you? Who sent you here?" he demanded.

"I AM sent us. We are messengers of the true and Holy God," Elijah boldly replied.

Angrily, the soldiers drew their machetes, but before they could raise them, Elijah lifted his rod to Heaven and called on the wrath of God. Paradise responded by thunder. An eclipse overtook the sun, casting complete darkness upon the region and blinding all except the witnesses. A shooting flame struck the center of an eight-meter Baobab tree a few yards away, engulfing it in flames. Its intensity was unbearable and pushed the mob back.

Once again, Heaven's fury unfurled, hurling down grapefruit-sized hail. Blinded and unshielded, they scrambled aimlessly about until there was silence. Once more, Elijah lifted his rod to Heaven and the sky, and its components returned to their original state. Hefty balls of ice, marred by blood and dirt, lay mixed among portions of cleaved human flesh and battered and bludgeoned bodies.

In the aftermath, left kneeling was one soldier paralyzed by fear whose eyes beheld the carnage surrounding him. Fearing the power of his enemies, he cautiously backed away, and after deeming it safe, turned to flee but stumbled over a ball of hail that landed him atop of his battered and bloody comrades. Springing to his feet, he jetted like a bat out of Hell to inform his commander. Extending his hand forward, Enoch motioned for his staff. Its sections revolved together and then mended. With one last glance, the prophets proceeded on their way.

Reappearing in Zimbabwe, Tanzania, Kenya, and then Somalia, they continued onward. Not to their surprise, the natives stood eyeing them from a distance and talking among themselves. After a subtle signal, several young, malnourished, teenage males ran like men on a mission, only to return with the militia who watched from a distance. The media stood well back, broadcasting their every movement and message.

"The Man of Sin hast been made aware of our presence," Enoch warned. "Time draweth near."

They made their way deep into the rugged terrain of the Karkaar Mountains where they settled down to rest under a large boulder that shielded them from the grueling heat of the sun. After retrieving a piece of unleavened bread from his garment, Enoch offered half to Elijah, and together, they reclined on the hard surface. Reminiscing on Biblical times, they chuckled at the way they arrived in Heaven. Having never tasted death, Enoch giggled at how one second he was on earth, and the next, standing at the Pearly Gates, staring up into Michael's radiant face. And Elijah described the elegant, horse-driven chariot of fire manned by angels that whirlwind him off to Heaven, leaving Elisha to carry on.

"As the younger heirs say, it's all a master plan," Enoch quoted as they laughed and thought about home.

The loud echoes from their laughter made them realize just how noisy they had become. They hadn't heard the faint weeping of a young woman nearby until a downward flow of loose gravel and rock from the shifting of her body brought them to their feet. Scaling a bit further into the mountains to investigate, they found the expectant mother sobbing in the arms of an older woman almost twice her age, whom she resembled. Next to them were several small children all huddled together, and close by was the silhouette of a younger child whose body was veiled beneath a dirty, floral blanket.

"We heard you speak of Heaven, did you not?" the older woman inquired in a quiet tone.

"We didst speak of home," Enoch replied. "Why doest thou ask?"

Pausing momentarily, she looked at the blanket. "God is a healer and a miracle worker, isn't He? He can do all things—even raise the dead after two days." She sobbed.

"Doest thou truly believe this?"

Closing her eyes, she shook her head and then rocked back and forward. "I do."

"Take thy grandson into thy arms," he instructed.

"My prayers have been answered," she yelled, crawling over to the body, knocking the younger woman backward. Throwing the blanket to the side, she grabbed the boy's nude body and cuddled it firmly in her arms as if he was full of life. After kissing his stiff little fingers, cheeks, and forehead, she glanced up at Enoch in anticipation, awaiting his next command.

"Place thy lips to his and breathe into his mouth."

Widening his mouth with her fingers, she took a deep breath, and with her lips pressed tightly against his, exhaled with all her might. With his staff raised to Heaven and in the Hebrew tongue, Enoch called upon Jehovah. A quiver shot across the body, followed by the movement of the child's fingers. His abdominal cavity rose for thirty seconds and then lowered, and his dirt-covered eyelids slowly parted, exposing his dark-brown eyes. His finger touched his grandmother's tear-stained lips.

"Granny," he softly whispered.

"Glory be to God Almighty," she cried. "Glory be to the Creator of life. Thank You, Lord, for restoring my broken heart."

"Your faith hath healed your grandson, woman." Enoch bequeathed her a friendly grin.

"Touch him! Touch him!" she frantically waved her hands at the rest of her grandchildren.

Obediently, they heeded her command and swarmed around Enoch. Grasping any part of his body that their hands could seize, they gazed up at him with hope in their eyes.

"God will heal them also?" Wiping the tears from her reddened eyes, she nodded at Enoch with immense joy tattooed on her face and waited patiently for his authorization.

"Thy faith hath already healed them from cholera."

"Yes!" she concurred.

"Yes."

She held her arms for them to run into. Clutching them like a hawk, she passionately kissed each one. As she did so, Enoch noticed a large, greenish-colored wound on her upper left arm that trickled down a yellowish, thick puss.

"It happened while we were escaping the militia. But I have no worries for myself. All that matters to me has been healed. By the grace of God, this is nothing."

"Thy faith and unselfishness hath also healed thee," he replied. He reached out and placed his hand over her wound, and upon removing it, her flesh was restored.

"When you return home, tell Jesus that I'm sorry I fell asleep, but my house and I will be prepared to meet Him this time around. Tell Him that my every hope and dream is built upon His return. Tell Him that we long to be with Him just as much as He longs to be with us. Tell Him that I wait the day when I can kneel down before Him on His throne and shout my praises unto His Holy name. Tell Him that Anna loves Him, OK?" She formed her hands in a praying position and smiled.

"I shall surely remind Him when I return home."

"Tell him! Tell him!" Anna instructed the young woman. "You must tell him. You must have faith."

Shaking her head no and cradling her bare stomach, she buried her face into the gravel and cried out in despair.

"She is with child, but the baby hasn't moved for days. She believes it is dead. She fell hard against the rocks while climbing the mountains trying to escape the militia."

Enoch, handing his staff off to Elijah, rested his palm on her belly and listened. Sitting her up, he spoke, "Thy daughter is lifeless."

"Bring her back, please," she begged.

"It be not our Lord's will." Placing his hands on her belly once more, her stomach flattened. "Thy daughter be now taken to Paradise for a short while."

Dropping her head into Anna's lap, she mourned.

"Blessed are they that mourn; for they shall be comforted," Enoch reassured her.

After providing an abundance of nourishment and drink, they continued on their journey to Sudan, Sierra Leone, and then into Egypt.

"It's changed quite a bit since we last saw it," they joked. "Remind me to ask our Lord why we didn't have cars. It would have made travelling a lot easier," Elijah laughed.

They journeyed into Istanbul, Turkey, Ukraine, Sweden, and then across Canada, preaching the message of hope. From Wyoming to New Mexico, Missouri, Tennessee, and Florida, they preached repentance but found that sound doctrine had been replaced with foolish beliefs and untruths.

⋆⇥▪▬ ▬▪⇤⋆

"They aren't coming back, Connery. If they were, they would have returned by now. You know what's happening on the other side of those doors."

Stanton spoke between quick, shallow breaths followed by episodes of whooping cough. Dark globs of dried-up blood speckled his tongue. His sunken cheeks and ashy, dry skin lay under beads of perspiration, and his frail fingers trembled at his side. Slowly, his hand inched midway to his distraught brother whose face lay buried in the sheets, but his weakened state made it extremely difficult to shift any further.

"Don't cry for us, big brother."

"I promised Mama that I'd take care of us," Connery whispered.

"You have. Now you need to take care of yourself. We're OK. Harper and Mabrey died in Christ; they are OK. They're asleep. And I lie here in peace. It's funny, Connery; Mom was at peace on her death-bed, and at the time I couldn't understand why. Now I understand. I understand why she wasn't afraid to die." He paused in reflection. "She was worried for us; you know that, don't you?

Connery didn't respond but stared off into space.

"She didn't want to die without seeing us change our lives. She knew that we were standing in danger of judgment. That's why she stayed on us as she did. That's why she prayed for us so." Through the painful expression on his face came a faint smile. "I thank her for that now. She prayed for us, Connery, because we were too foolish to pray for ourselves. She prayed for our souls." He held his palm open for his brother to take his hand.

"Connery, I see things clearer now than I ever have before. Ma always said that when you become a child of God, He gives you the wisdom to understand what is and what isn't. I see things from a spiritual perspective now, Connery. I know now to look behind the scene at the bigger picture, and behind it, this world we live in is nothing more than a battleground. And a vicious war is being waged right under our eyes—a war not between lands as most have been deceived into believing but a spiritual war. It's a war between God and Satan—good and evil. It's a war over souls—our souls. We now have to pray for ourselves—for our own souls. Ma can't go to God for us; we have to go to Him for ourselves. I went to Him to save myself." He paused momentarily.

"Connery, you blame God for my sickness. Why? God didn't do this—Satan did. Before I came to God, Satan had no worries about me because he had me conquered. But when I turned to God, he became afraid because he lost my soul; therefore, he came after me from every angle. This is Satan's way of attempting to turn me back to him and away from God. But God's wisdom, big brother, is power. God gave me the power to understand and overcome."

"I need to get you—" Connery started to say, but was cut off by his brother.

"No! You need to get yourself right with God, right now. That's what you need to do. Get right with God. I'm going to die right here, and you'll bury me in the backyard."

"I'm not burying my brother in the backyard."

"Why not? I won't be there. My soul will have sought higher ground behind the altar of God Almighty. Connery, you once declared that you made your own way in life, and I believed you to the point I patterned my life after your motto. But Reverend Charles Stanley once stated that 'if our way isn't God's way, then we're going the wrong way because God's way is the only right way, and all other ways lead to destruction.'

"I look back, Connery, on my life. 'How arrogant was I to think that tomorrow was always promised to me—not knowing if it was God's will. I lie here today thanking Him for saving me from myself and loving me in spite of my iniquities. I thank Him for not taking me before I was ready to meet Him. Connery, what if I hadn't awakened and had never seized the opportunity to repent? What if I had been killed but hadn't gotten my house in order? It's scary to think that so many of us today are still unprepared to meet Jesus because we are deceived. Our souls are at stake, Connery. Our eternal lives are hanging in the balance.' If we only knew the suffering and torment that awaits us in Hell." Stanton's voice began to fade.

"Stanton!" Connery called out, leaning over his brother. "Stanton!" His voice cracked.

"Don't cry for me, big brother, cry for yourself. Cry for yourself." His voice became even fainter. "Talk to God while you're still able. He'd rather you talk to Him when you're angry than you not talk to Him at all. But God will never force Himself upon you," Stanton mumbled under his breath. He slowly released Connery's hand. "It's your choice. He's still holding onto you, Connery. Grab hold of Him and never…"

"Stanton! Stanton!" Connery yelled. His limbs gave way, and his body fell at the edge of his brother's bed. "Stanton, you're all I have left. You're all I have left in this world."

For hours following Stanton's death, bellows of anger echoed through the empty house. Connery attempted to cope with his pain. He sat bedside, glued to his brother's body, not wanting to depart from it. The untimely deaths of his beloved brothers combined with the rapture of Ellen and Wentworth, which he never fully came to terms with, struck him all at once like a ton of bricks. Never before had he felt so abandoned and helpless.

"I need to bury you, Stanton," he muttered to himself.

As he walked through the house, bittersweet memories reached out to haunt him from every room. Stopping at his mother's bedroom door, her loving voice seemed to speak to him from the other side. Memories of her beautiful smile struck him hard. The contents of her room remained untouched. Her Bible still sat on the nightstand beside her bed. Picking it up, the intimate talk about Christ that he last shared with Wentworth preoccupied him.

"What more can You do to me?" he angrily asked Jesus Christ, looking up at the ceiling. "You can't hurt me any more than You already have. You can't take anything more from me," he heatedly blurted out. Tears swelled up in him. He sealed his lips tightly together. "Everything I loved in this world—everything that meant anything to me, You ripped it away from me. What did I ever do to You?"

Fuming with absolute anger, his whole body trembled. Overtaken by pure hatred, he flung his mother's Bible across the room and against the wall, where it came to rest on the floor.

He hesitantly returned to Stanton's bedroom. For a while, he stood in the doorway staring at his peacefully resting body. By no means did he want to depart from his much-loved sibling, but he knew that his corpse couldn't remain in the house. Struggling within himself, he made his way to the bed to begin the distressing task of covering Stanton's Caucasian-colored skin in the damp, solid-white sheets.

"What more can You take from me?" he blurted out.

Carefully lifting his brother's stocky frame, he struggled to support it on his shoulders. Making his way downstairs, he realized that Stanton no longer reeked of alcohol, as he had given it up after turning his life over to Christ. He approached the front door in time to see a stream of headlights glaring, followed by a muddy, gray World Militia jeep that was inhabited by four heavily armed soldiers. It dawned on him that his brothers never returned with their mother's vehicle. A feeling of helplessness and defeat overcame him as his options dwindled down to only one: the backyard. Stanton's words stung him like a bee. Anguish and despair started to eat away at him.

The brief stretch of area leading to the rear door seemed to take hours to cover, and every step became harder and harder to take. After placing Stanton's body on the kitchen table, he retrieved an old, rusty shovel from the basement. He laughed at himself after missing the first two steps and tumbling down the rest. His shoulder took a bit of a bruising, but the humor of it all made it worthwhile. After a quick peek out of the kitchen window, he waited. He figured that his neighbors had accepted the symbol of the beast because they travelled about without worry. After seeing no one in sight and with the highest level of precaution, he made his way to the darkest area of the yard with Stanton's body cradled in his arms. Digging blindly into the earth in the dark, he kept his clamor to a minimum and kept a watchful eye out for the militia and neighbors.

Though the resting place was not as deep as he would have liked, he deemed it acceptable. After wiping sweat and smeared dirt from his face with his soiled shirt, he scooted Stanton's body into the hole and concealed it with loose soil as best he could. Not being able to give his brother a decent burial ate away at Connery. Unable to bring himself to say good-bye, he scurried back inside the residence and collapsed on the kitchen floor in mourning.

He thought back on parts of his last conversation with Stanton: eternal life, spiritual warfare, Satan's deception, and doing things God's way. He thought about his mother's Bible that he had thrown down in rage. Out of nowhere, a soft, calm, powerful, and loving voice started to speak to him from within. He wanted to move but found himself paralyzed on the floor and unable to get up. A gripping, paralyzing fear seized him, but that calming voice quickly stepped in and assured him not to fret. Another failed attempt to stand alerted Connery that he was up against a force that rendered him totally powerless.

"What did I ever do to You?" Connery shouted after realizing that he was in the presence of God Almighty.

Instead of responding in anger, the tender, sweet voice answered, "I love you."

"You took everything from me that mattered," he cried.

Again, the calming voice responded with affection. Then, out of nowhere, a loud, intimidating, and forceful voice invaded the conversation and spoke to Connery from within. The voice was less powerful than that of God Almighty; however, it was powerful.

"If Emmanuel truly loved your brother, why would He allow Stanton to suffer so? Why is He allowing the world to suffer? Is that love? Why doesn't He do something?"

Connery paused to entertain the thought. Why had Stanton been made to suffer, he thought? "I have nothing left in this world," Connery shouted at God.

The soft, sweet, and merciful voice never changed. It responded and invited Connery to come unto Him, and he would find everything he needed to survive in the world.

"Do you really need Emmanuel?" the intimidating voice spoke louder and attempted to persuade Connery. "Haven't you made it this far without Him? What need do you have of Him now? You've always made your own way in life, haven't you?"

"What do You want from me? I have nothing to give You," Connery shouted.

God's soft, sweet voice made it known that He wanted nothing; instead, He had something to offer.

"I've never felt so alone and so scared," Connery wept.

God's calm voice responded, and a feeling of security came over Connery that totally overpowered his feeling of abandonment.

But Satan's cunning, clever voice became more menacing. "Emmanuel said that He would never leave you alone, but where are

Mabrey, Harper, Stanton, Wentworth, and Ellen?" Satan continued to attack. "Emmanuel took all of them away from you in such trying times, did He not?"

Connery reflected on Satan's deception and trickery. "I need them," Connery declared.

A picture of Calvary immediately flashed in Connery's mind, and God's voice alerted him that who he needed hung on the cross.

"I've always taken care of myself."

A period in Connery's life from two decades earlier resurfaced, and he saw himself gravely ill in a hospital bed with an illness that left doctors completely baffled. He envisioned angels standing bedside administering to him. The gentle voice informed Connery that during the lowest moments in his life, he had been cared for.

Sensing that he was beginning to lose the battle for Connery's soul, Satan became spitting mad. "Why would Emmanuel allow you to become so ill in the first place? Remember how distraught Ellen became?"

"I'm so angry with You," Connery admitted.

When God's voice informed Connery of just how much he was loved, his hatred and anger started to wane.

Connery started to focus totally on God and tune Satan out totally. "I threw Your word on the floor."

Once again, the calm voice spoke and informed Connery that He was willing to forgive anything.

With nothing left to argue, Connery opened his heart to Heaven, and the power of God released him. Like a newborn, he curled up in a fetal position and cried out, releasing all the hurt and pain that possessed him. For the first time, he recognized the true authority over his life.

"I'm sorry. I'm sorry, Lord, that I denied You. Please, forgive me for my sins. I submit to You fully, and I ask that You take control of my life. I know now that I can't make it without You."

Connery was reassured that he had been forgiven, his name had been written in the Book of Life, and Heaven rejoiced over his coming to Christ.

Satan was steaming with absolute anger. After being defeated by Almighty God, yet again, and being forced to realize that he had no control over Emmanuel, he departed Connery's presence.

-→═◉ ◉═◄-

"Boo! Boo! Boo!"

The sound of laughter once again spread across Paradise. After the heartbreaking departure of Elijah and Enoch, Jesus sought to bring joy back to the hearts of His children and happiness back in Heaven. What better way, He thought, than to have a Gong Show.

After He appointed a comedian to emcee the humorous occasion, the event took off with a blast. With a no-holds-barred stipulation in effect, everybody, including Jesus, was a target. Of course, the Creator was off limits. Act after act, with few surviving the demanding audience, many found themselves booed and then escorted off the stage by Temple, the angel. Laughter roared across Paradise.

Finally, it was Jesus' turn to take the stage, and His entrance prompted a standing ovation followed by the shout-out of His name. He chose to sing for His children. A bit nervous because of the tough crowd, Jesus sighed deeply, laughed a bit, and then gave it a try. After hitting His first note, He inventoried the audience for a response. An immediate hush fell over them. They started to eye one another and then flash a false smile. After observing their expressions and knowing their thoughts, Jesus giggled and then continued on. A third or fourth off-note prompted some of His children to tuck their heads while others buried their faces in their hands. Jesus kept going. A not-so-right high note finally brought about a response.

"Boo!"

The response apprehensively and subtly started from the center of the audience followed by laughter. Jesus joined in and then kept right on going.

"Boo! Boo!" They moaned a bit louder and laughed a bit harder.

"We love You, Jesus," someone yelled, which made them laugh even louder.

Although knowing that His time on stage was winding down and His chances of conquering the difficult crowd was hopeless, Jesus kept going. He laughed the hardest because it delighted His heart so to see His children happy again.

"Boo!" The moan became continuous.

With his head down and a smile on his face, Temple entered onto the stage. Jesus laughed until tears ran from His eyes and so did the heirs and the angels. Temple kindly escorted the Messiah off the stage, and the comedian returned. He paused momentarily, looking out at the audience with a half grin on his face.

"Evidently, some of y'all must have forgotten just who He is, didn't y'all?"

Jesus, along with His children, burst into laughter.

"Let me see if I understand this right. Y'all just booed the Lord off His own stage. Lord, I think they have lost their minds."

Again, Heaven erupted into laughter.

"I see some repercussions behind this. Lord, are there going to be some repercussions behind this?"

"I see a great famine falling over Paradise," Jesus responded jokingly.

The heirs laughed until they almost cried.

"The Lord is going to stop feeding us. The Lord gonna let y'all starve. Ugh, Lord, I didn't boo You; I clapped."

Everybody laughed.

"Lord, that may not be such a good idea. You may want to rethink this for a minute. These kids of Yours gonna start clowning, complaining, and showing out. I can hear them now; the Lord done got mad and stopped feeding us. I thought this was Heaven, but this feels more like the People's Temple. Are we in Jonestown? Where's Jim Jones? They gonna start stealing up here. You may want to rethink this, Lord."

Jesus couldn't respond for laughing.

"Lord, Your kids are going to tear up these gold streets, sneak down to earth, and barter for food. They gonna wait until Michael walk away from the Pearly Gates and then try to climb back over here. Some of them gonna have the nerve to come back in here with that sign on their hands hoping that You don't find out. And Lord, don't let them find the tree of knowledge of good and evil. That tree will be bare by the time Your kids finish with it. They're gonna find them some shade underneath that tree and pull out their paring knife. Hulls gonna be laying everywhere. You gonna have to put all us out of Heaven."

The heirs fell out laughing. They hadn't seen Gabriel when he approached the Messiah and whispered in His ear. It wasn't until Jesus rushed toward the Pearly Gates with Gabriel in tow that they stopped to take note. Seeing that He was deeply disturbed, they rushed after Him and found Him standing outside of Paradise, looking down upon the earth.

Next to an open food market on a busy, unkempt, downtown street in Cairo, Egypt, were the remains of Elijah and Enoch. After preaching the Gospel throughout Mexico, the Greater and Lesser Antilles, Central and South America, and then across the South Pacific, they returned to Egypt. After keeping a watchful eye on the witnesses, it was there that Drexter ordered their execution. Surrounded in the busy street by the World Militia for all to bear witness, the media broadcast the horrifying event as they were beheaded. Their eyes were gouged out; their spines were coiled around their rod and staff and had been mounted as tombstones before their mutilated remains. Around the gruesome scene flowed a river of precious blood. Their garments had been ripped from their bodies and torn to shreds. The races applauded the militia after they raised their machetes to the sky, and skipped, danced, and chanted

Drexter's name. Men, women, and children across the globe paraded the streets in celebration of the grotesque murders. Because they marveled over their murders and greatly despised the men of God, the witnesses' remains were left in the street.

A very boastful Drexter took to the media, flashing another devious grin intended to taunt the Messiah. Laughing and joking, he joyfully expressed his genuine hatred for Heaven's witnesses and his contentment over their mutilated bodies. Cunningly, he mocked and sneered at the Messiah and then declared to the races to be the sovereign force of the universe.

Jesus fell to His knees, bowed His head, and wept bitterly. The heirs rushed to His side.

"Lord, we can't heal Your pain or restore Your joy, but You can lean on us if You'd like."

Surrounded by His children, Jesus found solace on the lap of a seven-year-old girl who cuddled him tightly with her small frame. Together, with the heirs and the angels, Paradise mourned for the longest time. He commanded the Seraphim Angel, Magi, to earth to guard over the bodies. The powerful angel, who possessed four heads, eight arms and legs, and eight eyes, immediately left Paradise. Within seconds, he hovered over the bodies so that no man, beast, rodent, or insect was allowed to desecrate the precious remains. For three and one half days, their remains lay in the street where passersby cursed the sight of them.

Jesus spent most of His time in God's Holy Temple talking to His Father and at other times looking down on the earth. After three and one half days, He stood outside the Pearly Gates looking down on His beloved prophets whose deaths, according to God's will, had been prolonged for centuries in order to fulfill scripture. With one mighty breath, He breathed down on the prophets, and life entered back into them.

The markets were jam-packed with consumers buying and trading goods. The streets were congested with motorists going about their daily routines, and the media continued their coverage of the horrifying sight. Sneers could still be heard from every angle as pedestrians stopped to stare, and motorists hurled insults in passing. A hush readily fell over the region when thunder abruptly clashed across the Heavens, and a glistening of light from Magi cascaded down on the remains. Fear ran through the hearts of man, and panic spread when they witnessed the mutilated bodies take back their original form. The river of blood that once streamed from their bodies now receded back into their veins. With their limbs once again intact, their organs functioning as new, their hearts beating to the rhythm of the Lord's, and their garments of sackcloth now shining, snow-white robes, Elijah and Enoch stood up. Gazing out at the races with forgiveness, their hearts ached because of God's pending judgment against them.

Pedestrians scattered in every direction, looking for a safe place to hide. Motorists quickly sped off and then stopped at a distance they deemed safe to watch. The busy area quieted down like a ghost town.

"Come up hither," a mighty voice, also like thunder, called out from Paradise.

With God's work completed on earth, and with their staff and rod in hand, the faithful servants ascended on a cloud into Heaven.

From the luxury of his private quarters, Drexter and Priest Batteast sat in the presence of Drexter's father and watched the resurrection and ascension of the witnesses. Hatred once again flared within Drexter for the Messiah and all covered under the blood. That ultimate feeling of supremacy that he had emitted less than four days earlier had now dwindled down to feelings of inadequacy. It finally set in that his dominion over the world might be quickly terminating and that a new Heaven on earth was forthcoming—one ruled by his most despised adversary. Out of rage, he flipped his desk.

Dismissing himself from his father's presence, he found his way to the veranda of Mount BoeYourne. Gazing up into the sky, only he could see the Messiah standing on a cloud looking down. Standing beside Him were Elijah and Enoch, and in the rear were Michael and Gabriel. It startled Drexter. Their eyes locked, and for the longest while, the Supreme Being and the powerful force of evil exchanged stares.

Without warning, all entrances and exits to Hades, as well as portals, were sealed and locked for a short while, trapping Hell's occupants. Like the calm before the storm, the universe stood still. With a single flash of lightning, Hades violently quaked, as did Rome and Egypt. The wrath of the Lord unfolded. From Hell's deepest depths to the earth's infrastructures, nothing was left undisturbed. The earth's core fractured, and parts gave way. Egypt's highest mountains plummeted, and its oceans swelled to form waves in heights never before imaginable that invaded and demolished fragments of its land. Demons screamed in agony when they were tossed and hurled about and torched by their own flames. A snarl rumbled from Mount BoeYourne; Satan sat seething and powerless. In the aftermath, one third of Rome and Egypt lay in ruins, and thousands who bore the sign of the beast were slaughtered. But God's children remained unharmed.

After making war in righteousness, the Messiah entered the Pearly Gates, and Heaven kneeled to give glory to Him. Afterward, Jesus and all of Heaven's residents embraced each other for the longest time, and then another celebration commenced.

"Lord, I have a message for Thee from Anna. She has repented of her sins, and she and her house will be prepared to meet Thee. Her every hope and dream is built around Your awaited return. She waits the day she can kneel before Thee on the throne."

"I know Anna loves Me," Jesus smiled at Enoch. At that very moment, He blessed Anna and her house.

"Guess who this is?" Ellen interrupted, walking up behind Enoch, carrying a baby girl.

"Might this be?" he replied.

"This is. I named her Sarai, after Sarah, because she's beautiful."

Taking her into his arms, Enoch cuddled and kissed the beautiful soul.

⇢═◉ ◉═⇠

Drexter picked himself up from the buckled stairs, dusted the soil and debris from his suit, and nursed one of several minor wounds on his hand. Inventorying the irreversible damage that had been done to his dwelling, he cursed the Heavens.

After making his way inside the building, he found that his father had returned to his domain, and Priest Batteast was buried under the contents of what was once his quarters. He was disoriented but alive. Drexter helped him to his feet.

"Deploy more troops into the Middle East. Destroy the people of Israel. Bury them in my father's kingdom," Drexter commanded.

Chapter 11

"WE'VE LOST SEVERAL of our battle tanks. We can't hold them back. I repeat, we cannot hold them back," an Israeli Defense Forces captain frantically transmitted over the clamor of exploding grenades and heavy gunfire to colonels at the command center.

Within minutes, two of Israel's six districts, Haifa and Northern, had come under heavy firepower from the militia deployed into Turkey and Syria. Bombers and fighter crafts bombarded the tiny nation with specially-designed, highly-advanced Anti-Tank Missiles (ATM) and Air-to-Surface Missiles (ASM), and battleships positioned off the shore of the Mediterranean launched a round of Tomahawk missiles, crippling their military operations. Attacking Central, Tel Aviv, and Jerusalem Districts, along with the West Bank, were Syria, Iraq, Iran, and Jordan, with the aid of more battleships in the Persian Gulf. Southern District and the Judea and Samaria Areas were under savage attack by Saudi Arabia, Sinai, and Yemen. Cruisers and warships in the Red Sea and the Gulf of Aqaba were also firing rounds of missiles, and ground soldiers were awaiting orders to invade. Israel's Caterpillar D9 Armored Bulldozers and tanks were bombed, many of its structures toppled, its nuclear sites had all been taken out, and dire demands for reinforcements blared from every radio frequency.

Prime Minister Zebulon and Defense Minister Meers listened on as colonels ordered their soldiers to retreat if at all possible. Israel's disadvantage came as no surprise to the ministers. Not only were they outnumbered and outgunned, their warships couldn't be deployed due to enemy ships occupying nearby seas, their fighter crafts were shot down immediately after takeoff, and their weaponry greatly lacked in comparison to the World Militia's cutting-edge technology. They lowered their heads, signaling defeat as the number of casualties and collateral damage increased, and the blood of innocent men, women, and children stained the streets of every district.

Sneaking away from the command center, Prime Minister Zebulon felt the need to be alone with the Messiah. His mother's teachings struck him. She had also told him that there are every day prayers, and there are prayers for the upper room. When your enemies mount up all around you, persecute you, and all seems hopeless, it is then that you need to go into the upper room. You need not cry out but one word: Jesus. He already knows why you're there. Just cry out His name. There is unrestrained power in that name. The power to move mountains is in that name. Cry it out, be still, and then watch Jesus make a way out of no way at all.

Making his way to the upper level of the command center, he found a dark closet. Barricading himself inside, he laid flat with his face to the floor, submitting himself entirely to God, and wept. "Jesus! Jesus!"

For twenty minutes he prayed and cried in God's presence until the sound of feet scrambling caused him to raise his head. "Prime Minister! Prime Minister!" the familiar voice called out. The footsteps hurried past the closet door and down the hallway. "Prime Minister! Prime Minister, where are you?"

Leaping to his feet, he emerged from the closet, almost giving the young soldier a heart attack.

"Something's happening!" he yelled, nearly out of breath.

"What?" Prime Minister Zebulon asked puzzled.

"I don't know, sir. I can't explain it. The wind—it's moving."

"What?"

"Come see."

For a minute, he stood watching as the soldier dashed for the stairs until a weird-sounding ruckus diverted his attention. Returning to the command center, he found his dignitaries frozen in their seats.

"What is it?"

"We don't know," Defense Minister Meers replied.

"What do you mean? What the hell is happening?" he screamed. His patience had completely waned, and his frustration with his defense and security forces boiled.

"Something is attacking the World Militia, sir. I repeat, sir, something is attacking. The wind—it's moving."

The urgent broadcast from the front line brought a hush over the command center. Minute-by-minute field reports transmitted one over the other. Soldiers from every district attempted to describe the chaos over the upheaval in the background that rattled the entire nation.

"What's happening?" a colonel demanded information from frontline defense.

"Sir, their battleships are exploding. The wind, sir."

"What unit is firing?"

"No one, sir. No one is firing," he screamed. "We have nothing left to launch. All of our defenses are down, and our resources have all been depleted."

Making his way outside the command center with Defense Minister Meers on his trail, the prime minister was knocked down by a strong gust of wind. His eyes made contact with an enormous, peculiar-shaped, white cloud in the heavens that spanned the entire diameter of Israel and rained down on the nation sparkling dewdrops. Its spiraling, transparent funnel descended and expanded out into a solid, drum-shaped column of vigorous, rotating wind. Spiraling faster than the human eye could track, the powerful whirlwind of destruction travelled at a rate of speed immeasurable by man, and with a thunder so ferocious, it deafened everything around Israel and could be felt almost around the globe.

Powered by the wrath of God, the mesocyclone obliterated everything in its predetermined path as it repeatedly encircled the perimeter around Israel. The display of detonating bombs and weaponry made for a spectacular, firework-like illusion, but the mayhem and carnage left behind painted an entirely different picture.

In a matter of minutes, the indestructible wall of wind started to diminish and lose its energy. Entering into Israeli territory, it passed through the land like a breeze of fresh air and made its way into the city of Jerusalem where it concluded its course in front of the Holy Temple. The once transparent column of wind was now glowing and forming huge, blood-soiled, white wings. A pair of muddy feet, covered in metal, human tissue, and body fluids protruded from under its stained, tangled garment and touched down on land. Coming to a stop on one knee with his head bowed beneath his wings, the Angel of Death spoke not one word. The Israeli people frantically looked on from a distance, pointing their fingers, and whispering among each other. Blood on the angel's wings gradually dissolved until they were flawless and downy. The seams of his cleaved garb reattached, allowing his garment to flow loosely down his side, and bloody battle stains ebbed until his body was once more heavenly.

"Come hither," a mighty voice called out from the heavens.

Obeying the Lord's voice, he spread his wings and soared into the sky. A mild windstorm blew across all of Israel.

After the dust settled and deeming it safe to do so, the Israeli people came out of hiding to examine their land. Casualties of war, toppled buildings, the lifeless bodies of innocent children, and the splatter of blood spread throughout Israel. Mourning befell the tiny nation. Without delay, they began the troublesome task of rescuing their injured and burying their dead. The death toll rose astronomically, but even in sorrow, they praised the Messiah for His deliverance of their nation. A praise of thanksgiving travelled throughout the districts like lightning and unto the Lord. His name was glorified and lifted up.

Directly outside of Israel's borders lay a far more heinous scene. Across the continents of Europe, Africa, and Asia, and from one body of water to the other, was a bloodbath with little land left unsoiled. The scattered and unidentifiable remains of millions of decapitated soldiers blended among shreds of tattered clothing, fragments of armor, twisted metal, rock, glass particles, arched iron, and other mangled elements. It was a mass destruction that would take months to remove.

Circling the Holy Temple and finding not one inch marred, Prime Minister Zebulon marveled at the power of God Almighty. Rushing inside, he headed for the Mercy Seat. Sitting Indian-style before the throne, he felt the need to ask the Lord questions that he couldn't answer.

"Lord, why do You love us as You do?" He paused as if waiting for a verbal response. "We are undeserving of Your love, Your grace, and Your mercy. But for whatever reason, You always find fit to continue loving us, and Your grace and mercy are without boundaries. Why? Father, I trust in everything that You say. You have always kept Your word. You said that in the end You would deliver Israel, and Israel remains today only because it be Your will. I don't feel that my gratefulness is enough, but Father in Heaven, thank You. Thank You!" He stated with passion. "Israel thanks You."

⊷▬◉ ◉▬⊶

The Pearly Gates swung open, and Heaven's residents greeted the Angel of Death with smiles and plenty of hugs. Standing in the main pathway was the Messiah, to whom the angel bowed down immediately.

"Well done," Jesus spoke and embraced his shoulder. "Now rest."

Obeying the Messiah, he sought comfort near the center of Paradise with other angels who sustained him.

"My precious Son," God's precious voice rang out across Heaven. "Come."

Heeding His voice, Jesus turned immediately and headed for God's Temple. Angels stood guard outside the door, refusing entry to all. Equivalent to the next seven days, the Creator spoke intimately with His son.

Upon exiting the Holy Temple with a blank facial expression, Jesus went straight to work. First, He ordered all of His Archangels to assemble with Him in the Garden of Calvary. Kneeling before the Master, He gave specific instructions concerning Heaven's occupants and preparations for their journey. The Archangels exited the garden like lightning, assembling their legions of angels and laying out the Messiah's instructions. Soon Paradise was full of activity with angels rushing to and from to complete their tasks. For a while, the heirs of Paradise looked on but knew not to disturb them at their work.

When completed, Heaven's residents, with the exception of the Throne Angels, the Angel of Death, and the Elders sitting before God's throne, came together for a meeting. With Jesus ascended in the midst of them, the Good Shepherd's calm, soft voice travelled across Paradise.

"The time of man hast come to an end. I shall establish my kingdom on earth, and ye shall dwell with Me eternally."

Smiles graced the face of every heir. They jumped to their feet, kissing and hugging one another, and the angels also rejoiced over the good news. Jesus explained in depth the events that were to take place at His second coming. After observing worry on some of their faces, He assured them that they had nothing to fear. He spoke more on His thousand-year reign, Satan's return for a season and demise.

"Behold, I make all things new. I shall wipe away all tears from your eyes. There shall be no more death, nor sorrow, nor crying; neither shall there be any more pain, for the former things are passed away. The sun shall forever shine, and darkness shall cease to exist. I am Alpha and Omega, the beginning and the end. Through Me, all things are possible."

"Thank You, Lord. Hallelujah!" Tears of happiness swelled in their eyes. It was what every child of God longed to hear. "We'll follow You anywhere, Lord," they yelled.

"What about God the Father? Is He coming, too?" A juvenile female asked her mother.

"He'll be there, sweetheart," she kissed her forehead. "Just like now, He's everywhere."

"When do we leave, Lord?"

Jesus smiled. "Behold, I come quickly."

They laughed.

⊷≡◉ ◉≡↢

With nearly all of Drexter's army annihilated, word reached him via the media as news crews took to three continents to cover the gruesome scene. God's sovereign authority and His wrath were made clear to Drexter, who stood speechless while watching correspondents scale through the aftermath firsthand from directly outside the Israeli borders. Inside the borders, the Israeli people graciously and patiently waited in line to give their account of what transpired and to give glory to Christ. Immeasurable joy filled the atmosphere as they strolled peacefully about without worry. Even while burying their dead and laboring to again beautify their land, they sang beautiful hymns of peace, love, and thanksgiving. Happily, children ran to and fro, occasionally pausing to pose for the cameras, while the elderly and rabbis paraded the streets, holding up crosses and other religious symbols that represented Christ.

With no one else to tackle the massacre outside their borders, they emitted the willingness and dedication to engage the trying mission.

Inside the Holy City of Jerusalem, Prime Minister Zebulon was swarmed by media. He spoke openly of God's promise to deliver Israel and to make Jerusalem the future city that the Messiah would rule from His throne. In the background was the Holy Temple, and inside, the cameras spotlighted the Mercy Seat that sat awaiting the Messiah's arrival.

With a wave of his hand, Drexter froze his television and for a bit stood mesmerized by the throne. His eyes examined every detail of the elaborate seating. He allowed his imagination to run away from him. He pictured himself seated with the world kneeling at his feet.

"My throne," he mumbled.

Priest Batteast didn't respond but looked on.

"The time has arrived, old friend."

"And your army?" Priest Batteast inquired.

"We don't need an army, old friend. We never have," he spoke quietly. "It's my throne. I will take my place on it, and you shall stand beside me." He spoke deliberately.

"What shall you have me do?" Priest Batteast asked.

"Prepare for Israel. Once I'm seated on the throne, I shall rule from Jerusalem, and the world shall serve me."

"And the people of Israel?"

"Leave Israel to me."

Exiting his crumbling quarters, he stated, "I shall return."

"Where will you be?"

"On an important call. This observance requires my father's presence, don't you think?"

Chapter 12

PUBLIC AND PRIVATE facilities closed earlier than usual on the sunny Friday afternoon for the weekend festival. The Israeli people all migrated to the Holy City for the official kickoff of the Thanksgiving celebration, turning the other districts into ghost towns. Palms were thrown in the streets, and white Easter lilies decorated the windows and doorsteps of just about every home, business, religious, and public structure. The savory aroma of authentic Hebrew and Arabic dishes, mixed with the delectable scent of lamb, chicken, and venison roasting over open flames, could be smelled for miles around, tempting even the finickiest of taste buds.

Their democratic way of life showed in their many cultural, religious, and political beliefs, which were accepted by all. Jeans and T-shirts were the popular choice of the younger Jewish generation, while the older generation and Muslims opted for attire reflecting their religious and ethnic groups. Most noticeable were the Orthodox Jews who were adorned in their customary black attire. A new multicultural genre of music pleased the ears of the younger generation and fancied the ears of the elderly as well.

Lines at the Wailing Wall were three times their usual length. The history of the three thousand year old Holy Shrine was instilled in Israeli youths of every culture. Standing and kneeling, the nation approached the ancient temple wall with hearts of gratitude and words of extreme joy.

But in the cemetery on the Mount of Olives where Jesus Christ once sat and spoke of the Olivet Discourse to James, John, Peter, and Andrew, stood the Great Imitator and the False Prophet. Standing among the dead, they looked out on the Holy City, and in particular, at what they had come to claim. As always, its beauty stood unmatched and like a magnet, drew Drexter to it.

The Man of Sin turned back to the iconic site where his adversary once walked. The thought of Jesus once blessing it with His presence angered him, but the joyous celebration below angered him more.

He and Priest Batteast disappeared into thin air and reappeared in Bethlehem of Judea on the Grotto of the Nativity, the site where Jesus was born. They attempted to imagine the tiny manger filled with hay, the barn-like structure, the crowded and noisy inn, and the animals that must have been near to witness the miraculous birth.

"So, this is where it all began," Priest Batteast sighed.

"Yes, and if Herod the Great had done things correctly as my father intended, this is where it would have all ended," Drexter replied. His voice trembled with anger. "And had their God not intervened and warned the Magi in a dream, they would have returned with word of His whereabouts just as my father had planned." He paused. "Salvation wouldn't have been possible."

His hatred turned toward the three magi who had chosen to disobey Herod's orders and had, instead, followed God's and taken a different route home. Allowing his thoughts to escape back to biblical times, he imagined all the things that he wished would have happened to Christ at His birth.

"If only their Christ had been one of the many males slaughtered by Herod's army, it would all be over. My father would already be seated on the throne and I at his side. My reign on this earth would already be in existence."

Sensing the hatred swelling in his master, Priest Batteast resorted to humor. "I see that not much has changed since the beginning of man."

"Not quite what one would expect for a king, is it?" Drexter mocked.

"We've seen worse," Priest Batteast kidded.

Drexter laughed. "Are you being sarcastic?"

"Perhaps I am," he chuckled.

"When this is all over, perhaps, I shall send you back home, or to worse as you call it."

"You're not that powerful, Young Master."

At the blink of an eye, they disappeared and reappeared in Nazareth, Jesus' childhood dwelling.

"Jesus of Nazareth," Drexter uttered bitterly. "Jesus of Nazareth."

He studied the land where Jesus played as a child with His siblings and grew into manhood. His thoughts turned to the many prophesies that the servants of God had spoken of thousands of years before Christ's birth and how each one had come to pass just as described.

In a flash, they appeared on the River Jordan in Judea. Drexter and Priest Batteast walked on the surface of the water, visualizing John the Baptist sitting by the river, wild in appearance and dieting on locusts and wild honey. John's words about the coming Messiah stung Drexter's ears. He knew that the Creator had sent John ahead of time to pave the way for Christ's ministry. It infuriated him that God was always steps ahead of his father.

Like lightning, they vanished and then came back into view on Skull Hill in Golgotha, just outside of Jerusalem. A feeling of defeat came over Drexter—the same feeling that his father had experienced thousands of years earlier. It was the site of the most selfless and loving act that his father had fought tooth and nail to prevent.

"Calvary," Priest Batteast whispered.

"It was you, old friend, who informed me of what transpired here—you and my father's demons. Do you remember?"

"I do."

Humbled, Drexter looked at Priest Batteast. "Even now my father speaks not much of it. He has never really gotten over the defeat he suffered here. I can tell."

"Perhaps not, Young Master."

"He fought viciously to prevent this."

Priest Batteast didn't respond; instead, he nodded his head.

"You said that my father stood among the crowd, watching and hoping that their Messiah would come down from the cross, but He wouldn't. He wouldn't because of His love for them. And because He wouldn't, my father was forced to alter his course of action."

Priest Batteast stood silent while his friend finished venting.

Three images of wooden crosses flashed in Drexter's mind. The sorrowful cries of a few and the joyful yells of the vast majority from the crowd blasted in his ears, along with the cheerful faces of the soldiers casting lots for the Messiah's clothes.

"Death could not hold Him, they say. Death could not hold Him. He conquered death. He conquered sin." His voice started to blare with rage. "He rose with all glory and power in His hand. He rebuilt the temple in three days. His heirs marvel over that, don't they?"

Priest Batteast looked on in silence, not wanting to spark more rage in his friend.

"Upon His death, He walked into my father's kingdom, did He not?" His voice intensified. "He freed all who chose to leave with Him. He took my father's souls while my father and his demons stood helplessly by and watched, trembling at His sight."

Priest Batteast embraced Drexter's shoulder in an attempt to calm him down.

"He died to save them," he frowned. "He died to save them."

"Young Master."

"They aren't worth saving," he abruptly yelled out to Heaven. "You love them, but they deny You. You supply all their needs and wants, and they still complain. You gave them commandments, and what do they do? They break each and every one of them over and over again. They steal and lie. They murder, commit adultery, bear false witness, worship idols, and covet over and over again. You tell them to honor their parents; instead, they rise up and slaughter them." He paused. "They go astray, stumble and fall, and then run back to You because they know they can. They crawl back on hands and knees with repenting hearts and a couple of tears in their eyes, and You fall for it every time—You forgive them. They are worthless, do You hear me? They are worthless, but You cherish them. They deserve death, but You choose to give them life. They are deserving of Your wrath; yet, they have Your grace and mercy. They are deserving of my father's kingdom, but You postpone Your judgment that they may escape it." He swayed his head in disgust. "They are deserving of death, but You see to it that they have ample opportunity to live. Why? Why? They aren't worth saving. They aren't worth saving. My father and I shall have no mercy on them. I shall not spare one of them. My hatred for them consumes me. My father and I shall see to it that they get what they deserve: the harshest of judgment, never-ending torment, torture, and destruction."

Eager to abandon Golgotha, he and Priest Batteast faded into thin air and materialized atop the Wailing Wall. Curling his perfectly manicured hands into a clenched fist, Drexter peered straight down at the congestion below. Like a hawk stalking its prey, he zeroed in on the small pieces of folded prayer paper that believers had deposited into the wall's crevices. From an aerial view, his eyes scoped the rocky, short trail that led up to the open doors of the Holy Temple where he calculated the ten bodies entering the temple and the six exiting it.

A startling scream caught the Israeli people off guard. Believers at the wall halted their prayers and praises, and a horrified woman nervously pointed to the top of the wall, alerting them to the presence of evil. Sudden panic struck God's people. They immediately backed away, yelling "blasphemy" in their highest tone. No longer hidden in plain view, the men of evil began their descent on the nation. With his hands extended at his side, Drexter's poised frame drifted downward alongside the historic wall with Priest Batteast at his side. His razor-sharp fingernails screeched against the ancient stone, creating jagged, vertical incisions two inches into its structure.

When their feet touched down on the pavement, Drexter gawked and snarled at God's people. Out of fear, they increased their distance. He pulled the hood of his robe over his bowed head to where it cast a dark shadow over his face. His hands and feet turned reddish with scales and wrinkles for several seconds before taking back their original form. Tracking the palms that led up to the Holy Temple, he started barefoot up the path.

"Antichrist," a middle-aged man yelled out. "You will never defile our Messiah's throne."

Like a madman, he lunged toward Drexter with a raised fist, losing his hat in the attempted ambush. After accomplishing four steps, he stopped abruptly as if his body had collided with an invisible barrier. His eyes blinked wildly, and his rigid body flew twenty feet into the air. Pure horror covered his frightened face. He struggled to move but was unable to escape the unseen force restraining his immobile body. His body soared like a jet engine in the air and crashed violently against the Wailing Wall, creating a depression of his skeletal makeup. His corpse snapped in half, and every bone in his body cracked. Blood stained the ancient shrine when he slid down its rocky structure and landed face down on the ground. Fearing for their lives, some of the Israeli people backed further away while others sought safety in homes and businesses.

A slight smirk covered Drexter's face as they commenced their trek toward their destination. A handful of Israeli soldiers hurried toward the commotion with large rocks in their possession. They cast them at the rulers of darkness, but the stones were deflected by the powers of Hell. Like the clatter of balloons popping, the soldiers burst into intense flames. Spinning in circles and flopping on the pavement, their cries rang out over the blaze. Onlookers rushed to their aid to smother them with garments from their bodies and with rags, but the flames burned more intensely. The heat became unbearable, and the smell of searing flesh sickened their stomachs. Distraught, they withdrew. Within minutes, the soldier's incinerated remains turned to ashes.

"Go back to Hell where you belong," a teenage boy yelled in rage and then charged toward Drexter like a raging bull.

Laughing at his oncoming threat, Drexter casually waved his hand. His young assailant's spinal cord snapped from his neck springing around midway. Blood spurted from his mouth and ears, and his limp body dropped to the pavement like a load of bricks, bursting into flames.

"Their Messiah shed His blood; why shouldn't they?" Drexter advised his false prophet before continuing their walk toward the temple.

The clatter of millions of creepy, menacing voices resonated from beneath the earth. Acknowledging the cheers, Drexter stared down into Hell where a celebration was underway. Evil spirits and demonic forces excitedly danced and cheered for their prince. As an expression of their happiness, unmerciful and relentless pain and suffering was executed on the damned souls. The earth reverberated from the pounding of demons striking their feet against the base of Hell. Depressing pleas from the tortured sounded in unison underneath a frightening and thunderous chuckle that trumpeted over it all.

"My son," Satan called out. "My loving son."

Drexter grinned upon hearing his father's voice. Knowing that his father was pleased with him ignited immeasurable joy in his heart. Finally, he counted down the last steps that landed him in front of the temple.

"Jesus! Jesus!" the Israeli people screamed from the Messiah's temple.

They knew that they were no match in power against the Antichrist, but that mattered not. Their devotion to Jesus was all that mattered, even if it meant their lives in exchange. They used their bodies as human shields to barricade the entranceways.

"Unclean spirit," they yelled. "Depart from us in Jesus' name." Several of them spat angrily in Drexter's direction, hurled insults, and cursed Priest Batteast.

Their defiance toward evil, and their commitment to God had already taken its toll on the Man of Sin and had depleted him of all his patience. In Latin, he called upon the powers of Hell to bring judgment against them, and Satan granted his request. Hell's fury detonated, blasting the front section of the temple off its foundation. Disintegrated stone, glass, bloody clothing, and human flesh jetted in the atmosphere. God's children were tossed to their deaths; their bodies were ripped into pieces.

With nothing else standing in their way, Drexter and Priest Batteast advanced. As they crossed the threshold, the twitching hand of a badly wounded girl reached up and seized Priest Batteast's ankle. With very little life left in her, she utilized it in one last attempt to protect Jesus' throne. Clutching him with her four gory fingers, she refused to let go. Jerking away, he snarled at her and then kicked her severely wounded face as if she was trash. The fatal blow freed him from her grip.

Inside the temple, they made straightway to the Mercy Seat as if they had toured the structure a thousand times. Sitting behind the protective glass was what they had come for. Its magnificence stopped Drexter in his tracks. He could do nothing but gaze at its beauty. "At last, I take my place on my throne."

Delighting in his friend's pleasure, Priest Batteast held out his hand, beckoning for Drexter to proceed. Unwilling to waste another minute, Drexter penetrated the barrier as if it wasn't there and then started down the walkway. Priest Batteast followed suit, shattering the glass as he did so.

"Septem, sex, quinque, quattuor, tres, duo," the Man of Sin counted down the last few steps in Latin that led up to the platform. His moment had arrived, and nothing stood between him and the throne except one final step. The rhythm of his heart exploded, and his anticipation ran amok. Finally, the long journey was concluding as one foot landed on the platform.

"Evil stand where it ought not; for this place is reserved for Holiness. You dare desecrate it with your filthy presence."

From behind the throne came a commanding voice, challenging Drexter's claim of sovereignty. It was an accent he knew all too well; one that he was unable to mislead with his deception and trickery. Stepping from behind the throne, Prime Minister Zebulon closed in on his adversary. Their eyes locked, and for a while neither dared to blink.

"Do you really believe that you can stop me?" Drexter's words dragged out. "You know not what you fight against. You dare challenge the forces of my father's kingdom; you dare challenge the ruler of darkness?" The pitch of his voice strengthened.

"Though I walk through the valley of the shadow of death, I will fear no evil; for thou art with me." Prime Minister Zebulon paused. "You speak of the powers of your father's kingdom." A devilish grin formed on his face. "The devil believes, and he trembles," he taunted. "In the end, righteousness shall prevail. My Lord—"

"Your Lord! Your Lord!" Drexter barked.

With both hands, Prime Minister Zebulon suddenly grabbed his throat, frantically gasping for oxygen. The pressure around his neck made it impossible to breathe. The harder he struggled to inhale, the tighter his airways constricted. His skin tone turned a bluish tint. With every failed attempt to intake air, a high-pitched noise escaped his lips. Inch by inch, something was draining the life right out of him. Disoriented and weakened, he grabbed for the Mercy Seat but came up short. Collapsing to the floor, his racing heart stopped, and his skin withered like a rose.

Stepping over his nemesis, Drexter proceeded to the Mercy Seat where he proudly sat. "Leave it there," he ordered Priest Batteast who had started to dispose of the remains. "It shall serve as a warning to all who dare to defy me."

"So it shall," Priest Batteast agreed and then took his place on the left side of the throne.

Every portal between Hell and earth spewed with fire like volcanoes, and then came demons to the earth to praise their master. Satan sat on his throne looking upon the earth and delighting over his son. Without warning, the celebration came to a screeching halt when lightning flashed across the sky. The portals of Hell ceased to spit fire, Hell's residents froze in their tracks, and a standstill fell upon the globe.

The sky parted to deliver a glimmer of light, which gradually spread from the east to the west. Demons shivered with fear because they bore memories of its significance. Having witnessed it many times when they were angels in Heaven, some fled back through the portals to Hell where they sought refuge. Satan attempted to warn his son, but even he was subject to the authority of Jesus Christ; therefore, he was unable to speak. Unlike before, the eyes of every man witnessed the miraculous and glorious appearing.

Once more, Heaven's army stood on the clouds dressed in the finest of white linens. One horse stood out ahead of all others, and on it sat the Light of the World—the King of Kings—the Lord of Lords. Upon His head was a gem-filled crown of pure gold, not of thorns as before. There was a variance about Jesus this time. He was not the same king who had come to earth as before. The first time He came, He offered salvation and mercy to the world, but not this time. This time, He came to judge without mercy, to punish the wicked, and to rule with an iron rod.

"Rise!" Jesus commanded all the tribulation saints that had died for His namesake.

The earth rolled back its soil, seas ebbed, and boulders moved. Those who had been beheaded for being living testimonies for Christ got up. Those who lost their lives for refusing to accept the mark of the beast got up. Those who refused to worship anything but the true God got up. The Israeli people who had been attacked because of their faith got up. As before, they breathed the breath of life. Uniting with those who had remained upon the earth, they ascended on the clouds and sat on white horses with the heirs before them. But the rest of the dead who knew not Christ remained as they were until the second death.

"Go and gather the wicked before me," Jesus commanded His angels.

Armed with chains of great proportion, His archangels flew to all corners of the globe: Ariel hovered over the north portion, Raphael the east, Gabriel the south, and Michael the west. Remaining soldiers of the World Militia sought to do battle with them, but a single flash from the angel's radiant eyes robbed them of their sight. The wicked were all swept together and were delivered before the Messiah. Mercilessly, He gazed down on them with disfavor and then rebuked them. But instead of remorse, His wrath was met by snarls and hearts that had long waxed cold. They blasphemed, cursed, and denounced Him as king. Embracing their mark, they declared Drexter the Holy one and then sought to make war.

"Michael," Jesus yelled out angrily with the voice of many running waters.

The archangel drew from his scabbard a shiny, sharp sword, and with one mighty blow to the ground, caused it to tremble, crack, and widen to form a pit. Unmoved by this, the wicked still sought war. Jesus sought the power of Heaven, and it opened up. Down came a pouring of fire burning with brimstone that filled the pit. Upon seeing the lake of fire, the wicked turned to Drexter, believing that he would deliver them.

"Save yourselves," he uttered uncaringly and with a spiteful look on his face.

"The wicked shall have their part in the lake of fire," Jesus commanded His angels.

Having been deceived by Drexter into believing that he would deliver them and that they would thrive with him when he ruled from the throne, they had worshipped him. But now, reality painted a different picture as they stood in judgment.

"Jesus," they yelled and begged for mercy with insincere hearts, but mercy they found not.

Raphael and Ariel linked the chains together and bound them. After seeing their family members and loved ones standing in judgment, the saints lowered their heads in sorrow and wept; they knew what was to come. But their anguish was quickly overtaken by a sense of calmness. Jesus bestowed upon them His spirit of peace, which surpasses all understanding. Diligently, the angels dragged the wicked toward the flames. Their eyes fell upon the Messiah, and they screamed for tender mercy, but Jesus would not be moved.

The boiling inferno resembled a thick, black, molten lava-like substance with bluish flames and waves that pounded the edge of the pit. When the wicked were tossed in, it sizzled and popped, and an unappealing smell of steam rose into the air. Their skin dissolved on contact, and their flesh charred within seconds. All that remained of their form was a black, flaky, disfigured mass with eyes that tossed, tumbled, and wailed out in excruciating pain. The heat emitting from the pit, combined with the suffocating stench of burning human flesh, made it virtually unbearable. The damned sought a speedy death, but death came not. The everlasting flame, created for eternal damnation, would never cease to burn. Their souls were to be tormented day and night, never finding relief. After the last of the wicked had been tossed in, Jesus turned His attention to the Antichrist and his false prophet. Enraged, He rebuked them both.

Priest Batteast snarled in dismay. His facial expression displayed pure hatred for Christ. Relying on the forces of Hell, he, too, sought war against the army of God but was rendered powerless by a single blink of Michael's eyes. Seeing that his powerful prophet was also subject to the authority of Christ, Drexter became fainthearted. In the end, he, too, humbled himself before the Son of Man.

"Michael," the Messiah commanded.

At that moment, the archangel seized them with no resistance.

"Thou shall not deceive the world anymore. Thou, too, shall have thy part in the everlasting lake of fire," Jesus commanded.

After being secured by chains, Michael transported them over the fire, and upon reaching central point, released them. As did the wicked, they, too, screamed in terror when they plunged into the inferno. The saints all cheered, applauded their doom, and sang praises unto the Messiah for destroying the beast and his servant who had deceived and robbed so many of their salvation.

"My son," a distraught voice that was evenly balanced with Michael's called out from beneath the earth. The words were followed by heavy breathing and snorting.

The heirs' praises to Jesus ceased; they stared at Him. The pounding of heavy footsteps echoed out and seemed to near Michael's location. The howls of thousands of eerie, demonic pitches escaped from beneath the terrain. The army of God and the saints stood on guard for what was to come, and Christ awaited the arrival of His adversary.

Finally, the ground faltered and then gave way. A faint glow first appeared from within the break, followed by an offensive odor. Out of it rose Satan. His stature and form were equivalent to that of Michael's: towering and radiant, with the exception of his eyes, which were fiery, reddish tints. Many of the heirs were surprised by his outward appearance, having grasped the misconception that when he was cast down from Heaven his appearance changed. The Messiah and His angels knew differently.

Arrogantly, Satan stood within several yards of Michael. Stealing a quick glance at the clouds, he glared at the Messiah, His army, and then all the saints that he had feverishly pursued for their souls but failed to acquire. He peered intently into the lake at his beloved son while he roasted; his heart ached. The only person who genuinely meant anything to him, and who he had never lied to, existed no more. Immediately, he sought vengeance against the one responsible.

Again, he gazed up at Christ, and in doing so, quickly recalled a moment in time when he alone was able to prevent the Messiah from reaching Daniel for twenty-one days. He figured that he had a fighting chance of overthrowing Christ, but he would need some assistance. He knew that even with the combined force of his demons, he would still require a more authoritative power. Out of left field, he snickered. He hadn't been labeled the Great Deceiver and the Father of all Lies for nothing. Without a minute to waste, he threw his plan into action.

"My beloved brother, it's been awhile since our last encounter. I've missed you," Satan greeted Michael with a grin. "I have thought of you much. I still recall fond memories of our early days together. Doest you?"

Michael was unresponsive.

"I remember our long walks through the gardens of Paradise—how we would laugh, talk, and fellowship with each other. Doest they still appear the same?"

Michael wouldn't respond.

"We shared duty at the front gate. Doest you remember?"

Still, there was no response.

"All the angels looked up to us. They admired our beauty, our courage, and strength. To them, we were the most divine."

He attempted to bait Michael with the very sin that caused his downfall from grace: pride. The archangel was not moved.

"We were inseparable. We worked well together, did we not?" Satan paused for Michael's response but came up short. "We loved each other so, but our bond was broken out of jealousy, and we were forced against one another. I still recall our war in Heaven. It was one that I desired not. We waged war against each other, and I was forced to leave. But, look what I've accomplished." He waved his arms about. "You should have accompanied me. We could have acquired this together," he impatiently stated. "My beloved brethren, time hast not passed us by. We can join forces, and together we can rule for all eternity. I sensed that you desired not to respond and help your Lord when He struggled against me on His way to comfort Daniel. I understand that you were coerced and had no say in the matter. I never held it against you. Just think of what we could have achieved if our forces had been combined at that time."

Michael, being as intelligent as the dragon and knowing the craftiness of his tongue, knew not to make the same mistake that Eve made in the Garden of Eden: converse with him.

"Our Lord rebuke thee," Michael commanded.

Like a chameleon, Satan's true nature resurfaced and lashed out. "Then we shall wage war once more," he declared angrily and then motioned for his servants. "This time, I shall finish what I started in Paradise."

At that moment, his generals climbed from the hole and took their place behind him, followed by the rest of Hell's army.

"Michael," Jesus commanded.

The mighty angel drew his sword while Heaven's army gathered behind him. With a mighty yell and then a strike that landed within inches of Satan's body, the armies clashed. Satan and his demons fought, and Michael and Heaven's host fought back in an intense battle, but the dragon and his army prevailed not. One by one, Satan's army was overpowered, subdued, and then tossed into the lake of fire where they would never wreak havoc on earth again. When the last one had been pitched in, Heaven sealed the earth over the flames.

Heaven's host retreated to give way to Michael and Satan who fought a fierce duel. Satan soon realized that Michael, too, had grown more forceful. Satan began to wane and soon found himself to be no match against God's warrior. Satan was pinned to the ground with Michael's sword at his throat.

"You're my brother whom I adore. Conspire with me," he pleaded, making one last attempt with a look of sincerity on his face.

Once more, Michael rebuked him in the Lord.

Jesus spoke, and the earth opened up to form a dark pit. Its boundary was almost endless. Gabriel produced a key in his right hand and a huge shackle in his left. Satan was bound and then escorted to the edge of the pit.

"I shall resurface someday," he warned the Messiah. "Have thy time now, but my time shall again come about."

Heaven's hosts all rebuked him in the Lord, and Satan tumbled after being pushed over the edge. His squeals shook the earth, but the trembling diminished as he plummeted deeper. By the power of Heaven, the pit was secured so that the earth would be deceived no more until a specified time. Though the battle was intense, not one of Heaven's hosts was injured.

A hearty cheer sounded across the globe when Heaven's heirs and the angels rejoiced. They sang beautiful praises unto the Messiah and bowed down to Him. Jesus delighted in His children, and tears of joy streamed down His face.

With all evil wiped from the earth, there was one thing left to do. Turning to the tainted temple that had lost its splendor, Christ spoke a few words, and the remaining walls tumbled down, crushing everything that it housed. A storm of black-and-gray dust mounted straight up into the air, crystallized, and then solidified. Like glass, it popped, and cracks ran through it like spider webs. From within the cracks seeped a clear turquoise and bluish liquid. When it shattered, a breathtaking waterfall emerged. Water flooded the ground and then flowed outward across the globe, forming inviting new oceans, seas, lakes, streams, and ponds. Trees of all types were revitalized. They brought forth branches decorated with large, deep-green leaves and fruit of every kind. Bushes sprouted in full bloom and showcased petals of every assortment. The beautiful blue sky blended splendidly with the luminous sun, white, puffy clouds, and green grass that spread from the east to every end of the earth. Not far from the waterfall, a foundation formed that supported four extravagantly constructed marble walls that were crowned with a retractable, stained-glass dome. It rolled back to expose a new temple, one that outdid the first with its remarkable highlights. Amid its magnificence sat the main attraction: the Mercy Seat.

Christ's children watched as New Jerusalem formed all around them and then spread throughout the world for their enjoyment. Their hearts were filled exceedingly with joy. They fell down on their faces and praised the Messiah. After Jesus spoke, another celebration commenced. The races scrambled about joyfully in search of their kin and loved ones.

"Mama," a familiar voice called out to Ellen and Wentworth.

As she halted dead in her tracks, tears instantly swelled in Ellen's eyes. "Mabrey," she whispered.

Laughter from Wentworth prompted her to spin around where she discovered her two sons wrapped tightly in each other's arms.

"I made it, Mama. I made it," he yelled out before she embraced him.

"My baby," Ellen cried. "My son. Thank You, Lord," she shouted.

"Don't forget about me," another familiar voice sounded. "I'm your baby, too."

"Harper," she shouted, falling into his arms.

"You didn't expect to see me standing here with you, did you?" he kidded.

"I prayed, son. All I could do was pray for you. It was all in God's hands."

"Thank you for praying for me, Mama, when I was too foolish to pray for myself," he cried.

"It's OK, baby. It's OK."

"It was your prayers that saved our lives, Mama," Stanton stated, as he approached Ellen from behind, picked her up, and squeezed her tightly. "We're living proof that God loves us and can save even the worst of us if you just let Him."

"My baby," Ellen moaned in joy while she gripped his arms. "Thank You, Lord. I really do love you boys."

"We love you too, Mama," they replied simultaneously.

"Has anybody seen Connery?" Wentworth asked.

They started to scan through the ecstatic crowd. All around them, loved ones were crying while they embraced each other and gave thanks to the Messiah. Ellen started to wander a couple of feet outward until she observed Jesus approaching.

"Thank You, Lord. I love You. I asked that You bless me with at least one of my sons eternally, but You saw fit to give me all five of them. I am so grateful, Lord. Thank You." Ellen rushed to Him and gave Him a big hug.

"There are only four standing before you, Mary Ellen," Jesus softly replied.

"I know, Lord. But I trust in You. You delivered these four. I know that Connery, too, is here. Where might I find him, Jesus?"

Jesus looked at Ellen and saw that her heart was sincere even though she hadn't found her eldest son. He smiled.

"Lord, I learned from You that true faith—true faith—carries with it no worry," she continued. "Please, Jesus, point me in the direction among this crowd where I will find my eldest son. I know he's looking for us. I need to give him a hug," she begged.

At that moment, Connery stepped from behind the Messiah and kissed Him on the cheek. "Looking for me, old lady?" he joked, picked her up, and embraced her.

"My son is the evidence of my faith. Thank You, Lord." She hugged Connery a little tighter. "I don't doubt Your power for one minute. I know what You can do. You have never let me down, Lord. All things are possible through You."

"Lord! Lord!" a female voice repeated over again. It was Anna. As soon as she could, she ran to Christ and kneeled down at His feet. Gripping them with all her might, she kissed them tenderly again and again. "Thank You," she cried. "My family and I are with You today for all eternity. I'm all right now."

Jesus attentively helped her to her feet and embraced her with a hug and then a kiss to the forehead before they walked away.

⇢═ ═⇠

Christ returned as He had promised to set up His millennial reign on earth. As the generations passed, the earth was once again replenished. But as before, God's spirit would not always dwell with man. Man's heart would once again wax cold and thus begin the millennial breakdown. Satan would have one last opportunity to roam the earth and deceive souls, ultimately waging one last war against the saints. That, of course, is another story.

Author Biography

The author started writing poems and lyrics at an early age, which led to short stories. This is her debut novel. She was born in Tennessee and now resides in Missouri. She plans to write full time. Catch up with her on Facebook and Twitter.

Made in the USA
Lexington, KY
06 May 2015